"Maggie Brendan is adept at weaving a sweet love story, and *The Jewel of His Heart* showcases her penchant for capturing the Old West in authentic dialogue, in vivid descriptions, and in the struggle of two hearts destined to become one. Within these pages indeed lies a jewel."

Tamera Alexander, bestselling author of *From a Distance*, *Beyond This Moment*, and *The Inheritance*

"With its tender love story and vivid imagery of a time gone by, Maggie Brendan's gentle style of prairie romance is reminiscent of Janette Oke, capturing the heart of both the Old West and the reader with romance that will make you sigh."

Julie Lessman, author of the Daughters of Boston series

"For an action-filled historical romance, look no further than *The Jewel of His Heart*. Maggie Brendan blends colorful characters, lively dialogue, and intriguing historical details to create a memorable story of love and faith in the Old West."

Amanda Cabot, author of *Paper Roses*

"Maggie Brendan gives readers an authentic look into the past, painting a tapestry with words that draws us into Montana in the 1890s. This story has enough surprises to keep readers turning the pages, and the characters live on in our hearts long after we've finished reading the book."

Lena Nelson Dooley, award-winning author of *Wild Prairie Roses*, *Wild West Christmas*, and *Love Finds You in Golden, New Mexico*

"With the skill of an artist's brush, Maggie Brendan vividly paints the rugged Montana countryside and satisfies romance readers with the heart-touching story of a hardworking sheepherder and an independent woman."

Vickie McDonough, award-winning author of sixteen novels and novellas

D1022546

HEART
of the WEST * 2

The
JEWEL OF
HIS *Heart*

A *N*OVEL

MAGGIE BRENDAN

Garfield County Libraries
Silt Branch Library
600 Home Avenue
Silt, CO 81652
970-876-5500 Fax 970-876-5921
www.garfieldlibraries.org

Revell

a division of Baker Publishing Group
Grand Rapids, Michigan

© 2009 by Maggie Brendan

Published by Revell
a division of Baker Publishing Group
P.O. Box 6287, Grand Rapids, MI 49516-6287
www.revellbooks.com

Printed in the United States of America

All rights reserved. No part of this publication may be reproduced, stored in a retrieval system, or transmitted in any form or by any means—for example, electronic, photocopy, recording—without the prior written permission of the publisher. The only exception is brief quotations in printed reviews.

Library of Congress Cataloging-in-Publication Data
Brendan, Maggie, 1949–
    The jewel of his heart : a novel / Maggie Brendan.
        p.   cm. — (Heart of the West ; bk. 2)
    ISBN 978-0-8007-3350-6 (pbk.)
    1. Montana—Fiction. I.Title.
PS3602.R4485J49 2009
813'.6—dc22   2009015328

Unless otherwise indicated, Scripture is taken from the King James Version of the Bible.

Scripture marked NKJV is taken from the New King James Version. Copyright © 1982 by Thomas Nelson, Inc. Used by permission. All rights reserved.

This book is a work of fiction. Names, characters, places, and incidents are the product of the author's imagination or are used fictitiously. Any resemblance to actual events, locales, or persons, living or dead, is coincidental.

For Bruce, who gave me my beautiful Yogo sapphire ring from Montana, which inspired this story, and for my two wonderful children, Sheri and Jared. You bring great joy to my life! May God always fill your lives with love and hope as He directs your paths. And last but not least, in memory of Shebe, my brother's faithful Shetland sheepdog.

> He dams up the streams from trickling;
> What is hidden he brings forth to light.
>
> Job 28:11 (NKJV)

1

Utica, Montana, 1896

I need a wife.

Josh McBride rode down a grassy slope to the sparkling creek, allowing his horse, Pete, a drink while surveying with a keen eye the parcel of land he'd purchased three years before.

It's pretty here—the best spot on God's good earth.

But that didn't keep him from feeling lonely.

He was enjoying the beautiful Montana mountains this February morning, and the satisfaction of pursuing his own dream and place in the world instead of his father's. On these solitary morning rides, he treasured the peace and privacy with his Creator, feeling His presence.

He took his bandana from his neck and dipped it into the cold stream to wipe his face. The creek narrowed at this juncture to not much more than a trickle, or Josh might have missed the handful of small blue pebbles that had collected there. Reaching into the icy water, he scooped the pebbles up for a closer look. The sunlight reflected off the translucent blue pebbles, their hue unlike anything Josh had ever seen. Instinctively he knew these were not just blue pebbles or ordinary stones, but what he didn't know was how they would ultimately change his life forever.

Josh slipped the handful of blue stones into his leather vest pocket and mounted his horse. He headed back to the grassy rise overlooking the valley, pausing to gaze with pride at his sizable herd of sheep. Suddenly Josh's white and amber dog, Shebe, ran up to gaze at him lovingly, her tongue lolling from the side of her mouth.

"Hey, girl. Looking for me?"

Shebe's short bark was her answer, and Josh laughed. "We've sure been through some lonely times, haven't we, girl?"

"Boss!" Josh's young sheepherder, Andy, waved his hat at Josh and pushed his horse up the grassy ridge.

Josh called back a greeting and nudged Pete's flanks with his boot heel. He'd left his spurs behind when he rode off his father's cattle ranch. Besides, he and Pete understood each other perfectly. Josh sometimes thought Pete and Shebe understood him better than anyone else, and his affection for his horse and sheepdog ran deep. But still, he wanted a wife. A dog and a horse could not take the place of a companion to fill the lonely space in his heart.

"What's going on, Andy?" Josh reined Pete in next to Andy's horse.

"There's a grub-line rider down at the camp. Said he was passing this way from Lewistown. Think he said his name was Charlie."

"Does he want to join up, or is he just looking for a place to light for a few days?"

"I'm not sure, Boss. Reckon you'd better talk to him yourself. He's a bit different, and carrying some strange-looking canvas case with him." Andy folded his arms across his saddle horn, waiting for his boss's direction.

"All right, Andy. I'll follow you back to camp. You have the coffee hot?"

"Don't I always?" he said matter-of-factly.

They ambled along in silence. The worn leather saddle, with Josh's .44 Winchester rifle packed across the front, creaked under his shifting weight. Except for an occasional snort from their horses, it was a calm, still day. A lone eagle soared above the timberline, sending out its shrill call into the bright morning skies. Shebe was not far behind her beloved master.

As they entered the small clearing where the sheep wagon was parked by a bubbling creek, a handsome wrangler rose from a stump, a cigarette dangling from his lips. He wore a floppy hat pushed back at the crown, exposing a shock of long blond bangs that fell across his forehead. He sported a red sash around his neck.

"Howdy." He quickly threw the cigarette down, ground it out under his heel, and walked toward them.

"Hi yourself. What can I do for you? Our camp is quite a ways out for strangers." Josh dismounted, and Andy followed, taking the horses' reins. Josh was careful when strangers appeared, never knowing who to trust when someone dropped by unexpectedly.

The stranger stuck out his hand. "I'm Charlie Russell. Live over in Great Falls, just passing through. I saw your camp and thought a good cup of hot coffee would be mighty nice." His smile was warm and friendly, and he had a sparkle in his eyes.

Josh shook his hand. "My name's Josh McBride. I own the sheep, and Andy here is my sheepherder. Where ya headed?"

"I was over in Lewistown, and now I'm heading home. Crossed the Judith River and saw smoke from your campfire."

"Sit down, Charlie. Andy, how 'bout a cup of java?"

Josh felt an instant liking for Charlie. He was apparently friendly, and good-looking too. *Bet he has a way with the women. He could've talked Crystal into taking off to Montana, had he known her.*

Josh was startled by the turn his thoughts had taken. It had been some time since he had given Crystal any thought. He knew she was happy and that Luke adored her. Josh had finally come to terms with that.

Charlie sipped from the chipped enameled cup Andy had given him. "I may have to sketch you with that friendly dog you have there, Josh. What's her name?"

Josh scratched Shebe's head lovingly as she sat on her haunches next to her master, keeping a keen eye on Charlie. "I call her Shebe. She's my best friend, right, girl?" Shebe barked in agreement.

Charlie yanked open the black box he was carrying and pulled out a sketch pad and a box of pencil crayons. Josh started to move away. "No, just sit right there with Shebe. We can just talk, and you can tell me about yourself." He flipped open his pad to a clean sheet and outlined Josh and his dog.

"Not much to tell. I'm a sheepherder by way of Colorado, where my daddy is a cattle baron. I wanted to spread my wings and experience something different. Started out with a small herd of sheep that Andy mostly tends now. I've started bulding a cabin, and I hope to make it a real home soon. What about you?"

Charlie seemed eager to talk. "I'm an artist of sorts. Hung up my spurs in '92 after wrangling since I was sixteen. I used to be a horse wrangler with some of the best outfits around. I once worked at Judith River Basin as the night hawk. From time to time, I drew scenes of wrangling, calf branding, and cattle drives. I guess you could say I'm a self-taught artist. Once people actually wanted to buy my paintings, well, I decided to hang up my spurs and pursue my dream."

"Self-taught? Well, there has to be talent involved. I could no more teach myself to paint than design a ship that would hold up at sea." Josh fidgeted, shifting to a more comfortable position.

"Hold still, I'll be done here pretty quick."

Charlie's eyes twinkled, and he laughed as he deftly sketched an image that was beginning to emerge as Josh's face, showing him playfully touching Shebe's head as she lay curled at his feet. "Shucks, everything can be learned. I grew up in Missouri and left at sixteen to live out my childhood fantasy, but if it hadn't been for my good friend Hoover, I wouldn't have learned or experienced the ways of frontier life or being a cowboy. He took me under his wing and taught me the ropes." Charlie grinned at them. "Hey! That's funny. He did teach me how to rope." He chortled. "I did a little sheepherding myself for Pike Miller's sheep ranch near Judith Basin, but I didn't stick with it, and he was glad to see me go. But Hoover taught me a lot."

Andy, who was stirring up cornmeal batter, strolled back to where Charlie was adding the finishing touch to his sketch of Josh. "That name sounds familiar . . . Hoover." He walked behind Charlie and looked over his shoulder at the drawing. "Well, I'll be doggoned. That looks just like you, Josh." Andy just shook his head in awe. "I never knew an artist."

"I'm pleased you like it, Andy. Can't say I'm really making much money at it yet." Charlie dipped his brush into red pigment and mixed it with the black paint. "Hoover's a mountain man. He did a little gold mining too, but never struck it big. I lived with him at his cabin at Pig Eye Basin. His latchstring was always out. I think he really loved people, along with his habit of drinking. Hmm, I could use a drink myself."

"I don't drink." Josh cleared his throat. "So, you won't find one in my camp."

"No matter. I'm about done here. As I was saying, Hoover discovered sapphires near Utica, and I think he's formed a partnership to mine there with some investors."

"Wish I could find gold or somethin' somewhere," Andy said, pouring himself some coffee. "You staying for grub?"

"Is that an invite?"

Josh nodded, rising stiffly to peer at the picture Charlie had drawn. "Pretty good picture. Guess we owe you some beans and johnnycakes. You're welcome to stay."

"That's mighty kind of you, and I think I will." Charlie held out the picture toward Josh. "Here, you can have this."

"No thanks, Charlie. I have nowhere to put it right now. Keep it for your portfolio. Maybe you'll be famous someday." Josh lifted the lid on the pot of beans, and the savory smell wafted out into the chilly morning air. "The beans are close to being done. Andy, flip us some of your johnnycakes to go along with this."

Charlie stuffed the sketch and art supplies back in his canvas case. "Sounds good to me. Is there anything I can help with?"

"Nope," Andy said. "There's some oats over in that there barrel if you want to give your horse a nibble."

"Thanks. I'll do that."

Josh watched Charlie as he proceeded to pour oats in a bucket for his horse. He was an affable cowpoke, easy to talk to. Josh couldn't help but wonder what kind of skills he had as a cowboy but thought Charlie was at least a pretty decent artist.

The rest of the workday brought nothing unusual. Josh pulled a bleating lamb from a thicket, and it began frantically looking for its mother. Charlie tagged along. He talked the entire time, as if finding the whole realm of sheepherding interesting.

The sun was just beginning to slip behind the purple mountains of Tollgate Hill when Josh and Charlie tethered their horses. Josh removed Pete's saddle while Charlie gave the horses fresh water to drink.

"Mmm, I'm about to starve to death," Charlie said when they entered the campsite.

"Good thing, 'cause I'm just about to dish up the food." Andy flipped johnnycakes on the open fire with a flick of his wrist.

"Andy, you've turned out to be a good cook." Josh smiled at Andy. "I'm hungry myself. Hope there's some coffee to go with it."

"Matter of fact, I just made some fresh."

Josh looked at the young man bent over the fire. Andy made him smile inwardly with his eagerness to please. He was a runaway from a father who was meaner than a snake. Josh was glad he had hired him—Andy was worth his weight in gold. Josh had never had a younger brother, only his sister, April, and that was another thing altogether.

Later, Charlie wiped his mouth with the back of his hand. "Pardner, that was some fine eating I wasn't expecting out here tonight. Thank you, Andy."

"It's my secret ingredient."

"And what might that be?" Charlie laughed.

"If I told you, Charlie, it wouldn't be a secret anymore."

Josh chuckled at the two of them. It was getting dark now. He poked the fire, sending orange sparks upward and lighting the faces of Charlie and Andy. He suddenly remembered the blue stones tucked away in his vest pocket. He took another swig of his coffee, set his tin cup down, and pulled out the blue pebbles. As he held them in his palm near the firelight, they twinkled like distant stars.

Andy and Charlie stopped talking when they saw the pebbles in the firelight. Andy let out a soft whistle. "Hey, whatcha got there, Josh?"

"I'm not sure. Found these today in the creek bed when I stopped to let Pete drink. I just remembered." Josh was fascinated with the cornflower blue of the stones as his fingers pushed them around in his palm.

"If you find more, you may be able to build that home quicker than you think," Charlie said. "Remember my friend Hoover I told you about?" Josh nodded. "Well, these look like the blue stones he found last year at Yogo Creek. You ought to take those to Lewistown next time you're up that way and have 'em looked at. Could be you're holding your future in the palm of your hand, Josh."

Josh stared at the stones, then tucked them back into his inside vest pocket. He would definitely get them examined by an assayer. He would love to be able to build that house sooner rather than later.

When he'd left Colorado, he had not been on good terms with

his father. Jim McBride had told him that if he left the ranch, he would cut Josh out of the will. His father was a mighty powerful and wealthy cattleman. He used his influence to get what he wanted, when he wanted it. Besides, Josh had told his father he'd wanted to do something different and be responsible for his own welfare. Tempers flared and an argument ensued. Then, when the woman he was really interested in married another man, Josh decided it was time to leave instead of mooning over her and seeing her with someone else.

Crystal. He paused over the image in his mind. The pain was gone after three years, and he decided it must have been God's will for him. Another plan. Another life. Funny, when he thought about it. His sister, April, had been engaged to the man Crystal eventually married. What a strange turn of events.

He'd struggled in the last three years to make ends meet, and now he was beginning to reap the benefits. He wasn't wealthy like his father by any stretch of the imagination, but the way the price of wool was rising, he'd soon be able to show his father he could make it on his own.

Juliana Brady paused, pushing her thick, dark hair back from her face. She arched her back, stretched, and tried to rub out the stiffness. Bending over the miners' wash made her back hurt, but at least it was decent work for someone without any work experience, unlike the work of some of the "soiled doves" in town. Using a smooth limb from a ponderosa pine, she placed dingy clothes in the boiling kettle sitting atop the campfire. She moved the limb up and down and pressed the wad of clothing against the side of the huge black pot to loosen the dirt, then picked up a book of poems. She loved to read, and doing the wash was boring, so she tried to have a book of poems or good literature to keep her company.

There never seemed to be enough money, and it had been that way for as long as she could remember. She let her thoughts wander back to a few days ago. There had not been enough to pay for rent, let alone buy groceries, Mama had told her.

It pained Juliana to look into her mother's blue-gray eyes. She knew Mama was trying to keep her chin up, but declining health had plagued her recently, and Juliana had watched her mother's energy fall away the last few months.

It was hard keeping up with the miners' wash and the house-work. Juliana had insisted on doing it so her mother could rest. She admonished that hard work never hurt anybody. She had echoed that statement throughout the years, mainly toward her absent father, because he had chased the dream of striking it rich one day. Though Juliana loved her father, it broke her heart to see her mother struggle and carry the burden alone.

Maybe she would apply at the boardinghouse to see if there were any openings. She could read and write, but how could one use that skill? Around here, the only jobs she'd been able to find were cooking and cleaning.

She sighed, picked up the clothes by the end of the heavy, smooth stick, and lowered each piece into another kettle of clean water to rinse away the soap. Not many left, thankfully. After a few quick swishes, she wrung out all the water from each piece and placed them all in her laundry basket. By now her hands were numb from the cold water and the breeze that fluttered through the fir and pine trees. Juliana decided that if she was still doing this type of work in the summer, she would carry her laundry to the creek for rinsing.

When the miners' children were playing nearby in the woods, they would venture into the clearing around her wash fire as she sat on a stump reading. It wasn't long before she'd made friends with the curious children. Soon she wound up reading to them or telling them stories from the books she had read. Most of them had never attended school. When Juliana had lived in Kansas, she had attended school. After her father decided to go west searching for gold, her schooling stopped. Luckily, her mother had a good upbringing and education herself, and taught Juliana everything she could.

"Yoo-hoo, Juliana!" Her new friend Marion came springing into the clearing where Juliana worked on the laundry.

"Morning," Juliana called out. Marion was good-hearted, and Juliana was glad to have her friendship.

"Are you nearly through for the day, hon?"

"Soon as I hang out this basketful I will be. Good thing too. My back has had enough for one day."

"Great. How about going to lunch with me in town?"

"Oh, I couldn't, Marion." Juliana didn't want to spend her few precious coins on dinner in town.

"Nonsense, you'll be my guest. We'll go to the Stockton Hotel for lunch. I know the manager there." She giggled.

"But, I can't let you do that—"

"Sure you can. We'll get these hung in no time." Marion picked up the basket and walked toward the clothesline behind Juliana's cabin.

Juliana followed obediently, half-smiling. Her redheaded friend loved to be in control. Truth be known, she needed someone to make a few decisions for her right now.

Juliana's mouth watered at the thought of a good meal prepared by someone else for a change. She tried not to be envious of Marion's doting father, who just happened to be the manager and owner of the Stockton Hotel.

Marion prattled away as the two began hanging the clean laundry out in the bright sunshine. Her enthusiasm for life made her such a joy to be around. Bursting with energy, she was the apple of her father's eye, but she pretended not to notice, and it had little effect on her one way or another. She liked most people and seemed to feel it was her God-given authority to help others live out their potential.

Juliana wanted to be like her friend, who was always smiling. But she didn't have a whole lot to smile about. At least not right now. She couldn't remember the last time she felt happy.

After the last piece of clothing was hung, Juliana opened the cabin door, being careful not to open it wide enough for her friend to see inside the cabin. She was embarrassed at its bareness and didn't want Marion to feel sorry for her, or she might get it into her head to try to fix the problem herself.

She slipped in to tell her mother that she was going with Marion. Her mother stood washing dishes.

"I thought I told you to sit down and rest, Mama."

"Now, Juliana, you know I can't sit all day with you out there slaving over that hot kettle of wash. Besides, my joints feel better if I move around a bit."

"Mama, Marion wants to take me to lunch. Is that okay with you? I'm through with the wash and got it all hanging out."

"Baby, you don't need to be asking me. You're nearly eighteen. A grown woman. You go and enjoy a break—you deserve it." Juliana's mother dried her arthritic hands on the kitchen towel and reached over to touch her daughter's hair lovingly.

"Want me to bring something back for you?" She planned on returning with at least a roll from her lunch in her pocket.

"Don't worry about me. I'll have a cup of soup. Actually, that sounds tasty. Right tasty."

"Mama, you're too thin. Why don't you come with us? I don't think Marion would mind."

"Juliana, I couldn't impose. I'm fine." She shooed her daughter toward the door.

"I'll be back in time to get the clothes off the line." Juliana grabbed her cape off the peg by the door and skipped out the door and down the lane to where Marion stood waiting patiently. But she was feeling guilty for an afternoon off.

The walk to the center of Lewistown didn't take them long. Juliana noticed the usual flurry of activity in the small boomtown, which lent an air of friendliness to its huge flux of homesteaders coming west or those just passing through.

"I'm glad you came along, Juliana. We can talk girl talk and fill our appetites with some of Pierre's delicious cuisine."

"Thanks for asking me. I take it Pierre is a chef at the hotel?"

"Yes. Daddy found him down on his luck after coming west from France to seek his fortune. I'm sure when he has enough saved, he will open up his own little café. Just to warn you, he is quite the flirt." Marion giggled. "But pay him no mind. He talks to all the ladies in such a way that they nearly swoon."

"Interesting. I've never met a Frenchman before." Juliana held the hotel door open for her friend.

They were quickly greeted by Marion's father. "Marion, dear. I see you've brought your new friend." Marion's father was sharply dressed in a suit with his monocle hanging from his brocade vest. Juliana could detect a hint of aftershave as he reached out to grab her hand.

"Father, this is Juliana. Juliana, this is the world's greatest dad."

"Oh please, Marion, you're going to make me blush, to be sure." He twirled his mustache curl between his thick fingers, and his eyes twinkled.

"I'm very glad to meet you, Mr. Stockton." Juliana could tell by his manner that he was a sociable sort, and his stature was what

Juliana's mother would call "low chunky." The thought almost made her giggle. He would be easy to like.

"Come right this way, girls. I have the perfect table waiting just for the two of you near the window."

Following Mr. Stockton to their table, Juliana surveyed the rich furnishings of the restaurant with pleasure. Crisp white linen tablecloths with a rose in the center of each table lifted her spirits, along with the din of clinking glass, china, and conversation. She felt thoroughly out of place in her plain calico dress, but at least her brown woolen cape covered the upper part of her dress. Juliana felt the stares of the patrons but kept her chin up despite the butterflies in her stomach.

Beautiful artwork lined the walls above the tables, but one in particular caught Juliana's eye. Pausing to get a better look, she saw that it was a sketch of a man and his dog sitting in comfortable silence. The man had thick brown hair, but something in his amber eyes drew her closer. The irises were large, and she sensed a depth of softness in their expression. One hand lovingly rested on the shoulder of his dog. Somehow he reflected a man of character and one whose word would not be taken lightly.

"Ah, I see you like the newest piece I acquired." Mr. Stockton tucked his thumbs into his vest pockets.

"I do indeed, but I'm not quite sure why. Who is he?"

"I don't know him, but the man I bought this from said he was a sheepherder. The artist captured the very soul of the man through his eyes, don't you think? I feel very confident that this artist will someday be quite famous."

Juliana smiled at her friend's father. He apparently thought himself a connoisseur of fine art. "You may be right, Mr. Stockton."

Dragging her eyes from the picture, Juliana realized Marion was already seated by the window waiting for her, so she hurried to their table.

Mr. Stockton pulled out the chair for her and laid the linen napkin in her lap as if his daughter's friend were royalty. Juliana was very pleased he would show her such consideration, as though he were unaware that she was not accustomed to eating her meals out. But she was certain he knew otherwise.

"There you are. I thought I'd lost you, friend." Marion's silver-throated laugh filled the air.

"I was looking at the art your father has collected."

"Yes, well, he fancies himself a great art collector and then later sells some of the art to dealers or people looking to decorate their homes. But he starts with showing them right here in the restaurant." Marion opened her menu. "I'm starved. How about you? What are you in the mood for?"

"Mmm, just about anything." Juliana opened her menu, but in her mind, all she could see was the sheepherder's eyes.

They had scarcely finished their lunch when Marion's father hurried to their table with the town doctor, startling the two young women from their enjoyable conversation.

"Juliana, I'm sorry to interrupt, but the doc here says you need to come quickly. It's your mother."

Juliana stood, her napkin dropping to the floor. "What is it? What's wrong with my mother?" Her eyes sought the doctor's face.

"I'm Dr. Mark Barnum. Please, if you would, come quickly." The young doctor reached for her hand, guiding her through the dining tables.

"I'm coming too," Marion said, and fell into step with them as they made their way down the boardwalk.

Juliana's heart thumped in her chest. *I shouldn't have left her. I knew she wasn't well. Please, Lord, let her be okay.*

The doctor led Juliana and Marion to a small room at the back of his office, where Juliana's mother lay on a narrow cot. A thin blanket covered her slight form, and her gray-streaked brown hair spilled about her shoulders. She looked so frail that Juliana gasped. She reached out to pick up her mother's hand, but the doctor intervened, pulling her a step back.

In a hushed tone, he bid her to take a seat. Marion stood next to her. "Doctor, what is wrong with Juliana's mother? Is she conscious?"

The young man ignored Marion and looked right at Juliana. "I'm afraid your mother has suffered a heart attack. I want to be frank with you—I'm not sure she's going to make it. She's very weak and has been asking for you."

Juliana's eyes filled with tears, and she found herself staring at the top button on the doctor's coat. "How did she get here? She was at home when I left for lunch." This was all too incredible for her to take in. "Can I talk to her?" Juliana's voice trembled.

"A gentleman brought her into town to my office. He said he found her lying in the middle of the road on his way into town. When she wakes up again, you may have a moment with her."

He gave her a look with such tenderness that Juliana felt like crying. *He's trying to tell me she's dying.* Juliana could feel the warmth of Marion's hand stroking her shoulder through the thin material of her dress.

"I'll leave you alone with her," Marion said.

"Marion, please don't leave."

"Sugar, I'll be right outside the door if you need me. I wouldn't think of leaving."

Dr. Barnum took Marion's elbow, and they stepped back into his office, closing the door softly.

Juliana sat at her mother's side until the late afternoon shadows fell through the only window in the room. *Lord, please bring her through this. Touch her heart and make her well, if it is Your will,* she prayed.

Her mother stirred and mumbled something. Instantly Juliana leaned over close to her mother's pale face. Her voice was low, and Juliana didn't want to miss a word she said.

"Juliana, you're here."

"Yes, Mama."

"My sweet Juliana. You have your daddy's eyes." Her mother tried to reach up and touch her face, but Juliana caught her hand and pressed it to her lips.

"Shh . . . you don't have to talk, Mama. Just get some rest." Burning tears stung her eyes, and she fought the panic rising in her chest. How odd—her mother's normally blue eyes had changed to steel gray. Juliana heard her heart pounding in her ears.

"Just don't be dependent on any man. Find your own way in this world . . . not enough time to tell you how much I love you . . ."

"Mama, don't talk like that. The doctor is doing everything he can—"

"He loved you." Her breathing was shallow.

Juliana's hand shook as she lovingly pushed a strand of her mother's hair back from her forehead. "Shh . . . don't talk about Daddy right now. Save your strength."

"Don't be mad . . . he wanted the gold for you."

Juliana clenched her teeth. *Sure he did. That's why he never came back.* The gold fields obviously held more allure for her father than any real life with his wife and child. She thought again that her mother was so in love with her father that she always overlooked most of his faults, even now, when she was so ill.

"He'll . . . come . . . back," her mother whispered.

Juliana said nothing but continued to hold her mother's hand. The clock on the wall opposite her seemed to tick methodically like her slow heartbeats. She thought her mother was in a deep sleep when she suddenly stirred on her pillow.

"Don't stay in the cabin after I'm gone. It's too far from town for a young girl alone . . . It's time for me to go. The angels are coming for me now . . ."

Juliana thought her heart would break. "Mama . . . no . . . please don't leave me," she pleaded. Blinding tears covered her face.

"I . . . love . . . you." Her mother took one last deep breath and was silent.

Juliana flung herself across her mother's chest and sobbed. She couldn't bear the pain that tore through her heart. *Why, God? Why did You have to take her? I never really had a father, and now You've taken my mother.* In her anger, she pounded the edge of the mattress near her mother's still arm, then dissolved once more into hoarse tears.

The gulf between her and her mother seemed to be growing by the second, and she thought wildly of an escaping balloon she'd seen once in town. How she had longed to follow it on its ascent, but it was gone in moments. *Just like Mama*, she thought, and the enormity of her loneliness felt like stones on her shoulders.

After what seemed a long time, Juliana heard the door open behind her. She lifted her head from her mother's side, tears still streaming down her face, and saw Marion with the doctor. Marion reached out her hands and pulled Juliana into her arms.

"I'm so sorry, friend. Sooo sorry." Marion stroked her hair. "I'll help you take care of everything. Don't you worry."

When Juliana pulled away from Marion and lifted her eyes, she saw a stranger silhouetted in the doorway behind the doctor. His shadow fell across her face. She hadn't noticed him enter the room.

He lifted his hat. "Miss, I'm really sorry about your mother." He had a week's worth of beard on his face and dark, sun-streaked hair. He wasn't a large man, but somehow his presence filled the room the moment she heard him speak. His voice, a rich baritone, smooth as glass, resonated from deep within his thick chest.

"Juliana, this is Josh McBride, a sheepherder who works in the area. He's the one who brought your mother in," the doctor said in quiet tones. The man wasn't much taller than she, but broad across the chest, which hinted at muscles underneath the plaid chambray shirt and tan leather vest.

Juliana murmured her thanks, though it was barely audible. *Hazel eyes with a fleck of amber . . . Now where have I seen those before?* His look conveyed that he understood her sorrow, and his kind eyes matched his gentle voice.

"I am very sorry, Miss . . ."

"Juliana Brady," Marion answered for her. "And I'm Marion Stockton."

"If there's anything I can do . . ." He backed away toward the door, twisting his hat in his deeply tanned hands.

Juliana noticed that his hands were not large but were capable. Safe. Startled by her thoughts, she turned back to Marion. "What am I to do?"

Josh watched, feeling helpless as the sobs shook the girl's slight frame. She wore a faded blue housedress, the hem sagging near the back. The sharp curve of her shoulders blades poked out when she leaned over to hold her face in her red, chapped hands. When she finally lifted her head, the square angle of her jaw seemed in sharp contrast to the woman he had just seen crying. *I'll bet underneath that exterior, she's a fighter.* Something in the way she held herself, chin up, and her direct eye contact when they were introduced made him take notice. Her eyes were an odd blue with huge irises, and he could see himself reflected in them.

Dr. Barnum motioned to Josh and led him to the front door. They stepped out into the gathering dusk. Both men were quiet for a moment.

Gathering his thoughts, Josh thrust some bills into the doc's hands. "Here, take this and see that the gal's mother gets a decent burial. I'm just in town for a few days, so I don't usually carry much cash."

"I'm sure that will be a big help. From the looks of her, it doesn't look like she's had too many square meals."

"Do you know her?" Josh conjured up the vision of the dark-haired girl. She was tall and slender, but not delicate. She had the most gorgeous eyes and high cheekbones.

"Not really. I heard she lived with her mother in a cabin on the edge of town. She takes in miners' wash. Someone said her father, Davin, left for the gold mines in Colorado years ago and never returned."

"Well, guess I'd better mosey on and take care of my horse for the night. I appreciate you doing what you could for her mother.

If there's anything left over from the burial in what I gave you, just give it to the young lady. Maybe it'll help."

The two men shook hands and parted. Josh wondered if he'd see the young woman again. He knew he wanted to. But the question was, why? Was it her penetrating eyes that made contact with his soul? Come to think of it, they were the exact color of the cornflower blue stones that he'd fished out of the creek and now lay nestled in his vest pocket.

4

Grieving her mother, Juliana lay underneath a heavy quilt, her eyes tracing the wallpaper. The fancy print seemed elaborate after the simplicity of her cabin. She couldn't be more grateful to Marion and her father for giving her a place to stay.

Sleep would not come as she went over the funeral again and again. After the last shovelful of dirt had fallen upon the pine box, Marion had escorted Juliana out of the little cemetery back to the waiting carriage. The wind rattled the carriage awning and blew slanted sheets of cold rain against them.

Juliana felt that the tears coursing down her cheeks were the size of raindrops. It had been a sad and pitiful little ceremony paid for by a stranger, with few in attendance. She made a mental note to discover the benefactor the first chance she had.

She twisted the wet handkerchief in her fingers nervously. What would happen to her now? She had no family and didn't know how to reach her father, even if he was indeed alive. The Stocktons had told her she could stay with them indefinitely. But Juliana knew this arrangement couldn't last forever. Being too proud to take charity for long, she would earn her own way.

The cabin was little more than a shack, but she could continue doing the miners' wash. Then she would have to decide what to do.

Juliana turned on her side, pulling the pillow to her face to muffle her sobs.

Thank God for people like Marion and her family.

Morning's first light awakened Juliana, and she scrambled out of bed and poured water from the pitcher into the bowl on the nightstand to wash her face. Hastily she combed and pinned her hair into a tight chignon, then donned her brown gingham dress and white apron. She didn't want to appear to be lazy or to be taking advantage of her friend's hospitality.

She needn't have worried. A light rapping at the door sounded, and Juliana called out, "Come in." A young servant girl entered with a tray laden with a silver coffeepot, toast, and a pot of jam. She deposited the tray on the nightstand. Right behind her was Marion, sleepy-eyed and still in her robe and slippers. The maid curtsied and left.

"My goodness! You're up and about early," Marion said. "I wanted to bring you something in case you didn't feel like coming downstairs, but it appears you're way ahead of me."

"I'm used to it. Besides, I couldn't sleep."

"I'm sorry. I truly am. Maybe tonight will be better."

"I plan on going back to the cabin and pack up what little I have for now, since I promised Mama I wouldn't stay there. Then I'll try to continue with the miners' wash." Juliana looked down at her rough and dry hands with disdain.

Marion shook her head. "I'll help you pack up. I'll get some salve for your hands too."

"No, I really would rather do it myself, Marion. Honestly."

"All right then. Have it your way. But you needn't take in any more miners' wash. My father said you're welcome to stay right here until you know what you want to do. He meant that."

"I can't thank your father enough. But I must pay for my room and board somehow."

"But not now. We'll think of something suitable for you to do when we put our heads together. Try not to concern yourself with that right now. You've just buried your mother. You need some time." Marion poured hot coffee into a teacup and handed it to her friend.

"I'll try." Juliana watched Marion lift the lid off the silver dome, then smear jam across the thick toast. She handed it to Juliana, who wasn't sure she could swallow anything.

"Go ahead. Try to eat or you'll faint from sheer hunger. I noticed you didn't eat a thing the last couple of days."

The rumbling in Juliana's stomach surprised her, and though her throat felt constricted, she took a small bite.

Marion clasped her hands. "Wonderful. Now I'll leave you alone. I must get dressed myself. Let me know when you're ready to come downstairs. I'll get Louie to drive you to the cabin for your things." She patted Juliana's arm.

Before she could pull her hand away, Juliana stopped her. "Thank you so much for being such a wonderful friend to me. If there's ever anything, anything at all I can do for you, just ask."

Marion's eyes filled with tears, and Juliana was touched. "Bless your heart. I can understand your grief." She held Juliana's hands in her own. "I'd better get dressed. Go ahead and try to eat a little, okay?"

"I will. I promise."

The sign in the window of the town's local newspaper, *The Lewistown Gazette*, read, "Help Wanted, Inquire Within." Juliana stopped suddenly. She looked up and down the street, trying to decide if she should go in and ask about the job.

She had already returned her cabin key to the owner, and unless she wanted to be beholden to the Stocktons for free room and board, she knew she really had no other choice than to take a chance on the job. When she'd stopped by to thank the doctor for his care of her mother, Dr. Barnum had let it slip that the sheepherder had been responsible for taking care of her mother's funeral expenses. That meant one more person that she owed money to.

Her shoulders sagged. This job would be a sign from God, her mother would say. After all, she had been praying that something would come her way soon. Taking a deep breath, she pulled her shoulders back and adjusted her bonnet, then opened the door. The tinkling sound of a bell above the door alerted the shop's owner that someone had come in.

"May I help you?" A tall, rawboned man rose from his desk, pushing his spectacles up onto his thin nose. His shirt sleeves were rolled back, an apron was tied around his skinny frame, and his fingers were ink stained.

Juliana swallowed hard. Her mouth felt as dry as a summer day. "Uh, I . . . saw the sign in your window that you need help, and I am in need of a job."

"Well, I hardly expected a young girl for the job. Can you read and write?"

"Yes. I can do both, if that is what the job requires." Juliana held her breath, waiting for his response. He appeared to be in his late thirties and had kind blue eyes underneath his bushy eyebrows.

"Have a seat, young lady. I'm Albert Spencer. And you are . . . ?"

"Juliana Brady." Taking a seat near his desk, she sat straight and proper, remembering her mother's instructions on how to behave like a lady.

"What I'm looking for is someone to help with the newspaper. Your duties will be general chores such as organizing and filing my paperwork, ordering ink and supplies, and tidying the office. Can you do that?"

Juliana's heart hammered in her chest. "I think I could."

"What experience do you have?"

"To be honest, none at all, but I'm a quick learner, and I would work hard. Mr. Spencer, I'm in desperate need of a job."

In the distance, she heard the sound of voices coming from the street and the clip-clop of horses. This all seemed so unreal to her. Just a few days ago she would have been helping her mother with chores and peeling potatoes or perhaps chatting while they had an afternoon cup of coffee. And now here she was talking to a perfect stranger about a job, feeling totally insecure.

"To be quite frank with you, Miss Brady, I wasn't looking for a female. Tell me why I should give you a chance." He shuffled his papers into a pile on his desk without taking his eyes off her.

"Let's see . . . I've met a lot of the people here. I've been taking in miners' wash for a while, and I've gotten to know a lot of people

and hear a lot of stories. At the moment, I live right down the street at the Stockton Hotel and could be here quickly. I believe Mr. Stockton and his daughter, Marion, could vouch for me."
Please, Lord, let him say yes.

"Well . . ." Juliana saw a spark of interest in Mr. Spencer's face at the mention of the Stocktons. They were highly respected in the community. He reached for a thick book from the bookshelf behind him, opened it, and placed it on the desk before her. "Let me hear you read. Start here." He pointed to a passage of a poem.

Juliana started reading:

> I heard a thousand blended notes
> While in a grove I sate reclined,
> In that sweet mood when pleasant thoughts
> Bring sad thoughts to the mind.

Wonderful! Juliana had read this passage to her mother many times on cold winter nights. Wordsworth was a favorite poet. She continued:

> To her fair works did Nature link
> The human soul that through me ran;
> And much it grieved my heart to think
> What man has made of man.

"Perfect! Perfect indeed. I'm impressed with your reading skills, Miss Brady."

"Thank you, Mr. Spencer." His praise sent her heart soaring with hope.

"However, I'd like to have you write a couple of brief paragraphs of life in Lewistown after you proof this article that I wrote earlier," he said, leaning forward to hand her a handwritten paper. "Make yourself comfortable at the desk over there." He gestured near the front window. "There's pen and ink and paper there. Just take your time."

Juliana nodded, then stood on shaky legs, walked woodenly to the desk, and took a seat. It didn't take long to read over Mr. Spencer's article, and she found only one misplaced word. She marked it, then laid the article aside and pulled out a fresh piece of paper. What should she write about?

An idea came to her, and she jotted down her thoughts about the town, its shops, and the surrounding area, and ended it by describing in rich detail the Stockton hotel and its artwork. Once she looked it over, she walked to Mr. Spencer's desk and stood quietly, waiting for him to recognize that she was finished.

Mr. Spencer set his accounting book aside and took the paperwork from her. "Please, Miss Brady, have a seat," he said, smiling at her.

Juliana sat with her hands folded in her lap, her heart pounding hard in her chest. She hoped she looked calm and collected. She watched Mr. Spencer briefly look at her notes on his work and then turn his attention to her article. A big smile spread across his face, and he made a sound that sounded like a laugh as he continued to read.

He set the paper down, folded his fingers together, and rested his chin on them. He was quiet for a moment. "Miss Brady, I don't know when I've read a more vivid description of our town. It's simply delightful!"

Juliana tried to hide her surprise. "I'm not sure what to say, other than thank you."

"Just say that you'll come back in the morning at eight o'clock sharp. We'll see how you work out, but I won't make any long-term promises. You were not what I had in mind. Not at all. Still . . . I do believe in giving women a chance to do some things a man can do. That doesn't always make me popular with everyone. But then, surprises are best in this particular business," he said, smiling.

"I appreciate your forward thinking and would be grateful to prove to you that I am worthy of doing the job. Supporting myself is more important than finding a husband at the present time." She was so relieved he had agreed to give her a try that her shoulders relaxed, relieving the tension between her shoulder blades.

"I pay three dollars a week, with working hours from eight to five. Saturday and Sunday you will have off. Does that sound fair?"

Juliana couldn't believe she'd heard right. *Did he say three dollars a week?* That was twice as much as her mother received from doing laundry. Trying not to appear astonished, she willed herself to keep a straight face with her hands clasped tightly in her lap. "Yes, sir. Thank you, Mr. Spencer. That will suffice nicely."

"Good!" Mr. Spencer rose from his chair and extended his hand, and she held hers out for a firm handshake. "You're hired."

He escorted her to the door. Juliana could hardly wait to skip down the street to the hotel to tell Marion. This was too good to be true. No more sticking her hands in hot suds and scrubbing miners' uniforms. Maybe her hands would start to heal. She wished she could tell her mother, but somehow Juliana thought she knew.

5

A long soak in the tub made Josh feel human again. Dressed in faded Levis and a flannel shirt, he yanked his boots on, then slipped on his soft leather vest. He felt refreshed, though he hadn't slept much during the night, because the image of the young dark-haired girl had continually floated before him. *Wonder what she'll do?* He felt sudden sadness for her loss, and his reaction to it surprised him all the more. Why should he be concerned about someone he'd met only briefly? It made no sense.

Having enjoyed a hearty breakfast, he made his way down the busy streets of Lewistown. He passed the office of the *Lewistown Gazette* and made a mental note to himself to buy a newspaper to take with him before he left. Being out at the camp, he missed keeping up with current events. What he was looking for was an assayer. He wanted a professional to examine the blue stones. He wasn't sure they had much value, but according to Charlie back at the campsite, they were worth something.

Lost in thought, Josh collided with two young ladies coming down the sidewalk, knocking their parcels out of their arms. Quickly he reached down to retrieve the packages, muttering under his breath. Straightening, he recognized the girl he'd been thinking of so much lately. He realized he was only a few inches taller than she as his eyes met hers.

He stood awkwardly, holding the packages in his hands. "I beg your pardon." He nodded to her and her friend. "I guess my mind was somewhere else." Josh smiled at Juliana, whose full lips curved ever so slightly upward. When he realized he was staring, he dragged his eyes from her to smile at Marion.

"We meet again, Mr. McBride," Marion said. "Are you staying in town?"

"I am indeed. At the Stockton Hotel. Nice accommodations."

Marion's eyes were warm. Noticing how Marion linked an arm protectively around Juliana, Josh knew her friendship would be good for Juliana. He sensed it was her grief that held her back when he looked into her vacant eyes. He extended the small parcels to Juliana and felt a warm tingle pass through him as their hands touched for a moment.

"I'll tell the owner you're pleased." Marion flashed him a flirtatious smile.

"Oh, do you know him?"

"He's my father." She laughed. "We live at the hotel on the third floor."

Juliana shifted her packages to her other arm. "We should be going, but thanks again for what you did for my mother, Mr. McBride."

"I'm sorry she didn't recover, that's all." He couldn't take his eyes off her blue ones, which were framed with long, sweeping lashes. "I'd be happy to carry those back to the hotel for you, if you'd like."

"Thanks, but I can manage." Her voice was polite.

Josh tipped his hat good-bye. "Perhaps I'll see both of you later."

The two watched as he went up the sidewalk. Marion was the first to break the silence. "He's got his eye on you, Juliana."

"Hardly. He was just being polite." Juliana's eyes followed Josh until he faded into the crowd past the general store. There was something about him that held an odd attraction for her. Was it his thick, muscular physique? Though taller by only a couple of inches with longish hair, he certainly conveyed a commanding presence, and when he spoke, the rich sound of his voice intrigued her. The lingering smell of sheep had been replaced with the scent of spiced men's soap.

"I don't think so. He couldn't take his eyes off you, Juliana. We need to find out more about him." Marion stood staring after him with a strange look on her face.

"I'm not interested in the least." Was she protesting too much? "Besides, I have a new job that will require most of my attention. Now let's quit lollygagging and finish up our errands. I want to press my new gingham dress before work tomorrow." She pulled Marion by the arm, wondering about the rugged sheepherder in the back of her mind.

"If you insist." Marion fell into step with her friend.

Lewistown was burgeoning with activity, with mountain men, miners, and farmers pursuing the adventure nestled in the foothills of the jagged mountains. It was unlike the cow town of Utica near Josh's land, which was not more than a couple of buildings, and certainly not where one could stock up on supplies.

It was a cold day with low-hanging clouds clinging to the purple peaks. Josh was used to the unsettled weather, and he knew he'd left his flock in good hands, so he wasn't worried. He might hang around a few days before heading back to camp.

Up ahead, in the slight wind that threatened rain, he saw a sign swinging. Lewistown Assessor. Funny, it was the only one within a hundred miles. He strode into the store and greeted the shopkeeper, who had a balding head and slight paunch. The storekeeper moved stiffly from his chair, laying aside his jeweler's piece.

"What can I do for you today?" he asked, peering through his wire-rimmed spectacles.

"My name's Josh McBride." He smiled, extending his hand to the shopkeeper.

"Glad to meet you. I'm Will Smith. How can I be of help?"

Josh reached inside his vest for the small leather pouch. "I wonder if you'd have a look at these and tell me what you think."

The shopkeeper opened the bag, spilling its contents across the counter. He quietly examined the few stones with his eyepiece. "Some nice stones you have here."

"What are they?"

He looked back up at Josh, smiling. "They're sapphires. Not just Montana sapphires, but Yogos. Notice the color and clarity."

"I moved here from Colorado, so I'm not sure what Yogo means."

"Some say it's Indian for 'blue sky.' Where did you find these?"

"Out where I herd my sheep near Utica, where the Judith River dumps into a smaller stream." Josh was starting to feel excited by his find. He could tell Will was definitely interested in the small blue stones.

"Well, Jake Hoover discovered these particular sapphires last year near Yogo Creek. I recollect that he owns a Yogo mine and sent his sapphires off to New York to be examined by an assayer from Tiffany's. Man by the name of George Kunz. He thinks they'll become valuable because of their distinctive color and quality that's not found in other sapphires. Once the assayers cut them, they found out the stones didn't have the normal inclusions and flaws." Will examined the stones again with his eyepiece. "That makes them different from the regular Montana sapphires. Their color, while brilliant in sunlight, is not diminished by artificial light." He paused for a moment. "I'm not sure Hoover still owns the mine. He wasn't making any money and didn't consider it a sound investment."

"I see." Josh felt his excitement quell with Will's comment. "I'd like to contact him. Maybe I can find out if he's looking to add another mine. Since my land is situated between his and the Judith River, it'd interfere with his access and his ability to haul water to the bench lands for mine-site washing and tailing disposal. He might be interested to find out I discovered Yogos on my property. Do you know where I can find him?"

"I can give you the name of his partner, and you can contact him." Will scrawled a name and address on a piece of paper, then handed it to Josh. After placing the stones back into the leather pouch, Josh tucked the folded piece of paper into his pocket along with the pouch.

"I'd like to stake a claim on my property where I found these."

Will pushed a paper form toward him on the counter. "Just complete this form and sign it, and I'll file it for you."

Josh filled out the form, signed it, and dated it. "Thanks for the information, Will," he said, shaking his hand.

"Come back again. I'll look forward to doing business with you for the Yogos, whenever you're ready."

Josh stepped back outside and whistled as he headed down the street. He'd have to think about mining Yogos. He hadn't come here to do that. But it could be a possibility. Maybe he could become rich and show his father a thing or two. Then he'd have money to give Juliana anything her heart desired . . . Now what made him think of that? He barely knew Juliana. But he wanted to know her better.

Cold pellets of a passing rain cloud stung his face, and he lowered his head, thankful for his hat. He needed to pick up a few supplies, but he'd do that tomorrow. Right now he was going to shop for a new shirt and a pair of britches. If he ran into Juliana again, he didn't want her to see him in worn Levis and a frayed shirt. A haircut wouldn't hurt him either.

6

The cold, hard emptiness of the hotel room hit Juliana as she entered. She had slipped away from dinner early and knew Marion had watched her with concern. She ironed her new work dress, clean stockings, and underwear before getting ready for bed.

Juliana looked down at her hands, which were dry and scratchy from doing miners' wash. The delicate undergarments had caught on the rough skin of her fingers. Thoughts of an indoor job away from the cold and wind provided a glimmer of hope for the future. She had never had it easy, and neither had her dear mother, God rest her soul. All they ever knew was working long hours—six days a week to pay the rent—and the little that was left over was used for purchasing meager food staples.

Juliana wondered where her father was, why he'd never sent for them, and why he'd sent them money in his letters only in the first months after he'd left. Had he forgotten them altogether? She had been only ten years old when he left, but she still remembered her mother clinging to him with such fierceness that he literally took both her arms and pried her off him. Words of promises—promises that her father would return—never kept.

A soft knocking at her bedroom door brought Juliana back to the present. Sighing, she opened the door to see Marion's face etched in the glow of the moonlight.

"I see you're all ready for bed. Are you all right?"

"I'm just getting my things ready for tomorrow." Juliana invited her in, and the bed squeaked as they both sat on its edge. "I want to make a good impression."

"And you will. Otherwise he wouldn't have hired you in the first place."

"Just think, Marion, I'll have a decent wage. I'll be able to pay for my room and board in just a few weeks, hopefully." Juliana was excited and nervous all at the same time, and giggled. What if she wasn't able to do the work expected of her?

"It's nice to hear you laugh again, friend. We're not worried about your paying your way just yet. Besides, the hotel isn't full, and we don't have need of this room."

"I don't know how I'll ever be able to thank all of you enough. I'm glad I'm not alone in that rented cabin at the edge of town." Juliana's voice quivered.

"I know this is hard for you to be without any family, but you have us, and we will see you through, with God's help. I promise."

At the mention of God, Juliana frowned. Where was He when her mother became ill? Taking a deep breath and exhaling to calm herself, she admitted her fear to Marion. "What if I fail?"

"Juliana, I believe in you. Besides, you read very well, and you're eager to learn. That's half the battle right there." Marion patted her hand. "I'm going to let you get to bed now. I just wanted to wish you good luck and tell you not to worry. There's someone who cares for you more than I."

Then where was He when my mama lay dying on the edge of the road? Juliana wanted to shout. Instead, she said, "That's easy for you to say, Marion. At least you still have your father."

I can do it, I can do it, I can do it. Juliana's heels beat out the cadence in her head as she marched down the busy sidewalk for her first day at the newspaper. Peering from under the brim of her bonnet, she looked this way and that before crossing the street. Men lounged against hitching posts dressed in cowboy garb, procrastinating the day's work, but to her, the day was a new, fresh start.

Her heart thumped in her chest with anticipation. *Just think. I have a job with a newspaper! Mama would be so proud . . . Well, hold on, I haven't even started. I might not be able to handle it.* She paused in front of the general store, glancing at her reflection in the storefront glass and adjusting the ribbons of her bonnet under her chin. The new dress with its row of tiny tucks at the bodice flattered her figure, and she felt quite professional. The last bit of the money after funeral expenses had gone to purchase the dress. Once she received a wage, it would be cheaper for her to buy material and make a couple of skirts and blouses. The clothes she used to wear for doing laundry had long since faded and were threadbare.

Thinking of her clothes made her think of Marion's finery. What in the world did Marion see in her? Marion had many other friends in her social circle who had money and standing in the community. Juliana felt a familiar pang. In every camp she and her mother had worked in, she had seen the stares from the womenfolk who thought they were above her.

The tinkling of a bell above the door sounded as Juliana entered the newspaper office. Mr. Spencer rose from an ink-stained work counter and removed his spectacles.

"Good morning. My, but you are punctual. I like that."

"Good morning, Mr. Spencer." Juliana stood before him, suddenly feeling helpless. Where had her confidence flown?

"Juliana, I want you to call me Albert. I don't stand on formality around here. Besides, that makes me feel sooo old." He quickly added, "And I am, but don't tell anybody."

She liked his sense of humor. That could make working fun— and anything was better than what she was used to doing. "All right, Albert it is."

Albert walked over to a small desk cluttered with paper and books, and Juliana followed. "First we need to clean a space on this desk for you to work. I've sharpened some pencils." He motioned to the tin can holding them. "And here's a tablet and Noah Webster's dictionary. Any other reference material you need, just ask me."

Juliana pulled out the chair and took a seat, untying her bonnet and laying it aside on the desk that was old and scarred, but a desk nonetheless. She had always wanted one, but of course that was a luxury she could never dream of. "What exactly would you like me to do, Albert?"

"First thing I'd like is for you to proofread an article I've just finished about the town council meeting last night. I'll be setting the printing press for tomorrow's paper that I will put together tonight. But with you helping to proof what has already been written, it'll save me a lot of time. Then I'd like you to tackle that stack of papers on my desk and alphabetize them according to the title."

He handed her a sheaf of papers to read just as the tinkling of the bell above the door sounded again, and a tall cowboy entered, spurs jingling against his boot heels. Over his long legs he wore leather chaps. Juliana noticed the gun strapped to his hip. He smelled of outdoors, leather, and stale tobacco. His light brown hair was long under his Stetson hat.

"Wes, what can I do for you so early this morning?" There was no trace of the friendliness in Albert's face that she'd seen earlier.

"Well now. What do we have here?" Without waiting for an answer, the man said, "And where have you been all my life, beautiful?"

Juliana felt her face flush, and she stayed seated at her desk.

"Cut it out, Wes. This is a lady, in case you missed that little detail," Albert said.

"A lady? Someone told me she's a washer woman who washes men's drawers," Wes said. His long mustache curled up into a big S on either side of his mouth. Juliana didn't like the glint in his hazel eyes or the way he referred to her previous job.

"This is Juliana, my new assistant. Now state your business."

"Boy howdy! Assistant? Well, you sure can assist me. I'm Wes Owen." He bent downward, extending his hand toward Juliana. "Glad to meet such a gorgeous woman today."

Juliana squirmed in her chair. She did not shake his hand and spoke in a businesslike manner. "What can we do for you?" she asked, not knowing how to respond to his overt flirtations.

Wes pulled his hand back with a frown. "I want to run an ad in the paper for horse wranglers. I know a lot of the miners do a bit of both around these parts."

"Juliana, will you write up his ad? I'll see to it that it gets in the paper tomorrow." Albert nodded at Wes, leaving Juliana to take care of the matter.

Juliana swallowed hard, opened her tablet, and took a pencil from the tin can. "Tell me exactly how you would like the ad to read."

"Now, hold on a minute. We need to get acquainted, don't you think? Are you from these parts? I don't recall ever seeing you."

She swallowed hard and said, "I lived here awhile . . ."

"Well, your mama must have kept you under lock and key, or I would've come calling."

"Is that so?" Her heart lurched at the mention of her mama. "Now, tell me what kind of pay and experience you want placed in the ad," she said briskly, hoping he would drop the subject.

"Not so quick, missy. How about I drop by and take you to dinner at the hotel tonight? They have good food, and I'm not such bad company."

"Thank you, but no." She stared at the paper and started coming up with the verbiage for the ad. She could feel his eyes boring down on her. "Why don't you take a seat, and I'll write this up."

"Okay, have it your way." Reluctantly, he pulled up a chair and gave her the particulars for the ad. "You have beautiful handwriting, Juliana."

"Thank you. I'll read it back to you now." When she was through, she noticed Albert out of the corner of her eye appraising the situation but continuing to work. "How much do we charge for that, Albert?"

"Two bits for the week. Then if you need to run it again, you'll have to stop by and let me know."

Wes agreed on her short write-up and flipped two bits down onto the desk, all the while never taking his eyes off Juliana. He strode toward the door, opened it, and did a half turn. "I'm not giving up on that date, you know. I'll be back, rest assured." He tipped his hat without even looking at Albert.

"Good day, Mr. Owen," she replied. Relieved that he was finally gone, Juliana carried the write-up to her boss for inspection.

"Never did care for him much. Not exactly sure why," Albert said, taking the paper from her.

"He certainly is forward, and he made me feel a bit uncomfortable."

"I was watching and listening. You handled yourself very well, very businesslike. I think we will get along just fine." He read over the write-up. "I approve. You have a natural writing style."

His words warmed her heart. The rest of the morning flew by with few interruptions. Earl, the general store owner, wanted to run an ad of the newest sewing machine available, and a young boy of about twelve dropped by to see Albert about delivering papers.

Juliana left them alone to talk and went about tidying up the desk and surrounding area. Staying busy was best for her. It took her mind off her troubles and the future.

When Marion came by at noon, Juliana was surprised at how quickly the time had passed.

"I brought you some fried chicken and fruit because I know you wouldn't stop to eat otherwise." Marion opened the basket and started laying out lunch. "Mr. Spencer, I've enough for both of you."

"Thanks, Marion, but I promised my wife I would be home

for lunch." Albert paused. "I didn't know you and Juliana were friends."

Marion glanced at Juliana. "Yes, good friends. You'll find Juliana is a hard worker," she said while she spread a napkin across Juliana's desk.

Juliana felt pleased her friend would endorse her.

"I'll take your word on that, Marion." He winked, then lifted his coat off the peg by the front door. "You ladies have a nice lunch." He went out the door and disappeared down the sidewalk.

Marion couldn't wait to find out about Juliana's first day. "How'd it go?"

Flashing her friend a big smile, Juliana answered, "Wonderful, really." She decided it was best not to mention her encounter with Wes.

After work, Juliana walked outside and tied her bonnet while Albert locked the door behind them. When she turned around, she saw Wes watching them, but she looked away and fell into step with Albert down the boardwalk. Out of the corner of her eye, she saw Wes untie his horse from the hitching post and lift his hat in greeting. She didn't want to encourage him with even so much as a look, but she could feel his eyes on her.

7

Josh glanced around the dining room after being seated, unconsciously looking for the dark-haired young girl with the big
blue eyes. She had told him she was staying at the hotel since
her mother died, hadn't she? He unfolded his napkin and placed
it in his lap, thinking it would be nice to have dinner with her.
He should have already headed back to camp to check on Andy,
but he halfheartedly hoped he could connect with the girl. She
made him feel something he hadn't felt in a very long time. The
deep sadness in her large eyes conveyed a longing he felt an
urge to respond to. He figured she was quite a bit younger than
him, unless he missed his guess. What would she possibly see
in a short, stocky sheepherder and a man several years older in
the first place?

He did get his hair trimmed, but not as short as he kept it while
on his father's ranch. His hands were a lot rougher now from hours
spent building his cabin, shearing sheep, and mending fences. He'd
never worked so hard in his life before he moved to Montana.

On his father's big ranch, most of the really hard labor was
carried out by hired hands. But doing most of his own work gave

Josh a feeling of accomplishment and worth. He couldn't afford any hired help other than Andy.

A waiter came and took his order, promising to bring him a fresh cup of coffee, and Josh settled back in his chair, keeping an eye on the front door for Juliana. He was halfway through his meal of steak and potatoes when he looked up and saw her making her way down the stairs into the foyer, looking so young and innocent. He put his fork down, pushed his chair back, and hurried into the foyer. She was heading toward the front desk away from him, and he watched her from the back, admiring the gliding way she moved. She was light on her feet, and her skirts created a gentle whisper from the swaying of her hips. Her thick hair fell in lush, dark curls down her shoulders.

"Juliana," Josh called out.

Juliana paused, turning halfway. "Hello, Mr. McBride. It's good to see you again."

"Please, could you call me Josh?"

She smiled back at him. "I believe I can do that . . . Josh."

"Have you had dinner?"

"Matter of fact, I have." Juliana stood primly, holding her hands together.

"Too bad. I was going to ask you to join me." Josh couldn't believe those words had just tumbled out of his mouth. She didn't really know him. Why would she have dinner with him?

"Another time, perhaps?" Her lips curved in such a sweet way that he could only stare at her pink, upturned mouth. She seemed in no hurry to leave.

"I'm sorry. I guess I should have asked if you were on your way somewhere."

"Actually, no. I was just going to go sit in the parlor to get out of my room for a spell. There are a few books in there I'd enjoy reading."

Josh liked the fact that she was a reader. Many a night he'd sit by the fire after a long, cold day and read before going to bed. A hazy vision of Juliana sitting beside him reading, firelight illuminating her face, popped into his mind. He blinked his eyes and mentally shook his head.

"Well, then how about dessert? I hear the apple pie is excellent."

She gave him a lopsided grin. "You are persistent, aren't you?"

Josh cleared his throat. "Only when I need to be."

"And is this one of those times?"

Her blue eyes twinkled with delight at teasing him, as if it were the most natural thing in the world for her to do, making her seem older than her youthful face indicated.

"I eat alone all the time, except when I'm at the camp with Andy. So how about it? We could ask if they have ice cream to put on top of the pie." He hoped that might tempt her to come sit with him awhile.

Her eyes widened. "Now you're talking."

"Must be my lucky day!" Josh took a step forward, offered his arm, and guided her to his table, where the half-eaten steak lay waiting. He wondered what he would say to her now that she had accepted.

He ordered another piece of pie and coffee, then settled Juliana across the table from him. He noted that the tiny blue flowers of her calico dress brought out the color of her eyes. His eyes slid down to her hands, which were red and chapped. She had long, slender fingers with small oval nails. Fingers that shouldn't have to work like that.

Josh shook his head slightly to clear his head. What was wrong with him? She was just a mere slip of a girl, he would guess barely seventeen, but a woman just the same. Suddenly, Josh's throat felt tight and dry as burnt toast. He tried hard not to let his nervousness show.

"Will you be staying here or moving on now that your mother is gone?"

She clasped her hands on the table with a demure look. "I have a job working at the *Lewistown Gazette*." The pupils of her eyes were large with enthusiasm, and it was all he could do to drag his eyes away from them. He didn't want to scare her off. Not this sweet young girl. Her eyes spoke of past hurts in her life. She apparently needed something or someone to believe in.

"You don't say? That's great. I try to read the paper and catch up with all the news whenever I'm in town. Do you enjoy it so far?"

"I've only worked there a couple of days, but I find it very interesting, and I would much rather read and write than wash clothes!" She looked down at her pie, picking at the flaky crust with her fork, and added, "It gives me a feeling of security as well. I can't be beholden to the Stocktons indefinitely."

"You have a lot of pride for such a young woman."

"Mama taught me to work hard at everything I do and not to be dependent on others."

"'If a man won't work, neither shall he eat.'" Josh pushed back his plate and reached for his pie.

"What?"

"Never mind. I admire that in you, Juliana. It takes a tough individual with strong convictions to make a living here in Montana. Between the weather and the space, it can be a very lonely place." Josh was thinking of himself in the past winters. The brutal cold and harsh winds were trying things to deal with, especially without a partner to warm the lonely winter nights. "I'm surprised you intend to stay."

"I really don't have anywhere else to go. I have no family to speak of, and my father went to the Colorado gold mines a long time ago. Mother and I stayed in Montana. Ever since my father decided to mine for gold and left when I was ten, we never knew where our next meal would come from. So Mother took in miners' laundry to keep our heads above water." Juliana looked down at the table, avoiding Josh's eyes. "I don't want to have to live that way. Miners go from camp to camp. I would never want to marry a miner. The work is backbreaking, and there's little promise of any future."

Josh stiffened at her comments. Maybe he could be the one to change her mind about mining. "I don't know, some people have become very rich . . . So, you don't know where your father is?"

"I don't even know if he's alive, and I'm not sure it would matter now."

The anger in her voice surprised him. Changing the subject, Josh told her about his dog, Shebe, and how much she loved the baby lambs. He could see the relief on her face and was glad he hadn't asked more about her father.

They finished their dessert, and after paying the waiter, Josh insisted on walking her to the bottom of the staircase.

She paused before going up. "The dessert was wonderful. And thank you for the conversation."

Josh took a deep breath and exhaled. "It was my pleasure. I hope to see you again before I go back to the ranch."

"Good night, Josh."

He liked the sound of his name on her lips. "Sleep well, Juliana."

Back in his room, Josh peeled off his boots, placing them next to his bed. He stripped down to his long handles and crawled under the heavy quilts of the lumpy feather bed. Folding his arms behind his head, he wondered about the lovely Juliana. He'd met beautiful women before, and while he didn't consider her perfect in that sense, her lovely face reflected an inner beauty and strength, though he was sure she wasn't aware of it. That made her all the more appealing to him.

Maybe he would do a little investigating on his own about her father, or help her find any family that was left. She was all alone in the world. A bit like he'd felt when he'd left his family in Colorado, though it was his own choice.

Eventually, he drifted off to sleep with the image of Juliana's shining blue eyes floating through his thoughts.

8

"Juliana, I'd like you to attend the Lewistown Ladies Social Club meeting this afternoon at two o'clock, and try your hand at writing an article for tomorrow's edition." Albert hunched over his cluttered desk, trying to decide what his headline would be. "I've been thinking you may be capable of more than just running errands and filing. Think you can handle that?" He paused in his work as she hung her coat and bonnet on the rack near the door.

"I certainly would like to try. What is this about?"

"That's what I want you to find out. It's a small group of busybodies, mostly made up of the town's most influential wives. I try to give them a small column occasionally in the paper, mainly to publish what their next project for the town will be. It makes them feel good and puffed up with humanitarianism. But I'm thinking they need a female point of view for the column." Albert's eyebrows made a furrow in his forehead above his spectacles. "We want to keep them happy."

"We do?" Juliana detected a hint of truth to his humor.

"Indeed we do. There's nothing like a pack of women breathing down your neck. I think they're up to something."

Juliana bent her head down, trying to hide her smile.

"Where do they hold their meetings?"

"At the church three blocks down on the left."

"That should be interesting. I look forward to it. Are you sure you don't want to sit in on their meeting?" She giggled under her breath, walked over to the potbellied stove, and poured herself a cup of coffee. "Would you like more coffee?"

"Wouldn't mind if you'd pour me a fresh cup. I got busy, and this one is cold. The missus makes coffee, but since she brings it to me before I'm out of bed, I don't have the heart to tell her that it's weak."

Juliana envisioned a devoted couple from the few remarks he'd made to her, but she'd yet to meet his wife, Sally. Juliana and Albert had quickly become friends, and she was grateful to be able to work for him. She placed the chipped enamel cup before him and proceeded to her desk with her coffee.

Suddenly shots rang out, making her jump and splatter her coffee across the desktop.

Albert sprang from his desk and jerked open the front door, and Juliana was right on his heels. "What—?"

A horse flew past them and disappeared in a cloud of dust, its rider hunkered down low over the horse's back. Shopkeepers suddenly appeared on the sidewalks outside their storefronts.

"The bank's been robbed!" Glenn, the barber next door, shouted.

Albert and Juliana hurried down the sidewalk to the bank, where a crowd was beginning to form. "Anyone hurt?" Albert asked.

Glenn made his way through the bank's front door. Juliana could see past him to the banker, who was lying on the hard floor, blood oozing from his side. "Someone go fetch the doctor, and hurry before this man bleeds to death!" Someone in the crowd ran to do his bidding.

"Mac, can you hear me?" Albert knelt down next to the bleeding man. A moan was his only answer. "Do you know who did this to you?"

"I saw the man." A scared and white-faced man peeked out from behind the teller window. "Where's the sheriff?"

"On his way. You can give him your description." Albert nodded to Juliana. "Get a piece of paper off that desk there and take down any information you hear."

She hurriedly found pen and paper just as Dr. Barnum hurried through the door carrying his black satchel. He nodded in her direction. Pounding up the wooden steps behind him was the town sheriff, slightly out of breath, his silver badge displayed on his leather vest.

"Take it easy, Mac." Dr. Barnum knelt beside the man and ripped his shirt open to reveal a bullet wound in his shoulder.

"Who in tarnation . . . ?" Sheriff Ben Wilson tried to bend his stout frame over the wounded banker as far as his protruding stomach would allow. "Who did this to you, Mac?"

Mac tried to speak, but his breathing was too ragged. Dr. Barnum tried to calm him. "Mac, you're lucky. The bullet just missed your heart and lodged in your shoulder. You'll be okay." He turned to the crowd. "Can someone help me get him to my office?" Several of the men scurried forward to help.

The teller stared down in shock at his friend, his eyes stark with fear. It could easily have been him.

"Sheriff, there was only one. Older guy. I don't recollect ever having seen him around here before." The bank teller fingered his moustache with a shaking hand.

"Well now, exactly what did he look like?"

"Dark-haired, scruffy-looking with a beard, and kinda tall in the saddle."

"Humph! How much did he make off with?" Albert asked.

"Near as I can tell, about $15,000."

"Whew! That's a bundle for sure. I need to get a posse together and hit the trail before we lose him." The sheriff scratched his head in thought before turning to the crowd, his hand resting lightly on the gun strapped to his leg.

"How about it? I need five good men to ride with me."

"Sheriff, I'll go." A man standing nearby stepped up. "Just let me get my horse and rifle."

"Me too," another man said. Three more rugged townsmen spoke up, and they quickly mounted their horses hitched at the post in front of the bank. Sheriff Wilson nodded to Dr. Barnum before taking the lead.

"Take care of him, Mark." Sheriff Wilson reached over to the hitching post, untied the reins, then mounted his horse. "He's a good man." The posse left in a cloud of dust, choking the small crowd that stood watching.

Turning to Juliana, Dr. Barnum shook his head. "I hope they catch him."

As he worked on the man, Juliana, with trembling fingers, busily jotted down a few notes about the incident. She felt a little queasy seeing Mac in a pool of blood. She swayed momentarily.

"Are you okay? You look a little pale." Dr. Barnum reached out his hand to steady her elbow.

"I think so. It's not every day I see a man bleeding."

"Come on, Juliana. Let's get you back to the office," Albert said. "When I asked you to take notes, I never considered that it'd be tough for you. I'm sorry. I wasn't thinking."

She took his arm, and they headed back to work, with Albert talking the whole distance about how it wasn't safe around here anymore.

Before Juliana was to leave for the Ladies Social Club meeting, Dr. Barnum came striding through the door and stood before her desk. "I didn't realize you worked here until the shooting. I came by to see if you were okay."

"That's sweet of you, Dr. Barnum, but really, I'm feeling fine now. It was a bit of a shock. I guess if I'm going to be a reporter, then I might as well get used to seeing all sorts of things."

His smile was warm and affable. Juliana had never really taken a good look at the doctor, and she realized that while he was nice-looking, his countenance was serious.

"May I take you to supper sometime?"

Somehow that was not what she was expecting. She quickly filtered what this might mean. Two men in one week. Her tongue felt dry. "Well . . . I guess so." After all, there was no parent to ask permission now. How strange it felt to be alone with no family to care one way or the other what she did with her time.

"Wonderful! How about tonight?" When she hesitated, he added, "You have to eat, don't you?" His face softened, allowing the hard lines in his forehead to relax.

"That's true." Juliana saw his lips curve into a gentle smile across his clean-shaven face.

"Okay then. I'll meet you at the hotel at 5:30, and we can go over to Maggie's Café for some home cookin'. How does that sound?"

Juliana nodded. "I'll be there."

Juliana saw Albert watching her, and he nodded his head in approval.

"I'll be waiting. And please, could you call me Mark?"

Juliana nodded, and Mark tipped his bowler hat and stepped out onto the sidewalk.

It was a short walk to church, and Juliana walked past simple clapboard houses, whitewashed to match the fences, with her notebook tucked closely to her chest. The afternoon air was light and breezy and lifted her spirits. She let herself into the church vestibule that smelled of lemon and beeswax, apparently used to polish the dark wood pews and gleaming floors. Several ladies sat in the first two pews, and a stout lady with a round face and big blue eyes stood in front of them, laughing.

The chatter and laughing slowly died down as the women turned in the pews to see why their speaker had paused. Juliana felt her face flush with embarrassment.

"Please excuse the intrusion, ladies. I'm Juliana Brady from the *Lewistown Gazette*. I'd like to sit in on your meeting and write about your latest project."

"We weren't told of this." A plain, bony-nosed woman rose from her seat, visibly agitated. The lady who was sitting next to her reached out and touched the woman on the arm. "You weren't invited." She pushed her friend's hand off her sleeve.

"I—" Juliana sputtered.

The stout lady with the twinkling eyes walked toward Juliana, extending her hand. "I'm Helen Brown. We'd be delighted to fill you in on our club's activities." Her hand was soft and cool to Juliana's touch.

"But—" the plain woman began, but Helen shushed her. The others twittered in undertones and watched with interest.

"Albert did speak to me about creating a column that would be great advertising for our community endeavors. I just failed to mention it today in my haste to get started." Helen smiled at Juliana. "He did not tell me, however, that he had hired a woman to work for him at the paper."

"And such a young one too. Are you sure you can spell?" The plain woman looked down her bony nose at Juliana. "I'm Cynthia Hood, and this is Margaret Spencer—we all call her Miss Margaret—and her two daughters, Louise and Natalie." She indicated the other ladies clustered nearby, who nodded toward Juliana. Louise was slightly taller than her sister and wore an olive dress with leg-of-mutton sleeves, which ended tightly at her thin wrists with a tiny row of pearl buttons. Her sister wore a robin's-egg-blue dress with a matching bolero trimmed in tan velvet. The only adornment on each sister was a small string of pearls.

"And this is Esther White." Cynthia gestured toward a middle-aged lady decked out in black *peau de soie* and matching vest edged in lace jabots. Diamond drops hung from her ears and flashed in her rings on her hands. Juliana wasn't sure she'd ever seen someone dressed so finely.

Juliana nodded at the group. "How do you do?"

Natalie took Juliana's hand. "I'm glad you're here. Now maybe we'll be taken seriously." She laughed.

Juliana liked her immediately. "I'm not sure about that," she said. "I confess this is my first real assignment."

"It'll be better than the write-up we normally get, coming from another woman." Louise chuckled. "Women's social issues are really not Albert's forte."

"Marion Stockton is visibly absent today with who knows what. She is always prying into other people's affairs and neglects her own." Cynthia cocked her head sideways, making a *tsk* sound to indicate her displeasure at Marion's absence.

"Now, Cynthia, we don't want to give Juliana a bad impression of us by speaking unkindly of Marion," Miss Margaret said.

Esther added her two cents' worth. "Well, you know as well as the rest of us that what she said is true. She is just not dependable!"

Juliana bit her tongue. Should she say something? Tell them Marion was her good friend? Or just let them make complete fools of themselves?

"Please. Have a seat here next to me." Louise patted the wooden pew as she scooted to one side. Juliana took a seat between Louise and Miss Margaret, who was clearly the oldest one there. Her thin gray hair, though wound into a chignon, had strayed from its pins. She smelled of rose water and wore a beautiful embroidered white collar that was clearly old. Her watery, gray eyes smiled back at Juliana over her wire spectacles as she leaned over.

"Never mind Esther and Cynthia. They believe themselves to be above everyone else." The old lady patted her hand affectionately, and Juliana felt an instant kinship.

"Thank you, Miss Margaret." Juliana proceeded to open her notebook, clearly aware of the looks Esther and Cynthia cast in her direction. Juliana heard Esther whisper, "Didn't she used to do the miners' wash on the edge of town?"

Cynthia nudged her friend in the ribs. "Shh . . . she'll hear you."

Helen cleared her throat. "Ladies, we need to get started on the meeting and talk about our latest project."

Juliana felt entirely out of place. She would force herself to focus on what Helen was saying and forget about the snide remarks. Why did she think for one minute that by having a job at the paper, she would instantly make new friends? Helen seemed a friendly person and outgoing. She was probably middle-aged, though quite different from what Juliana was used to when she considered that her mother would have been about the same age. But apparently not all the women were as friendly as Helen and Miss Margaret.

"As I was saying, one of the most important things we can do for the future of our town is give our children a good education. But more importantly, we all know that down at the miners' camp, children are running around and playing like hoodlums without the benefit of a school."

Juliana's heart lurched at the mention of the miners' camp. Most of the children were little urchins who worked for their parents as they passed through to the next mining camp.

"What do you suggest we do?" Louise was the first one to respond, her big brown eyes conveying concern.

"We don't have the money to start a school, much less pay for

66

a teacher's salary." Esther leaned forward, her head cocked, to stress her point.

Natalie jumped up from her seat. "I think a school is an excellent idea! But how will we raise the money?"

"Hmm . . . that's the sticky part. I'm not quite sure. But"—Helen glanced in Juliana's direction—"with the column in the paper about our social circle, we could request donations."

"I like the idea, but we will need supplies, besides paying a teacher. How do you intend to do that when the school right here in Lewistown is crowded and could use more space?" Cynthia tossed her red hair so her shiny curls shook. "People are not likely to support another school for outsiders."

"I believe that to be untrue, Cynthia. Perhaps some of the books could be on loan. After all, we're not talking about a huge group of children. We wouldn't need much money. Just willing hearts," Helen said, her arms folded across her ample bosom.

"There are many in our community always looking for ways to serve the Lord," Miss Margaret interjected. "I believe we might find many willing hearts, if the need were known."

Cynthia fingered the broach at her throat, pulling her lips into a tight line. Her freckled fair skin turned a bright pink.

"If I may speak here . . ." Juliana nodded at the ladies. "I know I don't represent your club, but as Esther pointed out, I worked in the miners' camp. Helen's idea to bring education to these children, whose lives are so unpredictable, really warms my heart. I believe those miners who drag their families from one camp to another in search of instant riches would be grateful that someone took a genuine interest in them."

"Thank you, Juliana. Could you please convey that sentiment in your column?" Helen's round face lit up with enthusiasm.

"I will do my best, Helen."

The small circle of ladies clapped their approval.

"Now let's have our refreshments and then talk about ways in which to go about finding the appropriate teacher," Natalie said. She rose and gracefully walked toward the table laden with cookies, tea, and mints. The rest of the ladies followed, leaving Juliana to finish making her notes. Miss Margaret left the food table and shuffled her way over with her cane to Juliana. "How about some refreshments, dear?"

"Thanks, Miss Margaret, but I must get back to the paper."

"It was so nice meeting you, and don't worry about those other two." She nodded in the direction of Esther and Cynthia.

Juliana closed her notebook. "Thank you for taking my side. I hope to see you again." Juliana meant it. Miss Margaret seemed to be a wise lady.

Miss Margaret touched her arm and said, "I do too. Take care, dear."

Juliana could hardly contain her excitement about a school for the miners' children as she left the ladies and headed back to the newspaper office. Many a day as she washed clothes, the children would come near the fire, and she would talk to them about great literature she had read. They loved her stories and would sometimes pretend they were actual characters in the tales.

She hummed a tune, her step light, and people along the boardwalk stared at her. But her thoughts were on writing a good article that would do the Ladies Social Club proud.

9

Josh made his way past the whiskey barrels and stacks of flour to the cluttered counter at the general store, fishing his list from his shirt pocket. He saw several shoppers pause long enough in their shopping to give him the once-over, then turn away. Josh tipped his hat to them anyway. He knew sheepherders would never hold the same esteem as a dashing cowboy with his decorated chaps and wide-brimmed hat. He chuckled under his breath. *Wonder what they would think if they knew I'm a cattleman's son?* Working around his sheep, he found he had no need for chaps and spurs. He saved them for special occasions now, but still wore his cowboy boots because they were the most comfortable.

"Can I be of service to you, Josh?"

Josh smiled at Earl, a scrawny, pencil figure of a man, who looked like lifting a sack of flour could put him in bed for weeks. "Yes, sir. What do you have for dipping sheep?"

"Well now, let's see." Earl reached over to the shelf behind him and pulled out a gallon of dip mixture. "This here's the best. It's Semple's Scotch Sheep Dip. Seventy-five cents a gallon. Straight out of Louisville, Kentucky. I hear it beats 'em all."

Josh read the ingredients. "Strong Kentucky leaf tobacco and vegetable extracts." His brow furrowed in thought. "How many sheep can I dip with that?"

"It's concentrated. If you buy two and a half gallons, you can dilute it to dip a hundred sheep." The clerk peered over his wire frames at Josh.

"So . . . for three thousand sheep, I'll need seventy-five gallons?"

"Yep. A barrel holds thirty-one gallons. Let me go to the storage area and make sure we have a few barrels." Earl disappeared through a door behind the counter.

Josh pushed back his hat and leaned against the counter. He contemplated other items he would need after lambing season. He'd need a dozen pairs of shears and two long-handled hooks for grabbing the sheep's necks. Maybe a few leather aprons to protect him and Andy when they did the dipping, and several heavy knives for docking as well.

The bell above the door sounded, and he glanced to the front door to see Juliana enter. Instantly, Josh straightened up, feeling an unfamiliar warmth flood his face and neck. She saw him almost at the same time and flashed him a broad smile, exposing small but perfect teeth. He noticed her new brown dress that complimented her slender waist. In her hand she held a notebook and looked very businesslike for one so young.

"Hello, Josh. I thought you'd already left for your camp." She held her notebook to her chest.

Once again he smiled as his name rolled off her lips, like it was special.

"I had other business to attend to and decided to get supplies

70

rather than send Andy. I see you have a notebook there. Doing a little reporting?"

She flushed prettily as she walked toward him. "Matter of fact, I have been doing just that. I'm on my way back to the newspaper office, but I wanted to stop in and see if the ink order for the presses had arrived."

"Sounds to me like you enjoy your work so far." Josh thought she had the most beautiful eyes, like the blue Yogos. A light rose fragrance floated from her when she moved. He'd been in the valley away from women too long, he realized, and tried to concentrate on the purpose for his trip to the general store.

"I really am, Josh. Thanks for asking."

Earl cleared his throat behind them. "I have three barrels out back. We can have them loaded on your wagon in no time at all."

"Excellent. I have a couple other items I'll need." Josh handed his list to the clerk.

Earl's face lit up when he saw Juliana. "Miss Juliana, that ink didn't come in today. But I expect it tomorrow, if you could check back?"

"No problem, Earl. I was just passing by and thought I'd ask. Thank you." She turned back to Josh. "I need to get back now. I have a column to write."

Just as she turned to go, the shop door slammed hard, jarring the bell.

"Wes, what can I do for you today?" Earl asked, stopping dead in his tracks.

A tall cowboy entered the store, and when he saw Juliana, a ridiculous grin spread across his face, exposing slightly crooked teeth. He swaggered right over to her, apparently confident and unaware of anyone else. "Well, pretty lady. Nice seeing you here."

Josh saw Juliana's face tense up and her body stiffen. "I must be going now, excuse me."

Wes's long fingers grabbed her by the arm. "Now hold on there. We have a conversation to finish."

"What do you mean? We weren't talking." Juliana pulled her arm from his grip.

"Aw, you forgot already? Remember, I asked if I could take you out sometime? I'm still waiting for the answer." Wes shifted his weight to one hip.

"I've already told you." Juliana took a step sideways.

Wes leaned in a bit too close, and Josh stepped between them. "I think you'd best leave the young lady alone," Josh said, his face hot with anger. "And keep your hands off her."

Wes looked down at Josh. "Well, now. Just who do you think you are, mister?"

"A friend. That's all. But I can tell the lady doesn't want to be bothered by you."

Wes turned to Juliana with a smirk on his face. "Is that right? I think the lady can speak for herself." When he reached for Juliana's hand, Josh slammed his fist into Wes's jaw. Wes fell hard against the harnesses hanging on the wall, and the tack went scattering to the floor. He staggered momentarily, then lunged at Josh just as Earl intervened.

"What's going on here, Josh? Cut that out! You two break something, and you'll have to pay for it." Earl raised his skinny arm and pointed to the door. "I'm asking you to leave, Wes." He turned to Josh. "I don't hold to fightin' in my store. Either one of you leaves, or you take it outside. Your choice."

Josh held his clenched fists at his sides, trying to stay in control as his anger rose.

Wes straightened, holding his jaw. "I'm going. But you just messed with the wrong cowboy, sheepherder." He stormed out, his boot heels pounding hard against the hardwood floor.

Josh didn't bother to answer the insult. He turned to Juliana. "I'm sorry, but I couldn't stand by and let him try to manhandle you. You need to be careful. I don't trust him."

"Wes is just itching for trouble," Earl said as he placed the harnesses back on the proper hooks.

"He came to the newspaper office to place an ad and tried to get a bit too familiar." Juliana touched the top button of her blouse. "Don't worry about me, though. I'm stronger than I look, and I can take care of myself." Her smile went straight to Josh's heart. "But thanks for protecting me."

Protecting her was something Josh felt compelled to do. He took her arm and felt a slight tremble. He guided her to the door and out onto the boardwalk. She may think she was strong, but she was really no match for Wes. He could overpower her in an instant.

They paused outside, and Juliana looked up at him. "Will you be coming back soon?" she asked.

His heart thumped hard, and suddenly he had trouble breathing when he caught the gaze of her beautiful eyes. He swallowed hard, hearing himself answer, "In a few weeks, but I wanted to go ahead and be prepared to dip my sheep. Have you ever been near a herd of sheep?" Josh saw her eyebrow shoot upwards. Could she tell he was flustered?

"No, I haven't. Are they as docile as I've heard?"

"They are indeed. Say, why don't you ride out to the camp and see them firsthand? I'm near Yogo Creek. You might even decide to write something about them for the newspaper." Josh saw her look of concentration, as though pondering whether his suggestion was a good idea.

"I suppose I could. I would love to learn more about what it is you do. Maybe there's a story about sheep that needs writing."

"How about some Saturday afternoon? I can write down the directions for you."

"That would be perfect." Juliana smiled at him as he continued to look at her. "I need to be getting back to the paper. We do have a deadline."

"And I don't want to keep you from it. Good seeing you, Juliana."

Josh watched her leave, wishing he had more time with her.

Earl appeared, breaking up his reverie. "Are you about ready to load up?"

"Yes, I am. And I need one other thing—a wooden stamp for my sheep brand."

"Okay, you've got it. What do you want it to say?"

"'J' for 'Jewel.'"

"Now that's strange." Earl scratched his head.

"I'll have to tell you about it sometime."

10

Juliana sighed, rubbed the back of her neck, and stuck her pencil into her chignon as she read what she'd written.

The Lewistown Ladies Social Club met on Tuesday to discuss their latest project for spring. Helen Brown, president of the prestigious club of community leaders, challenged the members with plans for a small school to benefit the children of the miners at the outskirts of town. Education should be an emphasis to benefit the children who otherwise could not attend school. There was open discussion on how to obtain books and needed supplies and construct a small building. Another major concern was obtaining a teacher.

After much debate on the project needs and how to garner support, the club concluded enthusiastically to pursue this objective with the best intentions to help educate the children. As always, the members pride themselves on meeting the needs of the surrounding community. The ladies adjourned and enjoyed light refreshments. They were excited about the new project and about discussing fresh ways to implement their ideas.

Also present at the meeting were Margaret, Louise, and Natalie Spencer; Esther White; and Cynthia Hood. If you would like to contribute or donate your time for this cause, please contact Helen Brown.

Not bad, she thought. Glancing up at the clock, she was surprised to discover it was nearly five o'clock. She would just have time to turn her article over to Albert for tomorrow's run and freshen up for her dinner with Mark. She would have to ask Marion why she hadn't attended the meeting today.

It had been a busy day, but it kept her mind off her loneliness and her dear mother.

Her mind wandered back to the chance meeting with Josh at the general store. The way his amber eyes pierced her had made her feel giddy, and she had hardly been able to concentrate on why she was there in the first place. He was several years older than she, and he probably thought she was just a child. Maybe he looked at all women the way he looked at her.

She sighed wearily. What she really needed was to put him out of her mind. She couldn't trust any man. Her father was a good example of that. She would make a living for herself and not be dependent on a man for anything. That's what her mother had had to do, and Juliana would do the same. A man would not turn her life upside down the way her father had. She could be quite happy without a man. She had her books, her friend Marion, and her job, which would keep her plenty busy.

The encounter with Wes today was still very unsettling to her. His aggressiveness made her feel uneasy. His outright flirting put her on the spot, and she wasn't used to that.

"Shouldn't you be leaving now for your dinner date with Mark?" Albert paused over the printing press as he set the letters for tomorrow's paper. He glanced in Juliana's direction.

Juliana felt her face flush. "It's not a date—just supper. Matter of fact, I'm about to go. I was just looking over the column for tomorrow." She rose, handing him her article. She waited while he skimmed through what she'd written.

"Very good, Juliana. Now you go ahead and leave so you won't be late. You've had a busy day. Your headline about the bank robbery was pretty good, but I changed it a bit. By the way, there's a reward of five hundred dollars for the capture of the bandit." Albert turned back to setting the presses.

"I hope the sheriff catches him." She wanted to stop by to see Helen with a couple of ideas she had about a fund-raiser, so she grabbed her coat and waved good-bye to Albert, then hurried down the sidewalk to Helen's house. At the meeting, Helen had mentioned where she lived, in case Juliana had any questions concerning the project.

Juliana lifted the wrought-iron gate latch, startling a fat gray cat snoozing on the broad steps leading up to the front porch. The cat skittered away as she approached the sidewalk. Juliana smiled. She loved cats, and once she was settled, she planned to have one to keep her company.

She rang the doorbell and waited for someone to answer. Helen's home was a sprawling yellow clapboard, its porch dotted with flowerpots, with a cozy swing at one end. Rich, green ferns sat on either side of the door in beautiful ceramic pots. Juliana had never lived in anything so grand, and likely never would. She wondered what Helen's husband did for a living.

A young girl about the age of fourteen answered the door. Her dark hair hung in perfect ringlets, setting off the starched pinafore over her blue gingham dress. "Hello."

"I'm sorry to disturb you, but I wonder if I could speak with your mother. I'm a reporter for the *Gazette*," Juliana said.

"Well, I don't know. She's pretty busy right now. I'll have to go ask. Could you wait right here?"

"I can indeed. Tell her it's Juliana. And you are . . . ?"

"Marilee." The young girl smiled up at her.

"Nice to meet you, Marilee." She had a peaches-and-cream complexion and big green eyes. Pretty eyes, Juliana thought.

"I'll be right back." She left the door partially opened, and Juliana heard her call out for her mother.

It wasn't long before Helen stood before her, charming as usual. "Why, hello, dear. To what do I owe this unexpected visit?"

"I'm sorry for an intrusion, Helen."

"Oh, no bother at all. Pardon my manners. Please do come in."

She followed Helen into the parlor gaily decorated with rose chintz fabric. A portly gentleman rose from his seat, placing a teacup next to his chair.

"Harry, this is Juliana," Helen said. "She's doing a column on our Ladies Social Club for the *Gazette*."

"It's nice to meet you," Juliana said. "But I'm intruding. I'll come back another time."

"Not at all. I'm Harry, Helen's husband, and the mayor of this wonderful city." He extended his hand to Juliana's, shaking it firmly. "Join us, won't you?"

He seemed warm and easygoing, with a smile under his bushy mustache. He patted Helen on the arm, and she caressed his hand. It was apparent that they were very much in love.

"Sit right here, Juliana." Helen gestured toward the Victorian settee. "Marilee, please fetch another cup for our guest."

Marilee left the room momentarily and came back with a delicate rose cup and saucer. "I'm going over to Jane's, Mommy."

"Supper is soon, so don't be gone long, sweetie," her mother said. Marilee gave her daddy a quick kiss and was out the door in a flash.

Helen laughed, saying, "Ah, children. That one is twelve going on twenty." She filled the cup with tea and handed it to Juliana.

"I can't stay long. I'm meeting Dr. Barnum for dinner." As soon as the words slipped out of her mouth, she wished she hadn't said them. Surprise showed on Helen's face, but Juliana caught Harry's smile.

"Nice man, Mark. He's a fine doctor too," Harry said.

Juliana sipped from the cup of tea. "I really came to talk to you about an idea I had for your new project." She took a quick sip of her tea before continuing. "There may be a way to make money for the new school program."

Harry stood. "I'll let you two talk. I have an appointment at the courthouse, but I'll be back by suppertime." He winked at Helen. "Juliana, I'm sure I will see you again."

"I'll look forward to it." Juliana found herself smiling at Harry. She liked him.

Once he was gone, Helen turned to her enthusiastically. "So tell me, Juliana, what have you been thinking?"

Juliana could see she had Helen's full attention now. "I have some thoughts on ideas for a fund-raiser for the school."

"Any suggestion you have would be most welcome. Please share."

"Have you given any thought to an art show? I got the idea thinking about Mr. Stockton's vast collection of art he has hanging throughout the hotel." Juliana paused, waiting for Helen's reaction.

"Juliana, what a great idea! Who knows, perhaps we can persuade him to donate one or two." She laughed. "Although that'll take some convincing—"

Marilee burst into the room, her ribbon sash flowing below her dress hem and a hole in her stocking. "Mama, come quick!" She yanked at her mother's hand. "There's been an accident. Jane and I were running, and I chased her across the street, but then she slipped and fell, and a wagon hit her. Hurry, please!"

Shock registered on Helen's face, and she shot up out of her chair. She ran to the front door and down the sidewalk, with Juliana frantically trying to keep up.

Several neighbors were already gathered at the accident site, and upon seeing Jane's limp body, Helen cried out. She and Juliana quickly bent down to check Jane's breathing. "Thank God! She has a pulse." Helen began to loosen Jane's coat. A large purple bump was already forming over the girl's right brow.

"Do you think anything's broken?" Juliana asked.

"It's hard to tell, but she probably has a concussion. Has anyone gone for the doctor?" Helen asked, turning to her neighbors.

"He's on his way, and George ran to get Jane's mother," someone in the crowd responded.

"I don't think we should move her," Juliana said quietly, watching for any sign of motion in Jane's face.

Helen's neighbor ran up and stood next to them, wringing her hands. "That horse and buggy just roared right past Jane like she wasn't even there! I declare, I've never seen anything like it. He was in an all-fired hurry. I hope she'll be all right."

Marilee's eyes were as big as saucers, and Juliana got up to place her arm around the frightened young girl. "Don't worry, sweetie. The doc's coming."

Almost on cue, Mark hurried up to where Jane lay in the dusty street. He assessed her physical condition, looking for breaks, then pulled up her eyelids. "She's probably got a concussion. You did the right thing by not moving her, because she may have a broken leg. Are you her mother?"

"I am." Cynthia Hood rushed to the circle gathered in the street. Juliana recognized her as the snoot from the Ladies Social Club. Cynthia fell to her knees at her daughter's side, shock on her face. "Jane, please open your eyes." She felt Jane's face, gently nudging her, almost willing her to wake up. "What's wrong with her, Doctor? Is she going to be all right?" Cynthia frantically looked into his eyes.

"I think so." Mark turned to George, his next-door neighbor, and motioned for him to assist. "We'll need to get her inside and comfortable. Helen, since you're just across the street, can we move her to your house temporarily?"

"Of course, if that's all right with Cynthia."

"Oh yes. Let's get her off the street. Whatever you say," Cynthia said.

George and Mark scooped Jane up, supporting her neck and back, then carried her up the front porch into Helen's home.

"Take her up the stairs to that first bedroom. It's the guestroom. She'll be comfortable there."

Helen led the way. Juliana and Marilee stayed downstairs while Cynthia followed the men upstairs. Juliana gave Marilee a slight squeeze, and the girl leaned her head against her with a sob. "There now. Don't cry. Mark is a good doctor, and he'll know what to do."

"It's my fault. I shouldn't have insisted on chasing her. Mama said I should act like a lady. She's right," Marilee said with a hiccup.

"Let's go sit down and wait, shall we?" Juliana led her to the parlor, where earlier they had enjoyed pleasantries. How fast things could change.

It wasn't long before Mark and Helen came downstairs.

Marilee jumped up. "Mama, is she all right?"

Mark turned to her. "She should be, in a few days. She's going to have a bad headache, I'm afraid. And she'll need some quiet rest."

Marilee sighed deeply, looking pitiful with her tear-streaked face, trailing sash, and ripped stockings.

"Let's get you upstairs and into the bathtub, young lady, so we can have our dinner. Cynthia will stay next to Jane and alert us if there is any change." Helen pushed on her daughter's backside, moving her toward the stairs. "You two go on now and enjoy yourself." She nodded to Juliana and Mark. "We'll take care of Jane."

"I'll look in on her in the morning then." Mark turned to Juliana, elbow out. "Shall we?"

"If you're sure you don't need any help, Helen." Juliana said.

"Don't worry about a thing. We'll do exactly as Mark said. Now, I must bid you good-bye or Marilee will dawdle much too long with her bath." Helen flashed them a knowing smile.

11

Howling winds blew down from the craggy mountain peaks where gathering dark clouds hovered above. The wind kicked up the dust in the busy streets of Lewistown, and shopkeepers' signs rattled, their rusty nails squeaking against the weathered boards. The horses tied to hitching posts lowered their heads against the onslaught of dust in their eyes, while women pressed their hands down on their skirts to keep them from revealing the petticoats underneath.

Josh clamped down on his Stetson, pulling his duster together to keep out the sudden chill. This could be another storm brewing before the temperatures warmed to a comfortable level when the lambing season began. He thought fondly of his herd and the new lambs he and Andy would be handling.

A hot meal and a strong cup of coffee were what he was seeking tonight. Tucked under his arm was a copy of *Moby Dick*, which he intended to read while he ate his meal. Tomorrow he would head back out to his campsite with fresh supplies that should last a month or so. He missed Shebe and hoped Andy was taking good care of her. Next time, if the weather was clear, Shebe would come with him.

Josh was glad that at the last minute he had donned his nice woolen pants and shirt underneath his heavy coat, and shined his boots before he left for Maggie's restaurant. It was crowded tonight, and most diners were not dressed in their usual work garb. Maybe that was because it was Saturday. Out here, in the middle of nowhere, this was probably the highlight of the week for most people. He only had to look around to know that.

As the waiter showed him to his table, he nodded to Sheriff Wilson, who shared a table with a couple he didn't know. With the clatter of china, the clinking of glass, and the soft glow of gaslights, this would be a nice place to invite Juliana if he saw her again.

If? Make that, *he would* see her again if he had his way about it.

The small table near a window where he could look out onto the street suited him just fine. He placed his hat and book on the table, then peeled off his coat and waited for someone to take his order. He was mighty hungry, and the smells coming from the kitchen made his stomach sit up and take notice. He could eat a horse and snatch the rider!

Quickly the waiter took his order, promising to bring his hot coffee first with lots of cream. Josh settled back, pulled his book to him, and flipped it open to the marked page. He enjoyed reading but hadn't allowed himself the luxury of late because of his herd and the endless tasks that needed tending at his small ranch.

The coffee arrived, and he helped himself to cream and sugar, making the coffee the color of caramel. It tasted delicious. Almost as good as Andy's. After gulping down the coffee, he spied Juliana with Doctor What's-his-name . . . Mark? Yes, Mark Barnum. Well, he wasn't surprised. She smiled at Josh but then shyly looked away. He felt his face go warm despite the cold seeping through the windowsill he was sitting next to. A peculiar feeling inched its way up his chest, and he drew in a deep breath. My, but she was lovely to look at! She was laughing softly at something Mark was saying, and Mark's eyes were locked on her pretty face.

He quickly recovered and looked down at his book, suddenly unable to concentrate, though he continued to stare at the words on the page. How much did she like Mark? Maybe she felt friendship for him because he had tended to her dying mother. He stole a quick glance at the couple. Mark looked young and relaxed. He seemed to be closer to her age. Suddenly, Josh felt a bit old and tired as he compared himself to the competent, good-looking doctor. When he looked at Juliana, he couldn't quell his rising feelings of emotion. Feelings he hadn't felt in a long time.

Mark would be able to give Juliana the kind of life someone as lovely and unassuming as she was deserved. Right now, all Josh could offer her was a smelly herd of sheep, hard work, and a small house in progress, with hope for the promise of a better future. He looked down at his rough hands holding his book. He couldn't imagine touching her delicate, tender skin with them. The thought made his chest hurt. Better to get back to his reading while he waited for his dinner.

Sheriff Wilson approached his table and paused. "How ya doing this evening, Josh?"

"Doing pretty good, Sheriff. Got any leads on the bank robber yet?"

"None that panned out so far. I expect the culprits are holed up somewhere in the mountains." The sheriff ran his hand along the brim of his felt hat. "After trailing them all day, we turned up cold, but we'll head back out as soon this latest storm passes."

"It looks like we'll get something with the wind howling against the window here. Maybe a light dusting of snow. I've got to get back to my camp first thing tomorrow."

Sheriff Wilson shifted his weight and put his hat on. "Looks like your dinner's arrived." He moved aside to allow the waiter to place the order on Josh's table. "Keep a lookout for those varmints out your way. If you see anything, let me know."

"I'll do that, for sure, though we don't usually see many people out where we're sheepherding. The smell keeps most people away." Josh chuckled.

"You can say that again! Well, I'll get out of your way so you can eat in peace."

Halfway through his meal, the thought occurred to Josh that he was tired of eating alone. Not only that, but he was lonely, and he'd had enough of living alone. He laid his fork down, not hungry for the rest of his dinner. He stole another glance at Juliana, and his brow furrowed in irritation. She and Mark were getting up to leave, and he watched as they moved in his direction.

Mark held tightly to Juliana's elbow but paused when they came near Josh's table. "Hello, Josh. We meet again. You remember Juliana?"

"Yes, I do." He pushed back his chair and nodded to Juliana. His chest felt tight. "Lucky you, Mark. I would have asked this pretty lady out myself, but I figured, why would she want to go out with the likes of me, a smelly old sheepherder?" He chuckled as he rose from his chair, but his laughter sounded hollow to his ears.

Mark merely cleared his throat and appeared uncomfortable.

"Oh, don't get up," Juliana said. "And don't sell yourself short, Josh. You've cleaned up quite nicely, I see." She looked at his clean shirt and vest. "I thought you had already gone back to your campsite." Juliana's lips tilted upward at the corners, and Josh felt his heart skip a beat. Her pale blue eyes never left his.

"I will be, first thing in the morning, ma'am. I trust you both had a good meal. I'm afraid I was so hungry that the food didn't have time to hit the back of my throat!" Even as Josh said it, he knew it was a lie—most of the food was left half-eaten under his napkin.

Mark smiled back at him. "We did indeed. I'm just about to walk Juliana back to the hotel."

"Then I'll bid you good night. It was nice seeing you again." He bowed slightly at the waist, pretending to be unaffected. How could another human being that he barely knew invade his thoughts this way? "If you're ever out near my campsite, please stop by and have coffee with me and about two hundred fifty wooly beasts."

Juliana laughed. "I intend to do that." Her eyes lingered on Josh, and Mark gave her a quizzical look. "I want to repay you for what you did for my mother as soon as I receive my first paycheck."

"Please, don't concern yourself with that. I'm not worried about it."

"I insist. Thank you . . . We must be going. Good night, Josh." As Juliana turned away, the open lace loop of her crocheted shawl snagged on the back of Josh's ladder-back chair, pulling her backwards. She stumbled and bumped the table. The delicate water goblets and plates wobbled atop the table and threatened to hit the floor. Quickly she reached out to steady the glasses, while at the same time Josh stretched across her arm to lift the shawl off the chair's back. Somehow she fell against him, and they both halfway sprawled onto the table, landing in the leftover food as the dishes clattered to the floor with a loud crash.

Josh's face was an inch from Juliana's flaming cheeks, and time was suspended for a moment. He forced himself to refrain from reaching out to touch her high cheekbones. Her hair smelled like lavender, and he could almost visualize her washing her long hair and rubbing it dry with a towel. Placing her palms on his woolen shirt, she pushed herself away, then straightened her blouse.

Josh shook his head to clear the vision in his mind. "I'm so sorry. I was trying to untangle your shawl." His tongue felt thick in his mouth, but he scrambled to pull Juliana upright as the waiter came running up to help.

"It's okay. I thought I could prevent the glasses from toppling to the floor." Juliana brushed her skirt with both hands, dusting off bread crumbs. "How embarrassing."

The patrons in the restaurant had turned to see what the commotion was, but they turned back to their dining and laughter once everything was under control.

Mark grabbed a napkin from the waiter and gave it to Juliana to wipe her hands. "Here, let me get the back of your arm. Something is stuck to your shawl." He wiped it none too gently before dropping the soiled napkin in the heap on the table.

"Please, if you don't mind, I'll get this all cleaned up. Don't worry about a thing," the waiter said as he started picking up broken dishes.

Josh somehow managed to mutter a thank-you to the waiter. He already felt like a big clumsy oaf next to the polished city doctor, not to mention how he'd embarrassed the young lady.

Mark tugged at Juliana's arm, indicating he was ready to leave.

"We must be on our way now. Josh, maybe we'll see you the next time you're in town for supplies. I'll be sure to give you a wide berth." All three of them joined in a nervous laugh.

"You bet! I look forward to it," was all Josh could say. He watched Mark put a protective arm about Juliana's waist and guide her into the cool night air.

12

Juliana tapped the reins lightly across the hindquarters of her borrowed horse, Choco, as she headed across the valley floor. The air was crisp and cold, but she was warm under the layers of clothing Marion had insisted she wear. She'd borrowed a pair of faded jeans that made riding in the saddle much easier. She was certain that by afternoon she would be shedding the long woolen jacket.

It felt good to be riding with the wind pulling at the tendrils of her hair from underneath the cowboy hat and the feel of Choco's muscular body stretching out into a canter. This was real freedom, riding alone with the puffy white clouds draping like bridal satin across the ridge of the purple mountains to the west.

It had been a couple of weeks since her date with Mark. He was a very nice man, attentive and sweet to her. The townsfolk held him in high esteem. Whether it was because he was the only doctor around for miles, or because they truly liked him, she wasn't sure. But she figured the latter. Trouble was, even when she was thinking of him, the sheepherder's eyes came into sharp contrast, making it very difficult to concentrate on anything else.

She wasn't happy about this, because it interfered with her idea of the future. She wanted to have her own home someday and be able to dress like her friend Marion. Not worrying about where her next meal was coming from would be good too. Maybe the ladies at the social club wouldn't be so hoity-toity then.

Today she was going to take up Josh's invitation to visit his camp and ranch. More importantly, she would repay him the money for her mother's funeral. It made her feel good to be able to do that. She really never wanted to be beholden to any man like her mother was. Juliana intended to work hard at her job and make Albert proud.

She could smell the sheep before they came into view. She made out a wagon, a dog, and a couple of people around a campfire. They straightened and stood, waiting for her to draw closer. She recognized Josh because of his smaller stature and solid body, but the other man was tall and lanky. Josh's face lit up with a big smile as she drew closer, and he released the lamb he held in his arms, then mopped his perspiring brow with a somewhat dirty handkerchief. A dog Juliana guessed to be Shebe barked a friendly greeting, then moved to stand next to her owner with her tail wagging.

"Mornin' glory! What a pleasant surprise." Josh was quick on his feet and reached to help her, placing his hands around her waist to put her down into a crowd of mewing lambs. Though he was a little taller than she was, she felt like she could look almost directly into his eyes. He smelled of wet sheep and sweat. When she wrinkled her nose in distaste, he laughed.

"Sorry about the smell. We've been dipping and branding our lambs the last three days." He motioned in the direction of the troughs at the edge of the clearing. "Had you come a few days ago, you could've watched us shear their wool. That's a big undertaking, and we had to hire some help, or we'd have been here for a month of Sundays." He chuckled as he weaved through the lambs, tenderly touching a head here and patting a rump there.

Josh reached into a bucket of red paint, lifting a wooden brand. "Sheepherders use a more civilized way of branding instead of the red-hot branding iron that cattlemen use. I had this one made especially for me. But maybe that's more information than you came to hear."

Feeling out of her element, she stammered, "I hope I didn't come at a bad time." Juliana felt heat on her face, and it wasn't from the camp's fire. She couldn't help but notice how firm and hard Josh's chest muscles were as they strained against his chamois shirt. He probably was in great physical shape from working outdoors most of his life. Juliana tore her gaze from his amber eyes, which stared openly at her.

"No, no, this is a perfect time for us to stop, ain't that right, Andy? I didn't mean to rattle on." Josh turned toward the scrawny young man who gave Juliana a warm smile. "This is Andy, my right arm and cook."

Andy wiped his hand on his pants leg, then thrust it out to her. "Howdy. Shore is nice to have a visitor out here. We get lonesome out here, don't we, Josh?" He pumped her gloved hand up and down.

Juliana could tell he was curious about her, but when Josh didn't offer any information about her, she only laughed at his enthusiasm, and he finally let go of her hand, smiling all the while. He probably wasn't much older than she. His clothes were so worn that they were fraying at the pockets and the legs, where they met his worn boot heels.

"Well, speak for yourself, Andy, but you're right, we don't see too many people out this way. Most of them don't like sheep because of the noise and the smell." Josh indicated the sheepdog sniffing at her feet. "This here is Shebe—man's best friend."

Juliana pulled her gloves off and stretched out her hand to the dog so Shebe could lick her fingers. "I think I've just made a new friend." She scratched the spotted dog under the chin.

Juliana marveled at the soft furry little faces of the lambs and couldn't resist reaching out to touch the babies. "So adorable . . . and so soft. I think this is the closest I've ever been to sheep before. You have a lot of babies." A little baby lamb's damp nose nuzzled her fingertips, and the rest crowded near. Most of the sheep had been shorn fairly short but still had a small layer of fuzz. She noticed the red-painted brand in the shape of a "J"—for Josh's initial, she assumed—in the lamb's rump.

"It's real easy to get attached to them," Josh said. "They're not the smartest creatures in the world, but they'll do whatever you want them to. Sometimes when the ewe is lambing, she'll walk away from her baby, and we have to coach her to get the lamb to her teat. They're good at gettin' into trouble too. Like getting stuck in a bog or thicket. I've even seen a mama stand stark still, not making a sound, while a wolf carries off her lamb. Guess that's why the good Lord was called the Good Shepherd and we're called His sheep, because He lovingly leads us."

Juliana bristled at the remark. "Well, He sure led my father down the wrong path. Poor ewes are probably just afraid."

Andy's head snapped in his boss's direction. Josh squinted in the morning light, his bushy eyebrows furrowing beneath his hair, which was damp with perspiration. He turned to Andy. "Why don't you make us a fresh batch of coffee while I find the little lady something to sit on?"

Andy moved toward the campfire, grabbed the coffeepot, and poured out the dregs left from breakfast. "There's a little wooden stool in the back of the wagon, Josh. I'll go rinse this out and put the coffee on."

Soon the smell of rich coffee filled the sheep-laden area. Andy poured the strong liquid into thick mugs. "How do you like yours, Juliana?"

"If you have a bit of sugar, that would be nice, but I don't expect you have any cream?"

"Actually, you're in luck." Andy nodded his head toward a milk cow tethered not far away. "For all Josh's toughness, he has to have his coffee with both cream and sugar," Andy said, offering her a sugar cube and some cream.

Josh merely grunted. "'Bout the only way a man can stomach Andy's coffee is to doctor it up a bit." Josh grinned at Andy, and Juliana realized he was just teasing. Juliana smiled at Andy. "Thank you. I'm sure it will be better than what Albert brews at the newspaper."

"Speaking of that, how's the job coming along?" Josh asked, blowing on the steaming brew. He leaned against the wagon, propped his arm up, and casually cocked his head to look at her.

Juliana placed her cup on the ground and reached into her coat pocket for the envelope of cash. "The job is going very well, thank you. I brought the money you loaned me to pay for my mother's funeral. It was good of you to do that when you didn't even know me." A small catch threatened to crack in her voice, but she quickly cleared her throat, extending the envelope toward him.

Josh's fingers touched hers lightly, and she was stunned by the tingle that inched its way down her spine. She quickly drew back, but he pushed the envelope back into her palm.

"It wasn't a loan. I did it because I knew it was the right thing to do at the time. Don't worry about it. Save it. You'll be needing it."

Josh's look was so stern that she somehow knew not to argue with him, so she shoved the envelope back into her coat pocket. "Well, if you insist. Thank you again, and if there's ever anything I can help you out with, please let me know." Maybe now she could buy Choco from Marion and have a way to get around. She would check on that first thing when she returned.

"There is one thing I could use your advice on. If you have the time, we could ride up to the ranch. I've been building it in stages as I get the finances, and I'm ready to start on the inside of the kitchen. Perhaps you could help me with the layout. I don't spend much time cooking."

Juliana laughed. "I'm not much of a cook myself, so I'm not sure how much help I'll be, but sure, I'd like to see your place. I don't work on Saturdays, so I'm free all day today." As soon as she said it, she thought it made her sound desperate for something to do.

Josh's amber eyes danced when he looked at her, and she felt a nervous stirring in her belly. Suddenly she remembered the sketch of the sheepherder and the dog at the hotel, and with a start she realized the two were the same. The first time she had seen those amber eyes, her heart had lurched. *Don't forget you're going to be independent, make your own way. You don't need a man for that.*

"Well then, we'll both have to do something about that, won't we?" Josh downed the last of the coffee.

"I can finish up here, if you two want to go on. Just have a bit left to clean up," Andy offered. "Juliana, would you like to see inside our newfangled sheepherder's wagon before you leave? It's the latest thing straight from Casper, Wyoming."

"Sure, Andy. I've heard of a chuck wagon but not a wagon for sheepherders."

Andy couldn't hide his enthusiasm as he pulled her up into the wagon. "It's called a Candlish wagon, named after a blacksmith who got tired of hearing complaints of sheepherders' sleepless nights."

Juliana was amazed. The canvas covering was made tall enough for a man to stand up. It featured a Dutch door in front, a window in front of the bed, and a small cast-iron stove, which was vented through an opening in the canvas. A bed attached across the wagon's back housed a pull-out table, drawers, and cupboards, making them accessible from the outside. She saw a stack of old magazines and a few books.

"It's so compact and convenient," Juliana said, taking it all in.

"All the comforts of home, including a kerosene heater that keeps it snug," Andy said. "Mostly, I'm the one who stays here, but from time to time Josh will stay a few days, like when we're branding, because there's room for a pallet. It stays cool in the summer and warm in the winter."

She marveled at the structure. "It's quite cozy in here, almost like home." Maybe even better than the rented old cabin she and her mother had lived in. "It must have been quite expensive."

"I reckon so, but Josh has a fine stock of Merino rams that can fetch up to $1,000 a head, so he's doing all right."

"Is it okay with you, Juliana, if we go now?" Josh watched them from the ground and held out his hand to help her down.

"Sure, if you can set me on the right trail back to Lewistown from your place."

"No problem. Actually, there's a shortcut from the ranch."

"Juliana, it was good to meet you," Andy said. "Please come back when I have some apple dumplings to go with that coffee."

"That sounds good to me. Thanks for the coffee, Andy." She grabbed the reins and pulled herself up into the saddle. Josh unhitched his horse from the back of the wagon and led the way out of the camp, with Shebe following closely behind.

Josh was more than happy that Juliana was actually at his side at this moment. He had to admit it had been quite a surprise to see her riding up to the camp. He hadn't really thought she would come. The sunlight through the trees had bounced off her shiny dark hair falling in curls around her shoulders.

She was so unassuming, but he sensed her tough exterior. He knew she'd been hurt deeply, first by her dad, and then by losing her mother. Healing always took time. He should know. He thought about Crystal, the woman he used to love but had lost to another, and remembered his battle of words with his father, which caused a huge rift. He felt that leaving his father's ranch was the best decision he could have made at the time. But he knew it had hurt his mother.

"Sun's warming things up," he said once they were out of the camp's clearing.

"Yes, it is. I'm sure I'll have to remove this coat before too long." Their horses were only a handbreadth apart so they could talk comfortably. "How long have you been ranching?"

"Most of my life, but not always with sheep. I do have a few head of cattle, though. Just enough to have some fresh meat. Have you ever tasted lamb before?"

"Afraid not. It really doesn't sound appealing to me."

"Don't worry. I don't like it either. I raise sheep for the wool. Right now I'm looking into mining with a feller by the name of Hoover."

"Really?" Her eyebrows shot up.

"Yep. By chance I found some stones on my property, and then I had them appraised. I found out they're called Yogo sapphires. The only place in the world you can find them is here in Montana. I'll show them to you when we get to the ranch. Hoover already has a mine started and a few partners, and he needs the water from my property to work it. So I'm considering it."

" 'Make all the money you can' is my motto. You can never have enough of it." Her chin was set in firm determination, but the slump of her slender shoulders belied her confidence. "Sounds like it might be a good investment, but do you have to *become* a miner?"

"What's wrong with being a miner? Mining could be exactly what I need to set me up for life. I know money isn't everything." He thought about his dad. "I know of a few people who hoard it and never really live a happy life. A person needs to have money to travel, do some fun leisurely things sometimes, instead of just working their fingers to the bone. Mining will secure my future much faster than a sheep ranch."

"That's easy to say if you succeed. A lot of men die trying. Besides, mining is a dirty business and a dangerous job." Her tone sounded bitter.

Josh laughed heartily. "And raising sheep isn't?" He knew she was really thinking about her own father and probably carried a bad image of miners in her head.

Juliana bristled. "So what do you intend to do with the sheep?"

"Oh, I'll keep them too. I'll just hire more help. Not a problem with all the money I'll make from the sapphires. Wouldn't you like to have plenty of money?"

Juliana harrumphed. "Sure, I think about money, but I don't want it at *any* cost, and mining is a high price to pay. I've seen firsthand how it destroys families. I intend to earn money and save it to find my own place to live. I can't always live with the Stocktons. I'm not their responsibility."

"I'm sure they don't look at you as a burden but as someone they want to help and protect." *I could protect her and take good care of her, if she'd let me*, he thought. "The house is coming up just above the crest. I wanted it to overlook the valley so when I'm old and gray, I can sit on the front porch and watch the sunset. That time will be here sooner rather than later." He chuckled and looked into her cornflower-blue eyes for a reaction.

"You're not that old! At least you don't look old to me." She scrutinized his face from under her thick lashes until a smile tugged at the corners of her mouth, showing her white teeth.

"Well, let's just say I'm old enough to know better than to flirt with a pretty young lady like you."

She flushed pink and looked away quickly. "Maybe I'm older

than you think. I'll be eighteen in May. Maybe I could introduce you to Marion Stockton. She's probably about your age."

"You don't say?" He didn't know whether to be offended or not. She must think he *was* too old for her if she wanted to set him up with Marion. "I would have thought you were at least twenty-five," he teased. "I'm thirty. And I remember Marion from the hotel. Her father owns it. I'll have to keep her in mind." Josh trotted up toward the ridge with Juliana following suit.

His house had a magnificent view of the valley below and the mountain range to the west. Unadorned glass windows lined the front of the sprawling two-story clapboard structure with a large front porch, all in the final stages of construction. Several rockers were scattered about. He knew his unfinished home lacked a woman's touch and hoped Juliana could help him out with that. Perhaps she wouldn't be too disappointed.

Juliana's first thoughts upon entering Josh's home were that things were a little cluttered. A pile of boots and fishing gear sat in the foyer. The coat rack had one too many things hanging on it, and it threatened to topple when he took her coat to add it to the rest. It was obvious by the dust on the furniture in the parlor that the place was in need of cleaning, and his cluttered desk, tucked into a corner with stacks of newspapers, catalogs, and mail, was in need of attention. She tried not to act surprised. He was a bachelor, after all. What could she expect?

"Sorry, but I haven't been here the last couple of weeks to keep things tidy. I try to work toward that end on Sunday afternoons. I still have some boxes I've never unpacked," he said sheepishly. "Not all the rooms are completed. Come this way, and I'll show you what I've started with the kitchen."

Juliana followed him to the spacious room that would become the kitchen, which held a stove and a fireplace on one side. A table made of two-by-fours and two benches appeared hastily constructed. "You haven't always lived here?"

"No, I've lived in the house less than a year. I moved from Colorado nearly three years ago."

"I see. This is a nice-size kitchen. You'll have plenty of room for a large table." She walked to the large glass window, clapped her hands, and said, "Oh, this is a wonderful backyard with those big trees. I love it. This would be a perfect place for the sink when you get one, right under the window." She surmised that he was using the big tub on the floor to wash the dishes in.

Shebe ran past her straight out the back door when she glimpsed a rabbit, and Juliana and Josh laughed.

"I'm glad you like the place. Come on, let's have a seat at the table, and you can give me some more ideas about what I need to do with this place." Josh pulled out a chair for her, then came back with a pencil and paper. He drew the outline of the kitchen and indentations for the windows and doors on the paper and pushed it to her. "Show me what you would put in here and where."

"But I can't draw. At least not anything that's recognizable." She tapped the pencil on the table.

"Doesn't matter. Write it out for me."

Juliana placed a small rectangle where a new table should be and a circle to represent the sink under the window. Next to the fireplace, she drew a rocking chair and an overstuffed chair facing each other. Along one wall near the stove, she drew doors halfway down the wall to represent the cupboards. On another wall, she sketched several shelves to hold some plates or utensils.

She handed him the paper. "This is the best I can do, but you get the idea, don't you?"

"Not bad. I thought you said you couldn't draw."

"You're joking." She chortled.

"No, I'm not, really. What color should I paint the walls?"

"You could paint it a bright sunny yellow and trim out the woodwork in white for a nice contrast," she said, looking around the room.

"Mmm. Sounds rather feminine to me. Remember, there are no ladies living under my roof. I was thinking about a more masculine color."

"Well, from the looks of things, unless there's improvement around here, there won't be any females," she teased. Juliana enjoyed this comfortable bantering back and forth.

"Now look who's teasing," Josh said.

"Hey, I'd better get out of your way and let you do your planning." Juliana rose from her chair.

"You've helped me out a lot. I needed a different perspective. Next time you can help me with the bedroom."

Juliana felt her face go pink, but he continued to give her a playful grin while twirling the pencil in his fingers.

"By the way, I do apologize for that night in the restaurant," Josh said. "I didn't mean to be so clumsy."

"Don't even trouble yourself thinking that. It was entirely my fault," she said. "If it hadn't been me, I would have thought it was funny."

"Oh, I almost forgot." He reached inside his pocket and took out a small chamois bag, spilling its contents across the table. "These are the Yogo sapphires I was telling you about."

Juliana sucked in her breath and said, "Oh, they're beautiful." She picked up one of the stones and turned it to the light. "Such a beautiful blue. I've never seen that color before."

"I have," he said huskily.

"Oh, really? Where?"

"I'm looking at it now. It's the color of your eyes, Juliana. Beautiful and unusual."

She squirmed, not knowing what to say, while his small amber eyes looked squarely into hers, searching.

"I think I'll call you *Jewel* to represent these beautiful Yogos."

A sharp pang filled her heart, and she felt breathless with his face bending so close to hers. "What's wrong with my name? Don't you like it?"

"I like it fine, but I think you're rare like the Yogos." He said it so softly that she almost thought she'd heard him wrong. Josh reached out and squeezed her hand, which lay on the table. He leaned closer, brushing his lips against hers with a slight firmness. For a brief moment time stopped. The pressure of his warm lips against hers felt nice and oh so sweet. She wanted to linger there, but she pulled away, remembering where she was. She felt tongue-tied and swallowed hard. Why was she letting him get to her this way? She tried to find her voice, but when she spoke it sounded weak to her ears.

"I need to be going, Josh, and let you get back to your camp," she said, standing up. She couldn't discern what he might be thinking from the look on his face, but she didn't intend to marry a miner. Ever.

They stepped out onto the porch, and he gave her the directions for the shortcut through the woods back to Lewistown. She trotted down the path, turning around once to give a quick wave. She hoped he'd come up with an excuse to make another trip to town real soon.

The sun's glistening rays sliced through the spruce trees, creating a mottled pattern on the forest floor, and purple crocuses peeked their heads through the surrounding straw at the base of the trees among new sprigs of tender grass. Birds sang out as they flitted from tree branches back to their nests to feed their tiny hatchlings. Spring had arrived despite the shivering cold mornings, and Juliana lifted her face to the sun's heat, enjoying the moment. She loved the wildflowers scattered about, and she slid off her horse to let him graze while she picked a few to take back to her room.

The silence outdoors was a welcome sound after hearing the printing presses daily and the activity of busy Lewistown streets. She needed to do this more often and try to work something out with Marion for Choco if at all possible. She'd have to be able to keep him at Tom's livery if she was able to afford it. The prospect of owning something excited her.

She chuckled inwardly at the rough sketches she had made for Josh. It had been fun sitting there bantering with him, though she thought he used her input as an excuse to be with her. Being so near him allowed her to really get a close-up inspection of him. She thought about his wide forehead and bushy eyebrows and small eyes—unusual golden-brown eyes. His hands were not large but nice and solid, just like his barrel chest. His upper lip had a delightful curve to it, but she hadn't been expecting the kiss. She felt heat rising in her neck just thinking about it. So that's what it felt like to be kissed by a man. She had to admit she liked the way his lips tasted. The kiss had sent a thrill right through her.

The sound of crackling brush brought her back to the present. She looked around and hoped it wasn't some wild animal. Out of the corner of her eye she saw movement, and a rider appeared out of the woods, pulling his horse up sharply in front of her. Startled, she straightened. It was Wes.

"What were you trying to do, frighten me?" She tried to sound confident, but her heart thumped against her ribs.

"Well, lookee here. If it ain't Miss High-and-Mighty. Are you looking for an escort back into town?" He edged his horse closer. His stare seemed to go right through her prim cotton blouse, and suddenly she realized she'd forgotten the woolen coat she'd borrowed from Marion.

"Indeed, I don't. Just leave me alone." Juliana now wished she'd gone back through the camp instead of the forest. At least in the valley it was wide open. Here she was trapped.

"I think you just better start speaking a little more kindly to me. You're out here all alone in these woods." His eyes slithered over her body, making her feel exposed somehow. "My goodness, you're wearing men's jeans?"

"So what if I am?" Juliana shuddered slightly. "Out of my way, Wes, or I swear . . ."

"Or what?" He swung his leg across his saddle and slid off the horse's back. He reached out and grabbed her wrist.

Juliana winced. The tobacco smell of his breath disgusted her, and she stiffened.

He placed his hand on the back of her neck, pulling her close to his face. "I'll teach you to turn a man's kisses down twice!" He leaned down to kiss her, but she twisted against him, and the top button on her blouse popped off.

Her eyes narrowed with anger. "Stop it! Take your hands off me!"

But Wes only laughed and pulled her tighter. His eyes flicked over her again. She jerked away, trying to free herself.

"Feisty, aren't you? That just makes it all the more fun," he said.

Juliana yanked hard, and the two of them tripped, falling hard onto the ground. She felt a sharp stab in her shoulder. Wes's eyes showed surprise, probably at his good fortune to be lying almost on top of her. She thought she heard another person call out, or was it wishful thinking? Maybe it was Josh coming to bring her coat to her.

"Wes, get off her! Have you lost your addle-brained mind?" An older man dressed in miners' garb strode up next to them and yanked Wes back.

"Aw, just having a little fun, that's all. I was trying to steal a kiss, and we tripped over the rocks." He moved away, red-faced.

The older man reached down to assist Juliana up from the forest floor. She was trembling, mostly from anger.

"You all right, ma'am? He didn't hurt you none, did he?" The miner took a long, hard look at her. He had dark hair, a medium build, and a week's worth of beard and shaggy hair. But at least he'd stopped Wes.

"I–I think I'm okay." She rubbed her wrist. Her shoulder and arm smarted too, but she said nothing.

"Of course I didn't hurt her. I was just trying to teach her not to be so stuck up," Wes grumbled.

He looked madder than an old bandy rooster, Juliana thought.

"Wes, git on your horse and high-tail it outta here before I come after you myself!" The man waved his arm at Wes.

Wes turned to Juliana. "Uh, I'm sorry. I wasn't gonna hurt you, honest."

Juliana only glared at him. Wes shuffled toward his horse, picked up the reins, and was on the horse's back in a hurry.

"Here, let me help you get back up on your horse," the miner said, reaching out to her, but Juliana backed away.

"I don't need your help." Juliana scrambled back up onto Choco's broad back. She looked down at the older man, who had blue eyes beneath dark, worried brows. "But thank you for saving me from that reprehensible man. I do hope he is not your son."

"Fortunately, no, he is not. I never had a son. Just a daughter, and I wouldn't want her handled like that. He gets a little hot-headed at times, fancying that he's popular with the ladies."

"Don't make excuses for him." Juliana spat the words out like a bad taste in her mouth.

"I don't excuse his behavior. But I didn't get your name."

"It's Juliana." She held the reins in one hand and the top of her blouse in the other.

"Pretty name. I work in the mine over at Yogo Creek. I'm glad I happened along when I did. I really don't think he would have harmed you." He lingered, looking up into her face a little longer before mounting his own horse.

"You men are all the same, taking up for one another, but thanks anyway." She flicked the reins across Choco and tore through the forest, anxious to get back to civilization. She would never take this trail alone next time, if there was a next time. Her back was just starting to hurt when she realized she hadn't gotten the miner's name.

14

After leaving Choco at Tom's livery, Juliana practically ran down the boardwalk and up the hotel stairs to her room, then threw herself across the bed. She closed her eyes, wanting to dream about the kiss with Josh and how delicious his lips felt against hers. Gosh, it was wonderful. Had he thought the same about hers? She'd never felt like this before, and even now her heart skipped a beat when she remembered how he'd called her Jewel.

She rolled over and looked up at the ceiling, placing her hands behind her head. She wasn't sure what to think of Wes and his crazy way of trying to kiss her. She was glad that miner had come along when he did. Something was awfully familiar about him, but she couldn't think of what it was.

A gentle tapping at her door made her sit up on the edge of the bed, and she made an attempt to smooth her hair back in place. She didn't remember losing her hat. "Who's there?"

"It's me—Marion. May I come in?"

Juliana forced a smile as she pulled open the door.

"I wanted to see what you had planned for—" The look in Marion's bright blue eyes held surprise. "My goodness! What's happened to you? Are you all right? Are you hurt?" she said, reaching out to touch Juliana on her arm.

"If you'll slow down with the questions, I'll tell you. Choco threw me, that's all." She rubbed her sore backside.

"Oh really? That doesn't sound like Choco at all." Marion's eyebrow raised in question. "Let me see." She turned Juliana slowly around. "How did you get the tear in the back of your blouse? I can see blood through the material."

Juliana looked away with Marion still holding her arms. "It's nothing, really."

"Is that right? So why is the top button on your blouse missing?" Marion tapped the toe of her shoe against the hardwood floor, her hands on her hips.

Juliana looked down, unbuttoned her blouse the rest of the way, and removed it. Marion gasped when she saw her back.

"All right. I had a little scuffle with an odious cowboy."

"Let me get a closer look at that cut. You're bruised! Now tell me, what cowboy are you referring to?"

Juliana winced when Marion touched the spot on her shoulder. "His name is Wes. I rode out to Josh's camp to pay him the money for Mama's burial. Later, I was taking a shortcut from his ranch back to town, and Wes appeared from out of nowhere."

"What did he do to you?" There was fury in Marion's normally sweet voice. "If he harmed you, we are going to Sheriff Wilson right now!"

A nervous giggle escaped Juliana's lips. "He didn't do anything. He wanted a kiss because I turned him down for a date the other night." Suddenly Juliana felt the sting on her back.

"Oh, honey, come sit down. I think you're bleeding."

Juliana let herself be led to a chair by the window. Her arm was hurting as well, probably from when she'd fallen. Marion walked over to the pitcher sitting on top of the dresser and poured some water in the basin, then took a washcloth and began to gently blot her back.

"I'll be right back with some salve to put on that cut. Don't move an inch." She left the room but was back in two seconds with a jar of cream. It had a cooling effect on Juliana's back, and she let herself relax, closing her eyes to the ministrations of Marion's fingertips.

"There. I think that will help it heal quickly. So, tell me about Josh. Did he take the money?"

"He wouldn't even think of it." She took another blouse out of the bureau drawer. She was down to two now. Then she slipped her pants off and donned a skirt.

"I'm not surprised at all. I told you before that I think he likes you." Marion folded the ruined blouse neatly. "What are you smiling about?" she asked, looking at Juliana.

"Oh . . . nothing. But I forgot your coat at Josh's ranch. I'm sorry."

"What? You mean to tell me you went to the ranch? I thought you were only riding to his camp," she said with a demure giggle.

"That was my intent, but he wanted my opinion on the layout of his new kitchen." Juliana made a nonchalant half-twirl, the navy full skirt falling softly against her legs, and picked up her hairbrush.

"What would you know about something like that? I hope you told him you hardly ever touch a pot or pan unless forced." Marion laughed.

"Don't be silly. I can cook, at least a little." Juliana gave a pouting look to her friend. "Anyway, I gave him some advice about what to put where. He has a nice place, though it's a work in progress." She looked out the window.

"Is that all that happened?" Marion asked.

Juliana answered quickly, "Actually, no." But she was not about to tell Marion about the kiss or the nickname. "He showed me some sapphires he found. He might go into a mining venture with another fellow."

"Mmm . . . somehow I get the feeling you're not telling all there is to tell, my friend." Marion poked her finger into Juliana's arm teasingly.

"Nope. That's about it. I don't have time to be courting anyone. I have to make my way right now."

"What about Mark? I thought you liked him."

"I do, but as a friend. I enjoy his company, that's all. What about you, Marion? I told Josh you were available."

"You didn't!" Marion sputtered.

"I did. I think he's looking for a woman closer to his age. I'm just a kid to him." Juliana knew this was a half truth. She knew Josh liked her, or he wouldn't have kissed her or said those things. Would he? She knew very little about men, except that most were not trustworthy, and that one certain man had raised feelings in her she didn't know existed.

Marion's face went pink, and her blue eyes sparkled. "I can't believe you told him that. I don't need you to play matchmaker. I have to admit it, though, he's attractive in a strange sort of way."

Juliana was not expecting this reaction from her. For the first time she thought about her friend in a different light. Marion was a young, vivacious woman still in her twenties who would be interested in finding a husband.

"Marion, would you like to walk over to Helen's to see how her daughter's friend is coming along? I can fill you in on the last meeting of the social club while we walk."

"Are you sure you feel like it?"

"A little bruise is not going to keep me inside. I feel better now, and it's a beautiful day."

"I'd like that. Helen is a really nice lady. And I wonder how Jane is doing. I hope she'll be okay. She was hit pretty hard from what you told me. Hey, why don't we stop in the kitchen and pack up some of the fresh cookies that were baked today and take them to Jane?"

"Good idea. All kids like cookies. But I wish I hadn't left your coat at Josh's. I'm sorry."

"No matter. It'll give him an excuse to come back to town to see you," Marion said.

"I don't know about that. He may try to find you." Juliana flashed a grin and walked out into the hallway as Marion swatted at her in feign embarrassment.

It was a beautiful day for a walk, and the two chatted as they walked past pretty wooden homes, some of them painted white with picket fences around them. Neighbors called out and waved hello, and they returned the greetings. It made Juliana feel like she was a part of the community to be Marion's friend. Most people in the town hadn't known her until she started working with Albert at the paper.

"Marion, would you consider selling Choco to me?" Juliana asked with trepidation.

"Well . . . I might consider it. Why?"

"I'd love to be able to ride. He's pretty gentle and seems to like me, and since Josh wouldn't take the money I tried to give him for my mother's funeral, I thought maybe I could buy him . . . if you aren't too attached." She turned to get Marion's reaction.

Marion smiled back at her. "No, I'm not too attached. We have several horses. Yes, my friend, I think we could work something out with you where you could make a payment once a month." She squeezed Juliana's arm in her pleasant way.

Juliana stopped on the sidewalk, giving Marion a brief hug. "You're the best! I don't know what I would do without you."

As they continued on their way, she told Marion what she'd missed at the Ladies Social Club meeting.

"That's a marvelous project to work on," Marion said.

"To tell you the truth, Marion, I think you'd be an excellent choice as the teacher, and I intend to nominate you."

Marion seemed surprised. "Me? Why me?"

"Because. You're intelligent, articulate, and maybe it would give you something challenging to do when you're not helping your dad with the hotel."

"You may be better suited, although it would be fun to do something different, something I feel would be beneficial to young minds eager to learn. Reading and writing certainly will open up the world to the miners' children. It could give them hope that they don't have to follow in their dad's footsteps if they get an education."

"Exactly my point," Juliana said. "If it hadn't been for my mother's teaching me after we left Kansas, I wouldn't have a job right now, that's for sure. Then where would I be?"

"You would live as you are now, with us, then find a good husband who would take care of you," Marion answered.

"Marion, times are changing. Some women don't want to just automatically get married. Some are actually becoming doctors these days. That sounds exciting to me."

"Don't you want to get married and have a family?" Marion's voice conveyed complete shock.

"Someday, yes. But I'm not in any hurry. I'm enjoying writing articles for the newspaper. I don't want to repeat the same course my mother did, following my father's dreams only to be abandoned." Juliana didn't mean to sound bitter, but she believed her mother felt she'd had no choice, traipsing from town to town with her husband's great schemes to get rich.

"She did what she thought was best, Juliana. Could be that it turned out best for you."

"I don't see how that's possible, since my father left to go look for gold. He didn't care what happened or how we got by. A few times he sent money, but later, even that stopped. How can someone not want to see his wife and daughter? I just don't understand it at all." She shook her head in agitation, fighting back angry tears.

"But your mother took great care of you and educated you. She never left you. Yes, you didn't live the best kind of life, but you had a godly mother who was positive about life and you. I admire her for that. It couldn't have been easy for her."

Marion's reminder made Juliana feel very selfish. "You're right, of course. She taught me to believe the best in people and always give a lending hand. I guess since she died, I've gotten a little cynical, haven't I?"

"It's okay to question everything. It means you're seeking what's best in life for you. God has a plan for each of us. Trouble is, most of us don't ask and don't want to listen."

"You really believe that?" Juliana sighed. Maybe Marion was right.

"Yes, I really do." Marion paused in front of Helen's gate before opening it, then turned to Juliana. "If He cares about the lilies of the field, how much more does He care for you?" Without waiting for a reply, she swung open the gate for Juliana to pass through, then slipped the wrought-iron latch into place.

Juliana tucked the remark away for the time being. She didn't really understand it anyway.

The musky smell of sheep dung and the bleating of lambs woke Josh out of his deep sleep. The sun warmed his unshaven face through the crack of rough boards on the sheepherder's wagon. He smiled wistfully. He'd had a strange dream. In it, Juliana was reaching out to him, beckoning him to come closer. Her face was etched with concern, and her blue eyes exposed deep emotion and tears, but as he reached for her, she receded into the background of his foggy dream. He wanted to take away whatever was upsetting her. Was she in trouble? He hoped not.

He rolled over to the edge of the bed that was built across the wagon's back and sat up, rubbing his sleepy eyes. *May as well get started*, he thought, reaching down to pull on his boots. Shebe shifted, yawned, and stretched when Josh reached down to scratch her behind the ears. When she wasn't herding, she hardly ever left his side. "Morning, girl," he said. The soft brown eyes seemed to smile back at him, and she gave a small yap, then tore for the outdoors when Josh pulled back the door.

The first chance he got, he planned to seek out Jake Hoover about the sapphires he'd found a couple of weeks ago. Maybe they could see about working something out with mining the stones. When Charlie told him that Hoover and his partners had already washed the same sapphires out of the lower part of Yogo Creek last season, he'd wanted to know more about the stones. He figured there were more sapphires to be found.

"You up, Boss?" Andy stuck his head into the opening of the wagon, holding a steaming cup of coffee.

"If you want to call it that. Why did you let me sleep so late?" Josh asked, taking the proffered cup from the young man.

"It's not late. The sun just came up over those hills."

"Every time I sleep too long, I wind up having a bad dream." He blew on the hot coffee.

"Want to talk about it?"

"No, it was just unsettling."

"Okay, whatever you say, Boss. Hungry?"

Josh's stomach growled. "Yeah. Have any of those sausages left over? We could just stick them between a biscuit for now to have something quick."

"I've already thought of that." Andy stepped back down into the clearing. "They're in the skillet now just waiting for me to warm 'em up a little on the stove. I was waiting for you to stir. Tonight I'll fix us a right nice supper."

"Sounds good to me." Josh hauled his stocky frame down out of the wagon and donned his jacket against the morning chill. "Would you like to ride with me over to Hoover's place I was telling you about? It's about three miles. We won't be gone long, and the sheep seem pretty content today. I want to talk to him about the sapphires I found."

"A short break might be nice, if you think the lambs will be okay." He motioned toward the herd.

118

"Sure, for a short time. It's your call."

"Okay then. I'll just stick these on the stove to heat. It won't take but a minute, unless you want yours cold?"

"No, I don't. I'm not in that big of a hurry." Josh grinned at the young sheepherder, who scampered up the steps to the stove behind the Dutch doors. Andy was a real treasure, almost like Josh's own son. Like a gift from God. They enjoyed each other's company, and Josh reveled in the knowledge that sometimes they could go for hours without speaking and still know what was on the other's mind. The age difference didn't seem to matter to either of them.

Pig Eye Basin was on the Judith River, south of Utica and just west of Lewistown, not far from Josh's property. The warm spring sun had melted some of the snow along the eastern slope of the basin, and Josh could hear the gurgle of rushing creek water below from the melting snow. He enjoyed springtime in the mountains and watching the fledging meadowlarks. Tender green leaves of the cottonwood trees gave the impression they had unfurled from their deep winter's sleep. Josh looked at the towering ponderosa pine clustered near the grassy bench lands. The air was fresh and invigorating. It was a great day to be alive. Shebe was happy to be following along with him and Andy and would scamper off to investigate movement in the brush, then run back to catch up with them.

Josh and Andy followed the wagon road that led to Hoover's small ranch and were greeted by the yapping of a couple of dogs. They rushed up to greet the strangers, barking loudly at Shebe until a man opened the door and called the dogs off. They backed away with wary eyes but obeyed their master.

"Can I help you gents?" the man said, stepping out to the front porch. He had curly brown hair, a long, thick moustache, and several months' growth of beard, typical of a miner and trapper. He sported a flannel shirt and duck pants tucked into his boots.

"I'm Josh McBride, and this is Andy, my ranch hand." Andy nodded a hello. "I run sheep in the bench lands about three miles from you."

"I've heard of you, Josh. You filed a couple of claims after finding those Yogos, didn't you? Pleased to meet you. I'm Jake Hoover. Step down off your horses. The dogs won't hurt you."

"Don't mind if we do." Josh slid off his horse's back and lightly held the reins. Andy followed suit. "It was the Yogos I came to talk to you about. I met up with a friend of yours by the name of Charlie Russell, who was just passing through on his way to Great Falls, and he told me you were mining gold and knew about sapphires."

The older man scratched his head and laughed. "You mean 'the Kid'? He is forever drawing or painting. A better friend a man never had!"

"He said the same thing about you."

Hoover motioned for them to come in. "I've got a pot of coffee on the stove. We can talk sitting down."

They followed him inside the modestly furnished cabin. Josh noticed the usual tools of a prospector as well as a trapper scattered about the cabin. A low fire crackled in the grate. "Here, have a seat, and I'll dig up some cups." Hoover bustled around, whipped out three enamel cups, and plunked them down on the pine tabletop. Lifting the speckled enameled coffeepot with a folded dishrag, he poured the dark liquid into each of their cups.

"I first discovered gold at the lower part of Yogo Creek in '94. I knew what I'd found was gonna be more than me just using picks and pans to discover the extent of it." Hoover paused to take a swig of coffee.

"Do you have a partner?" Josh asked.

"Yes, I do. Hobson, a rancher and president of Fergus National Bank in Lewistown. My other partner is Bouvet, a veterinarian. Quite a combination, eh?"

"I'd have to say that's an interesting partnership," Josh said thoughtfully, and glanced over at Andy. *Bet Andy's enjoying someone else's coffee for a change.*

"They put up most of the capital for our promising mining venture, and we hired an engineer to dig a ten-mile ditch to divert water from the upper Yogo down to the lower end, knowing the strike was from a secondary deposit. It took us two months."

"So you struck it rich?" Andy finally spoke, his eyes wide with interest.

"Nope. Nothing like that. We spent nearly $38,000, and the rest of our capital was spent on laborers I supervised all summer long to build sluices, but it was a bust. We spent more than we collected." Hoover's eyes squinted as though recalling a bad misfortune. "Anyway, I began looking in the sluice concentrates for blue pebbles I'd seen earlier. Apparently they were washed out of the lower Yogo Creek. The dike cuts through the creek and washed the sapphires downstream, concentrating them with what little gold we found."

"So, how did you know they were valuable?" Josh asked, enjoying his second cup of coffee.

"When I first discovered the Yogos, I wasn't sure what I had. It took me awhile to collect enough stones to fill a cigar box to send to Tiffany's in New York. An assayer named Dr. George Kunz thought they were valuable enough to pay me quite well for them."

"Sounds like you'll need the right kind of equipment, not to mention financial backing." Josh lifted his cup, swallowing the last sip. "And you make a good cup of coffee."

"Glad you like it." Hoover paused to drink the remainder of the coffee in his cup, then wiped his mustache on the back of his hand. He set his cup down, looking directly at Josh. "From what the engineer says, your claim is situated between our properties on the Judith River. He said that would interfere with our access, and if we bring water to the bench lands to the site for washing, that's gonna interfere with disposal of the tailings. That'll involve a whole new set of problems."

Josh shifted in his chair. "What are you saying?"

"Are you interested in partnering?" Hoover refilled his own cup, then Andy's. "Could be that we hit it big, you know. We could both be wealthy men." Hoover smiled, his eyes flashing.

"I'll have to think about that." Josh was a cautious man. It sounded like a lot of work to him, and he wasn't sure it was worth the risk. It'd take money to invest, and right now he hoped to sell his claims and finish building his house—for a wife he hoped for soon. He was tired of living outside or in the sheep wagon.

"You ought to have some of those stones cut and polished by an assayer. Then you can really see their value," Hoover said.

"I intend to," Josh said, rising from the kitchen table. "We'd better be getting back to the herd." He motioned to Andy, who stood, pushing his chair back under the table.

"Nice meeting you, Hoover," Josh said.

"Thanks for stopping by, and we'll be talking further," Hoover said, shaking hands with Josh and Andy. He followed them out the door. "Give it some thought and keep in touch."

"I'll do that. See you soon."

Josh was pensive on the ride back to the camp, and Andy, who was used to Josh's habits, stayed quiet. Josh wasn't sure what to do. This mining venture could make him wealthy, a success in his father's eyes. Is that what he really wanted? He could give Juliana everything she ever wanted to make her happy. That, he knew he wanted. Yet taking up mining meant losing Juliana—and he didn't want to imagine life without her. Lots to think about.

Maybe on another trip into town he'd leave a couple of the stones to be cut and polished. He could probably pay the jeweler's fee out of the other stones if they were very valuable. Another great excuse to call on Juliana and return her coat.

Andy interrupted his musings by saying softly, "There's someone in our camp up ahead."

"You sure?" Josh slowed his horse, being careful not to make any sudden moves.

"Yes. I saw someone slip into the wagon. What do we do?" Andy shifted in his saddle to turn toward Josh.

Josh squinted to see if he could make out any movement. He saw someone step down out of the wagon, flinging the door back on its hinges. Josh eased his .44 out of its sheath and turned to Andy. "Easy and quiet now. Drop back a ways. I'll give that no-account something to think about before he goes plundering again." Josh gave his horse a slight kick in the side, with Shebe running close behind him. "Yee haw!" he yelled, charging toward the camp. Slowing at its edge, he fired a few random shots in the clearing to scare the person off. A dark-haired man ran from the wagon and hopped on his horse, ducking the flying bullets. He crashed into the woods.

Josh and Andy gave chase. They ran right through the herd, scattering bleating sheep. Shebe trotted over to the flock instinctively to calm the frightened sheep, swerving this direction and that and keeping them all together with her sharp barking. The man had a head start since he was on the other side of the sizable herd, and Josh and Andy lost his trail in the woods.

Josh pulled back hard on the reins. "Let's head back. He's long gone now."

"Wonder what he was after—money?" Andy turned his horse back toward camp.

"Probably. Guess he thought a sheepherder would be a good target, but he should've known there wouldn't be much for the taking."

"Maybe he heard you discovered the sapphires," Andy said, patting his horse, whose sides were heaving from the hard run.

"Could be. Even Hoover had heard the news. I guess word gets around somehow." *All the more reason for taking the stones back to the assayer now*, he thought.

Back in the clearing, they found the camp was a mess. The man had ransacked the wagon, apparently looking for something, but nothing was taken. Josh felt like Andy's suspicions were right. But it wasn't worth losing their lives over. Now they'd have to watch their backs.

Shebe was lying in the shade, her tongue hanging out from working the sheep, which she had managed to keep together. Josh brought her a bowl of water as his thanks. "Good girl, Shebe. I declare, you're the smartest sheepdog around," he said, watching her lap greedily from the bowl.

Andy laughed, slapping his thigh. "She's the *only* sheepdog around!"

16

Working at the newspaper gave Juliana a sense of being in control of her life, and she felt great satisfaction that she and Albert worked well together. No male had materialized to take her job, so she felt she could relax a bit. She had been allowed to not only write articles about the Ladies Social Club or the price of beef or sheep for the market, but also design snippets of some of the shopkeepers' ads, which helped bring in some more business. Coming up with a catchy phrase or slogan was fun and challenging. Many days she and Albert would spend part of the afternoon drinking coffee, laughing, and brainstorming their ideas while pouring over layouts for ads. She knew this was important because the cost of the ads paid to keep the newspaper in business.

Tonight Mark had invited her and Marion to supper at the hotel, and she was looking forward to spending Friday night over a good meal with friends. Maybe she'd even sleep late on Saturday morning. Now that would be grand. Something she had never done, actually.

The bell above the door jangled, and Mark gave her one of his warm smiles. "I've come to walk you home before supper."

"You didn't have to do that, you know. It's only a couple of blocks from here." She cocked one eye at him as she continued to tidy her desk. Juliana wasn't sure exactly how she felt about Mark, because for the first time in her life, she enjoyed her bit of independence. Finally she was being paid for something she actually enjoyed doing.

"I feel honored to be able to walk a pretty lady anywhere."

"Any lady?" she teased.

His face turned as red as a ripe tomato, and he ignored Albert's chuckle. "Correction—one pretty lady."

She could feel the pink creeping into her face, so she turned to gather her cloak hanging on the coat rack behind her.

"Here, let me help you with that," Mark said, reaching to drape the cloak about her shoulders. The act seemed intimate and brought his face close to hers. Close enough that she could smell his shaving lotion, and she noted his trim, manicured nails on long fingers. A surgeon's fingers. Any woman would be proud to become his wife. Josh's hands flashed in her mind. Strong, capable hands that were calloused yet gentle with his dog or a baby lamb. She turned the thought off as quickly as it came. It just wouldn't do.

"I'll lock up, Juliana. See you at church Sunday?" Albert's eyes crinkled with mischief.

"Yes, of course," she answered. She was going only to pacify Marion and get to know the townsfolk a little better. Church was a good place to meet new people. The ladies in the social club normally attended, so who knows, she might pick up a tidbit for the paper. Other than that, she found the minister's sermons boring.

"Ready?" Mark opened the front door and stood waiting for her.

"Albert, please tell Sally thanks for the muffins today." Juliana waved briefly before following Mark outside into the late afternoon. Albert waved back, grinning at the two of them. Albert was wise, and she respected him. It was apparent that he and his wife had taken a liking to her, and it warmed her heart. Juliana wished for a time like that with her own father.

Mark took her arm and steered her in the direction of the hotel. "I dropped by to check on little Jane this afternoon."

"I hope she's feeling better. Marion and I paid her a short visit recently." Juliana tried to match her steps to his stride.

"She is doing well. Her broken leg is curtailing her normal life, but it should heal nicely."

Juliana nodded. "I can understand how she may feel, especially for an adolescent who is normally busy with her friends."

The hotel was full of activity this time of day, with weary travelers checking in after a long day on the stagecoach or train. Marion stopped briefly from her work behind the front desk to say hello to them. Juliana went on upstairs to freshen up before dinner, leaving Mark to talk with a couple of local men in the lobby.

There was a note on her door and a brown package propped up on the doorjamb. Puzzled, she opened the piece of paper. It was from Josh.

Miss Juliana,

I brought your coat back since I was in town on business. Sorry I missed you. Maybe I'll catch up with you later. You need protection from the cold spring mornings!

Your friend, Josh McBride

Juliana reached down and picked up the parcel, holding it to her chest while unlocking the door to her room. A distinct scent permeated the package. Not unpleasant, but the kind that tells you it has been in the possession of another, and with a masculine appeal because of its clumsy wrapping in brown paper tied with coarse string. How sweet of him to return the coat.

She untied the string and shook the coat to release the wrinkles. She glanced over the note again. His handwriting was bold script, legible, but with short, distinctive loops and characters. She found herself sitting on the edge of the bed staring at it. Something about it held her, just like the eyes that had drawn her when she first saw the sketch of him and his dog. She could practically hear his voice in her head. But why was she dwelling on that? What was happening to her mind? After all, he had signed it "friend." What else did she expect?

She shook her head and sighed, folding the note and putting it aside. Time to freshen up and get back down to the dining room. She didn't have time for woolgathering. *Woolgathering . . .* She laughed. How appropriate that particular word would come to her. She remembered Josh saying that people need a shepherd, like sheep do. Was that from the Bible? She couldn't remember his exact words.

She smoothed her hair and washed her face and hands. Her hands were beginning to look softer. Where there were rough spots before, she now came home with spots of ink. But that didn't bother her.

A sharp rap sounded on her door, and she opened it to see Marion in a blue dress with long sleeves etched at the neck and cuffs with delicate cream lace. Her hair was pulled up by a matching ribbon. "Marion, you look beautiful!"

Marion blushed. "Why, thank you. Are you ready to go down and meet Mark? I hope you don't mind, but I invited Josh to have dinner with us too. He stopped by the hotel this afternoon."

"Ah ha! That's why you changed your dress—"

"No, not at all," Marion interrupted. "After working behind the counter all day, my dress looked a little the worse for wear. That's all."

"Well . . . what I have on will have to do." She looked down at her brown calico dress, pretending indifference. "Even so, you still look nicer than me." She grabbed Marion's arm as they headed down the stairs. "Let's go. I'm famished. What do you think Pierre has on the menu tonight?"

Juliana's mind was not on dinner but on how mousy she looked next to her friend. But why should she care? Hadn't she said a dozen times that a man was not a pressing need in her life just now? Survival was first and foremost.

17

Josh and Mark rose from their seats when Juliana and Marion approached the table.

Josh noticed that Marion had changed her work dress and looked fresh as a bluebell on the mountainside. But it was Juliana who drew his attention. She seemed somewhat quiet as Mark pulled out a chair for her, and she busied herself with adjusting her skirts before looking at him with a half smile on her lips. Maybe she was just tired. He'd get a full smile out of her.

Even though she was wearing a serviceable work dress, he thought her large, thoughtful eyes and dark hair framing her face were prettier than he remembered. She was tall and slender, almost too thin, but curvaceous enough in all the right places, and striking. That was the word—not beautiful but striking. He pulled out a chair for Marion next to him.

"Thanks for the dinner invitation. I hope I'm not intruding," Josh said, casting a thoughtful look at Mark.

"Think nothing of it. Now we're a balanced table." Mark turned to smile warmly at Juliana.

"Josh, thank you for bringing the coat to me." Juliana's eyes latched onto his, and his heart began to thump.

"I was afraid you might have need of it. The spring mornings are still cold."

"I will need it, but the coat is a loan from Marion, and I know she appreciates its return." She nodded toward Marion.

Josh directed his gaze to Marion. "You're a good friend to Juliana."

"It's easy to be her friend. Who wouldn't like Juliana?" Marion beamed at her.

"I'd have to agree with that," Mark said, giving Juliana's arm a squeeze.

The possessive touch did not go unnoticed by Josh, and he turned toward Marion. He hadn't noticed before how attractive she was. She had pulled up her cherry-colored hair, exposing her slender white neck with just a sprinkle of freckles on fine porcelain skin. Her hazel eyes sparkled with mischief, and she talked in an easygoing manner.

But all of it only made him think of Juliana's chestnut hair, large blue eyes, and creamy beige complexion.

"Josh, what brings you to town and away from your sheep? Don't the sheep need a shepherd?" Marion spoke teasingly, giving him her full attention.

"Indeed they do. I have a young fellow who works with me named Andy," Josh said. He didn't want to reveal too much. If he didn't know better, he'd think she was flirting with him.

After placing their orders for dinner, everyone relaxed. Juliana looked around at her friends and, with a reporter's eagerness, said, "Tell me all your news!"

Mark leaned in toward them. "I received news from a colleague of mine that Colorado has a new kind of photography. It's called an X-ray." Mark's face lit up with excitement, and he tapped his fingers on the table. "This is exciting news in the medical field."

"Oh, Mark, tell us all about it, please."

Josh watched as Juliana gave Mark her rapt attention. Maybe it was just the journalist in her. Or did she find his field intriguing?

"Yes, what does that mean?" Marion asked.

Mark had an audience now. "It's a way to take a picture of, say, your hand or another part of the body without the flesh, and one can see the bones underneath."

"Did your colleague discover it?" Josh's eyebrows lifted.

"Oh heavens, no. It was developed by a German physicist by the name of Roentgen last year. Then a professor at Colorado College, Dr. Cajori, and his associate, Dr. Strieby, read about it and decided to experiment for themselves. Other medical colleges were doing likewise. The first X-ray was done successfully at Dartmouth College in Hanover on the wrist of a fourteen-year-old boy." Mark paused and drank from his water glass.

At that moment, their entrées arrived, and for a moment it was quiet as they began to eat.

"So what do X-rays mean for the medical field?" Josh asked as he spread butter on his roll.

"It means we can take a picture of a part of the anatomy and be able to make an accurate diagnosis. Like a broken bone, or to pinpoint a bullet." Mark sliced the meat on his plate like a surgeon making his first cut.

"That's so exciting! That would have come in handy when Jane was struck by the wagon, right?" Juliana eyes widened. "I just had a thought. Wouldn't that same thing be useful somehow to check how deep a bad spot is on one's tooth?"

"I don't see why not. That's very astute, Juliana. I'll see what I can find out." His adoring look at Juliana turned Josh's stomach. She seemed to be basking in it since her cheeks were rosy. "In fact, I'm thinking of catching a train down to Denver to see it firsthand. This would be invaluable in treating my patients." Mark turned back to his dinner. "Delicious steak, don't you think, Josh?"

"Sure is. I couldn't have cooked it any better myself." Josh smiled at Juliana and wiped his mouth on his napkin, but she glanced away. He sensed her excitement but wasn't certain it was from the X-ray news or because she was happy to be with Mark. He thought Mark was a fine person and liked him, but not with Juliana. Very selfish thinking indeed, he admitted. He also knew Mark was a strong pillar in the community. Doctors were always well thought of because they were so few and far between in the West. He would make a name in society as the town grew larger and more influential people settled there. He was surprised Marion didn't show an interest in *him*. Even Josh could tell Mark was good-looking.

"Josh, I'd like to hear a little bit about you. You're not originally from Montana, are you?" Marion asked.

"No, I'm not. I was born and raised in Colorado."

Marion leaned in closer. "Oh? I've never been there. What made you leave?"

Josh carefully chose his words. "Well, I wanted to try something different before I got too old and ran out of courage."

"You aren't old. And are you glad you came to Montana?" Marion's eyes softened as she gazed at him, but Josh kept his guard up.

"Yes, yes, I'm very glad I did," he answered her with a smile,

134

and he noticed a faint pink stain her cheeks. *Gracious! I think she's flirting with me.* He was flattered, but he quickly directed his gaze to Juliana to get her reaction. She just sat there calmly picking at her vegetables.

"Anyone for dessert?" Mark asked, pushing away his empty plate.

Juliana regarded the connection she saw between Josh and Marion. Her friend was leaning in close to Josh and laughing at something he said under his breath. They seemed more suited to one another age-wise, so it didn't matter. Or did it? As she watched Marion openly flirting with Josh, she realized once again how lovely she was. Of course Josh would enjoy her company.

Juliana had a funny feeling in her stomach, and suddenly she wasn't very hungry. She felt hot underneath her calico dress. It was obvious Josh liked the attention Marion was giving him. Juliana breathed a sigh. Wasn't she the one who'd said they might be well suited when Marion had teased her about him? Marion had admitted there was something strangely attractive about Josh.

Josh shot her a glance, but she diverted her gaze, realizing she had been watching them openly. She turned back to Mark. "I'd like to write an article for the newspaper about the X-rays. May I quote you?"

Mark touched her hand. "That would be just great if you would do that. Our community needs to know about this wonderful discovery."

Josh could tell Juliana looked pleased that she had stumbled on a newsworthy article for the *Gazette*. That showed intelligence, and he admired that. So why did he have a sinking feeling in the pit of his stomach? Well, she hadn't so much as looked at him through the whole meal. Had he overstepped his bounds when she was at the ranch? He watched as she lifted her cup of coffee to her lips, and her sleeve fell away, exposing an ugly bruise. An old one, because the color was already turning yellow green. How had she gotten that? As if sensing his gaze, she quickly pulled her sleeve back down. He continued to look at her as if it would make her take notice of him.

Marion tapped him on the arm. "Would you like another cup of coffee, Josh?" She held a carafe in her hand, poised to refill his cup.

"No thanks, I'll pass. I'm going to go on back to the camp. I don't like to leave Andy and my flock for too long. If you all will excuse me . . . Thanks so much for including me at the last moment."

"Oh, so soon? Will we see you tomorrow?" Marion asked with obvious anticipation, her hazel eyes searching his face.

Josh pushed back his chair. "I can't leave Andy for too long to run things by himself. He might send Shebe after me."

"I see. I haven't heard you speak of her." Marion's face fell.

Josh winked at Juliana, and she finally smiled mischievously. "I didn't? Well, she likes to know my every move. You know how women are." Chuckling, he bid them good night and plunked down a few bills for dinner, and they murmured their good-byes.

Marion's disappointment was obvious by her deflated look. He could almost imagine what was going on in her head as she tried to figure out who Shebe was, and that rather tickled him. But then Marion was too much like his sister—a little pushy and controlling.

He smiled, thinking of his sister, April. In spite of her bossiness, he really missed her and her exuberance for life. He wondered how she was doing now that Crystal and Luke were married. He felt sorry for her, but that was in the past, and he was determined to keep it there. Now Josh was feeling sorry for himself. He had lost the love of one woman, and he didn't intend to lose Juliana's. He just wasn't good at conveying his feelings, and maybe he held them too close to his heart. He hoped it wasn't too late to let Juliana know how he felt. His heart felt full to bursting as the image of her floated across his mind, and he remembered how she'd looked at dinner tonight.

He headed toward the livery where he'd left his horse, enjoying the evening chill to clear the cobwebs in his head. The street was quiet with few people milling about. The moon had partially slipped behind the clouds high above the mountains, lending an eerie effect to the shadows of the clapboard buildings. He liked it best when the stars were out. He thought about how the moon always hung steadfast every night, and it reminded him of God's constant presence. Did Juliana believe that? Would time be able to heal her distrust?

As he stepped down to cross the street, he caught a flash of movement from the alley out of the corner of his eye. But when he turned to take a look, a hard blow at the side of his head made his knees buckle. As he sank to the ground, he saw some stars he didn't intend to as his eyes slid closed . . .

18

"Mister, can you hear me? Are you all right?"

Josh struggled to open his eyes, and a figure swam in his line of vision. What had happened? He shook his head and blinked hard until the person became clearer. Pulling himself up to lean on one elbow, Josh realized he was lying in the dusty alley. He had a sharp searing pain on the side of his head, and when he reached up with his hand, he felt a lump and wet, sticky blood. He winced, feeling woozy from the blow.

"Here, let me help you up," the stranger said, brushing the dust off Josh's backside. "Let's get you down inside the hotel where we can get you checked out. Looks like someone tried to rob you. Can you stand?"

"I think so." But as the stranger pulled him to his feet, Josh's legs felt wobbly. "I think someone took a swipe at my head." He had trouble focusing on the face before him.

The man steered him back toward the nearest door of the hotel and into the lobby. "I'm Albert Spencer, and you would be . . ."

"Name's Josh, Josh McBride. Thanks for your assistance. How long was I out?"

"I don't rightly know, but it looks like you might need a stitch or two on that head. I was staying late at the newspaper tonight and was walking home when I saw you in the shadows."

"Do you own the *Lewistown Gazette*?"

"I do for a fact," Albert said, guiding him to the settee in the lobby. "You rest right here, and I'll go fetch the doc."

"No, don't do that. I'll be okay once I sit a few minutes to clear my head. Could you please ask at the desk what room number Juliana Brady is in, and then go knock on her door and ask her to step down here?"

"Juliana?" A big smile split Albert's face. "You know her? She works for me at the paper."

"I just had dinner with her and Mark Barnum."

A sudden rustling of skirts came toward them. "Josh! What happened to you?" Marion bent down to investigate the large bump on the side of his head.

"I wish I knew. Someone came out of the shadows and walloped me on the head." He forced a lopsided grin. He was having a little trouble bringing her face into focus.

"Albert, why don't you take him to the library, and I'll fetch something cold for that lump." Marion touched Josh's scalp tenderly. "I'll be back in a moment or two." She scurried toward the kitchen.

Albert put his hand under Josh's arm for support, but he was able to stand without wobbling. "I feel okay now, I reckon," he said as they made their way to the library door. Albert swung the heavy oak doors aside, where inside a crackling fire popped and snapped. Josh took a seat in an overstuffed chair near the fire. The only other light was from the wall sconces, making the room cozy and appealing with its bookshelves lined with books and art adorning the wood paneling.

True to her word, Marion came back and stood over Josh with a cold rag in her hand, which she pressed lightly to his head. He got a whiff of a delicate rose-water scent that clung to her arms.

"Ouch!" He grabbed her wrist in midair.

"I'm sorry, I was trying to be gentle. Here, you hold the cold rag against your head and just lean back and rest." Marion's face was etched with concern. "Why do you think someone would do this to you?"

"I have an idea they were after something—maybe my money—but they found nothing." Josh didn't want to mention that they might be looking for the sapphires.

"I think I should go fetch the doc," Albert said. "Want me to fetch the sheriff too?"

Josh waved his hand. "No need, nothing was taken. Whoever it was is long gone now."

"The doctor could still be in the dining room. We all had just finished dinner moments ago when Josh left. Would you mind checking to see if he's still there?" Marion pleaded. "I'll stay with Josh."

"I'll do just that." Albert's long, lanky frame crossed to the door in two steps.

Josh held the cold rag to his head, rested on the back of the chair, and closed his eyes. He was very aware that Marion had taken a seat nearby. He was glad he had turned the sapphires over to the assayer's office, all except the largest one. That one he had left with a jeweler. He expected the sapphires were what the robber was after, especially after the incident at the camp.

He must have dozed a moment because the sound of Mark's voice woke him. He opened his eyes to see Mark peering into his face, with Juliana standing behind him. So . . . they had still been lingering over their coffee.

"How are you feeling? Are you dizzy, Josh?" Mark asked, examining the growing knot on his head.

"Mmm . . . only a little when I stand." Josh struggled to sit up straight. "I have a bit of a headache, though." His eyes traveled over to Juliana, who stood holding her hands tightly, a worried look creasing her brow.

Mark looked closely in Josh's eyes and felt his pulse. "You're lucky it wasn't any closer to your temple. It might be wise if you stay here for the night. I'm sure they have a vacant room, right, Marion?"

"I'm sorry, but we are totally booked. You shouldn't be walking anywhere, though. You might pass out." Marion was quickly at his side, taking the damp rag from him.

"Oh, no, I don't want to be any trouble," Josh said. Out of the corner of his eye, he saw Juliana lean in closer. Her shiny hair caught the lamp's soft glow.

"Josh, you can have my room. Marion, is it okay if I stay with you tonight?" Juliana's voice sounded like music to his ears.

"Certainly."

"I planned on riding back to my camp tonight," Josh protested, though he thought they might be right. His head was now throbbing something terrible.

"That's a good idea, Marion." Mark turned to Josh. "Come on, I'll help you up the stairs and then go collect your saddlebags from the livery."

Josh had never been fussed over, particularly by women. *Two of them! I could get used to this,* he thought. A little bubble of laughter came up his throat, but he stifled it.

"Not to worry, Doc. I'll go fetch his things real quick-like," Albert offered.

"I owe you." Josh nodded to the kind newspaper editor and followed Juliana up the broad staircase. Mark kept his hand at Josh's elbow just in case he started to fall.

Juliana unlocked the door and stepped aside quickly for Josh to enter. "Marion will be back with fresh linens." She walked over to the bed and started stripping the sheets off. "You can have a seat over there by the window, Josh."

Her room held little other than a bed, a desk, and a chair. There was a multicolored hook rug on the side of the bed that matched the quilt on top of the white iron bed. He felt a little funny about sleeping in her bed, but the thought of being where she had slept or perhaps read before going to bed was a pleasant one.

"I'm off now," Mark said. "Take this powder before you get settled in bed, and it'll ease that headache. I think you'll be okay with some rest. I'll stop by tomorrow and check on you right after breakfast. See you later, Juliana." It seemed he stood for a long moment watching her as she stripped the bed.

Juliana looked up. "Thanks for dinner."

"I sure do appreciate it, Mark," Josh said. "I'll need to get back as quick as I can before Andy starts worrying about what happened to me." He gave a slight wave to Mark as he left.

Juliana picked up the bundle of sheets, clutched them to her chest, and strode toward the doorway in search of Marion. Josh cast a glance at her, not wanting her to go just yet. "I couldn't help but notice that large bruise on your arm, but I didn't want to say anything at dinner in front of anyone. How did you get that?" His voice was husky with concern as his eyes narrowed.

"Oh, it's nothing," she said, looking down at her arm, but a pink flush crept across her cheeks.

"It looks like something to me. Did you fall off your horse?" He studied her face and knew she was hiding something.

"No, I . . ." She mumbled something inaudible, staring past him.

"Juliana, are you okay? Tell me what happened. You can trust me." His eyes latched onto hers, searching, as he got up and shuffled over to her.

"Is that so? My mother told me as she lay dying not to put all my trust in a man!" she snapped.

Josh regarded her with sympathy. He sensed her wounded heart and wanted desperately to build her faith. But how? "But did she tell you that you could trust in your heavenly Father? Not all men are like your father. There are still a few good ones around."

She looked down, studying the hardwood floor for a moment as if there were a message written on the worn planks. "And you're one of them?" Her dark eyes snapped as she looked up.

"I was thinking about Mark and Albert, but—well, yes, me too." He reached out to lightly touch the ugly bruise above her wrist. "I'm sorry for whatever happened, but if you want to talk about it, I'm here for you." Her skin felt warm and silky to his touch, and he felt a small shiver pass through her body. "God didn't intend for man to live alone."

"Well, where was He when my mother died, and all those years we were struggling and waiting for my daddy to return like he promised? Tell me that, will you?" Her voice was shaky, and a sob shook her thin shoulders, but she took a deep breath.

He dropped his hand from her arm. "He was right there, Juliana," Josh said. "We don't always know why things have to happen the way they do, but we must trust that He knows better than we do how it's all going to work out." Apparently he seemed to bring out her hurts easily without even trying. He didn't want to make her angry—far from it. He would have continued, but Marion walked up with clean sheets.

"Here we are. It won't take but a moment to throw these on the bed, Juliana. The maids have all gone home for the night. And Josh, you should be sitting down! What's gotten into you? You could swoon and hit the floor." She pushed him right back to the window seat, where he sat and directed his gaze to the two women making the bed.

Heaving a deep sigh, Juliana placed the handful of laundry outside the doorway and turned to assist Marion.

"I'm not helpless, just a bit woozy, but I'll get out of the way of a commanding female." Josh chuckled. He concluded that Marion was a take-charge, no-nonsense person. Again she reminded him of his sister April.

Marion rolled her eyes but said nothing, and in a flash she and Juliana had the bed sheets tightly folded under the mattress and smoothed out on top. "Juliana tells me you're halfway through building your house. That's so exciting. You'll have to tell me about it at breakfast tomorrow." With a flick of her wrist, she plumped the bed pillows and turned to him. "It's all ready when you are. Be sure to come down and have breakfast in the morning before you leave." She flashed him her sweetest smile. "A man like you needs a hearty breakfast to start his day."

Josh shot a look at Juliana, who hadn't opened her mouth since Marion arrived, and observed a thoughtful look on her pretty face. He watched as she walked over to the bureau and pulled out her dressing gown and a change of clothes.

"Take your time tomorrow. There's no rush. I have everything I need." Juliana gave Josh a feeble smile, perhaps to indicate that she wasn't angry at him. "That lump on your head has grown quite red and large, so just stay as long as needed."

"Thank you for allowing me to take your room for the night, Juliana. I'll have to think of a way to repay you." He threw her a mischievous look.

Marion snorted. "No need for that, is there, Juliana? *We* are allowing her to stay until she decides what she wants to do."

Juliana had a hurt look on her face but only said in a quiet tone, "Yes, Marion's right. I'm just charity." Then she stalked out of the room, her black heels making a pinging sound on the hardwood floors.

Marion shrugged her shoulders at Josh. "Whatever is wrong with her?"

Josh considered answering her question but thought he'd better keep his thoughts to himself.

After Marion left, he yanked off his boots and removed his clothes. He left his long handles on and laid his pants and shirt in the chair by the window. He reached inside his saddlebags and pulled out his Bible. The turned-down sheets looked inviting and his head still pounded, but first he took the powder with a glass of water before crawling beneath the covers. A faint scent of soap filled his nostrils, and it was a comforting smell. One he remembered from home and his sweet mother's attention to detail. He missed her and her fussing over him, and hoped the hard feelings between him and his dad would not keep her from visiting him. His mother was a gentle, kind-hearted soul who never stood up to his dad, though Josh knew many times she had her own ideas about things. One thing was for certain, he wanted his wife to be an equal partner with him. Not someone to boss around.

Leaning his head back on the fluffy pillows, he opened his Bible to the book of Psalms, one of his favorites. He read for a bit but was having trouble concentrating because of his headache—and the image of Juliana's wounded face and pinched lips earlier. How he wanted to wrap his arms around her and make her feel she was special and loved! Perhaps tomorrow he might push a little harder about the bruise if he had a minute alone with her.

He was sure Andy was wondering why he hadn't shown up tonight, but he probably wasn't too worried about him. The thief wouldn't come back to the camp a second time since he hadn't found anything.

Josh's head began to nod, and the Bible slipped out of his hands and slid to the floor.

19

Juliana followed Marion down to her room, a large corner suite. Her father had the exact same suite on the opposite corner on the third floor.

Inside Juliana was seething about Marion's comment to Josh about allowing her to stay. If her memory served her right, it was Marion who'd decided she should move into the hotel until she could get on her feet in the first place, despite her protestations. But from the way her friend was flirting with Josh and fussing over him, it seemed suddenly Marion wanted her out of the picture. Now she was feeling like a burden, and she decided it was time to see if she could afford to rent a small room in the boardinghouse. She was already making payments for Choco to Marion. Would she have enough left over for anything else? It was too soon to hope for any kind of raise from Albert. Maybe she should have just stayed at the shack near the miners' camp, but she'd made a promise to her mother.

Marion interrupted her thoughts, motioning to Juliana to enter her suite. It was a richly decorated room and sitting area illuminated by brightly lit wall sconces that cast a soft yellow glow. A beautiful brocade settee and English writing desk were placed near the large windows covered in heavy, cream-colored drapes. A small table next to the settee held a clock and a silver tea service. Marion's bed was covered with a cream-colored coverlet, and strewn against the headboard were ruffled and lacy pillows.

Such luxury Juliana had never seen. This was the first time she had ever been invited to Marion's personal room, and somehow she felt totally out of her element. She shouldn't be here at all.

While Juliana was agape, taking it all in, Marion pulled open the heavy double wardrobe doors. She removed her dress as she talked over her shoulder. "Josh is such a nice man, don't you think?" Before Juliana had time to answer, she went on. "Such muscles—my goodness! And those eyes! They look clear to one's soul." She turned toward Juliana. "You're not listening. What's wrong?"

"I feel like I'm inconveniencing you by sharing your room. Are you sure there were no vacancies? I don't want to put you out any more than I already have," Juliana said, her feet rooted to the floor.

"Now what's that supposed to mean? Yes, I'm afraid all the rooms are booked tonight."

"Well, it's just that . . . you made it clear I was a charity case." Juliana's breathing felt constricted. She always felt this way when she was anxious about something. It was never pleasant to tell someone how she felt if she was upset.

"Oh, that . . . Well, we both know it's temporary," she said. She stripped down to her chemise, then pulled her nightgown over her head. Tiny blue ribbons edged the delicate, rounded yoke, while fine Hamburg-embroidered tucks fell clear down

148

the front with ribbon insertions and embroidery on the cambric gown. Juliana was sure she'd never seen a nightgown quite like it before. "I thought you were jealous of how Josh was giving me his undivided attention," Marion continued.

Juliana had looked away, but she snapped back around to give Marion a chilly stare. "I'm not jealous! Josh doesn't belong to anyone, as far as I know."

"Don't be so touchy. We have to share this bed tonight." She made a clicking sound with her tongue against her teeth, then started pulling down the comforter and pillows. "Well, don't just stand there. Change your clothes and get comfortable. I'm sure someone is still in the kitchen. I'll ring us a pot of chamomile tea." She reached for the fabric braided rope as she put on her slippers. "It'll settle your nerves."

"There is nothing *wrong* with my nerves!" Juliana stalked over to a chair in front of Marion's dressing table, sat down, and began removing her shoes.

"So you say." Marion's left eyebrow arched. She stepped over to the window and looked down at the streets below, where the gaslights created soft shadows.

"I guess it's time I look for some other place to stay. I've been charity long enough." Juliana slipped on her nightgown of rough muslin, knowing full well it paled in comparison to Marion's. The hardwood floor was cold on her bare feet, but she didn't own any slippers. She wished she'd grabbed a pair of stockings earlier.

"Are you implying I want you to leave, Juliana?" Marion cocked her head and regarded her. "I never said anything of the sort. You're my friend," she said, pulling her robe on.

"Nonetheless, I feel clearly that I'm in the way, and I shall look for something tomorrow that I can afford. But I don't want to sound ungrateful. I appreciate what you've done for me by allowing me to stay here. I'll figure out some way to pay you back once I pay off my debt for Choco." She thought she glimpsed a slight curve bordering on a smile on Marion's lips. *Ah ha! She was hoping I'd leave.* How quickly their relationship had changed once a man entered the picture. One more reason to stay away from men.

"As you wish. You seem a bit miffed that Josh was being quite nice to me. Is that what's upset you?"

Juliana rolled her eyes. It had been apparent to her that Marion was gushing attention on Josh, to the point it almost embarrassed her. "That has nothing to do with anything. I didn't act any different than I normally do. So what are you trying to say?"

A knock on the door stopped Marion from replying, and she opened it as the maid carried in a pot of hot tea and placed it on the table next to the settee. "Here you are, mum. You're in luck—I was just about to close up the kitchen. Your favorite chamomile tea, and I brung along a couple of sugar cookies too." The young girl bobbed her head at Marion and then at Juliana.

"What a dear you are. Thank you, Nellie," Marion said. The maid lingered a moment or two, waiting for a tip, but when none was forthcoming, she left in a flash, no doubt tired from her long day at the hotel. Juliana felt uncomfortable for Nellie and wished she'd had her coin purse with her. She knew what hard work for little pay was like, and she figured Nellie counted heavily on her tips from the hotel's patrons. Maybe Marion figured since her father owned the hotel, no tip should be expected.

"Please, Juliana, sit down, and I'll pour us some tea."

Juliana hesitated briefly. A cup of tea was very tempting, so she padded over and sat down while Marion poured the two cups and offered her sugar and lemon. She shook her head at the lemon but placed two sugar cubes in the delicate china cup.

"Back to our conversation. What I was trying to say was that Josh is fair game. Before, you told me you weren't interested, but I couldn't help but detect a certain way you look when you're around him. I'm not sure he shares the same sentiment as you, dear friend. You're a little young for him." Marion stirred her tea, gazing at Juliana. "He needs someone a bit older. Maybe someone like me."

Juliana almost choked on the sip of tea. "I never indicated he needed someone older, Marion. I do like him. He's a very nice gentleman." Her heart pounded against her ribs. "You're right. He was looking at you intently. You're a nice-looking woman, have a viable standing in the community, and are closer to Josh's age." Marion flinched. "Could be he is interested. Maybe he'll ask to come courting." She eyed her friend. "Is that what you hope for?"

Marion shrugged her shoulders. "I won't deny I find him attractive. I wouldn't want to step on your toes if you have feelings for him, but you can't have Mark and Josh. That just won't fly." She waited for Juliana's reaction.

Juliana stared down into her teacup. What *did* she feel for Josh? Truth was, she was very attracted to him and felt her insides tremble whenever he came near. She felt comfortable with Mark, but more like friends than anything else. Was she unconsciously leading Mark on? She hadn't meant to.

"Marion, I like Josh and Mark as friends, nothing more. Besides, they're not really interested in me. I think they just felt sorry for me when my mother passed." But even as she said it, Juliana was thinking about the kiss in Josh's kitchen. In fact, she had been thinking of it earlier when Josh touched her arm, which had set off an alarm throughout her body.

"I wouldn't be too sure of that, especially where Mark is concerned." Marion dismissed the subject with a shake of her head. "Now that that's settled, let's have a cookie before lights out." She munched on her sugar cookie as she sneaked a peek at her friend.

Juliana remembered how Josh's eyes had seemed so full of compassion when he asked her about the bruise. She wondered what it would feel like to have his strong arms around her, holding her close enough to hear his heartbeat . . . Ah, she'd never know. She'd observed the way he looked at Marion, who had so much more to offer. It was clear that Marion had designs on him too. Josh must think Juliana was merely a child.

Still, there was that kiss . . . But she didn't want to get too close, or her heart might be broken.

For hours Juliana lay in the dark, listening to Marion's deep breathing. She was unable to sleep and stared out into the darkness, playing everything over again in her head. Her friend was a take-control kind of person and relished it. She was sure Marion didn't mean anything by that. It was just the way she was.

Face it, Juliana! Josh and Marion would make a nice couple. He had seemed intrigued with Marion this evening as she plied her charms and fussed over his injury. Why would he bother with Juliana, who was poor as a church mouse, when there was pretty, wealthy Marion just dying to give him all the attention he wanted? *If I were a man, I would be fascinated by her too.*

A little knot lodged in her chest, and a tear slid down her cheek. She brushed it away, sighing deeply, and hid her face deep into the down pillow.

The early breakfast crowd was keeping the waiters hopping this Saturday morning as Josh sipped hot coffee after placing his order for eggs and biscuits. His head felt clearer and had finally stopped throbbing, so he would eat as quickly as he could and then head on back to the camp with his supplies.

He glanced around the dining room, hoping Juliana would appear before he left. He was kind of glad he hadn't run into Marion this morning, because he wanted to speak with Juliana. Marion struck him as someone who took her time with her toilette and probably was used to sleeping a little later, though he knew she helped her father out at the front desk from time to time.

Since it was Saturday, Juliana wasn't working. Otherwise he'd have had a good excuse to walk her to work. Was she sleeping with her beautiful hair spread out across her pillow? Or choosing what dress to wear? He had noticed that since he'd first met her in that pitiful, threadbare blue dress, and after she started her job at the newspaper, she had bought a couple of new dresses.

He was glad he'd met Albert, who seemed a likable fellow and protective of Juliana. He wondered how Juliana would spend her Saturday. Josh and Andy usually made it to church on Sundays, but sometimes not, depending on what was happening with the herd and the weather.

He paid for his breakfast without catching so much as a glimpse of Juliana and was in the lobby just as Marion came hurrying over to him.

"Good morning! How's your head? I see it's purple and blue now." Marion drew closer, inspecting the wound on his head.

"Much better. Thanks," he said, taking a slight step back.

"Have you had breakfast? I was just about to go find a table." She was impeccably dressed in a crisp white shirtwaist and navy skirt. Her hair was swept up into some sort of roll, and when she moved her head, her black earrings bobbed against her jawline. She looked professional but approachable.

"Yes, I've already eaten. I'm about to start back to camp. Thanks for taking care of me last night."

"Oh, I was hoping we could breakfast together." Her bottom lip pouted. "I wanted to hear all about your new home. I'm quite the decorator, having had this entire hotel to do, both upstairs and down." She straightened her shoulders with pride.

"You've done a magnificent job too. I'm almost finished with my house. When it gets completed, I'll have you and Juliana over to have a look. You could bring Mark along too. By the way, have you seen Juliana?"

Marion stiffened. "Why do you ask?"

"I just wanted to thank her for allowing me to use her room last night on a moment's notice."

Josh watched Marion purse her lips in a tight line before answering. "She was gone before I was up this morning."

"So early? She doesn't work today, does she?"

"No, she doesn't. I think she has her mind set on finding another place to live." Marion made a pretense of adjusting the cuffs on her sleeve.

"I see. Well, I must be off now." Josh doffed his hat to her and was aware that she stood watching him leave.

The sun had long been up and dissipated the clouds that had drifted in over the mountains the previous evening, and the morning was bright and clear. When Josh stepped out onto the boardwalk, he saw Juliana at the corner of the street, tying her bonnet under her chin. She paused as if to decide which way she should go. If he hurried, he could reach her before she crossed the street.

Shifting his saddlebag across his shoulder, he jogged over to her. "Howdy, Miss Juliana."

Startled, she turned to see who was next to her. "Hello, Josh. I thought you'd left by now." She tilted her chin up to meet his gaze.

"I'm on my way over to the livery to get my horse and wagon. I thought maybe I'd catch you at breakfast." Their eyes locked, and finally she looked away as though something across the street had caught her eye. Underneath the serviceable bonnet, her face looked tired and drawn.

"I wasn't hungry, so I skipped breakfast this morning because I have something I must do." She offered him no explanation. "Marion was looking for you, though." Her voice trailed off.

"I saw her as I was leaving. But I wanted to let you know how much I appreciated the use of your room for the night. It was quite pleasant knowing you'd slept there," he teased. "May I walk with you?"

"Yes, all right. Is your head feeling much better?" She stole a glance at him.

"It is, though it looks pretty ugly. Mark told me it could have been much worse if the blow had hit my temple. So I'm grateful for that. Nothing was stolen, but I have an idea what the thief was after." He matched his stride to hers. "Where are you heading?"

"I'm looking for a room to rent. I can't stay at the hotel forever. I fear I've worn out my welcome, so I thought I'd try the boardinghouse up the street."

"How could a sweet thing like you ever wear out your welcome?" Josh asked. Instantly her cheeks flushed prettily, making her all the more desirable.

"Let's just say I have my moments," she said quickly, seeming to recover from the compliment.

"Apparently. Did you get into a tussle with someone to receive that ugly bruise? If someone is giving you trouble, I'd like to know."

"Why, Josh? You're not my protector."

"I'd like to be if you'd let me, Juliana."

"You don't give up, do you?" She slowed her pace in order to look up at him, but her eyes held a twinkle that indicated she wasn't trying to be too resistant.

"Not when it involves you." Josh paused in the street, shifting his weight to one hip. "Did you know that when you look up like that, your eyes sparkle just like those Yogos I showed you?" Josh could hardly believe he'd blurted that out, but that's what she did to him whenever she was around—she stirred up his senses with feelings that had been long buried. It was all he could do not to reach out and touch the bruise, then pull her to his chest, which now felt tight. His eyes swept over her lovely face as surprise registered in her eyes.

"Josh, please. You're making me blush." She jerked her eyes

156

away and looked down at her shoes. The morning breeze tugged at a few strands of her hair that had escaped her bonnet and drew them across her face. She reached up and tucked them back into place.

He reached out and grabbed her hand. "It's true, Juliana. I wasn't trying to embarrass you." He noticed that she let him continue to hold her hand in his. While she still had a few calluses, they were softer than before. He wanted to kiss each of those hard spots, but not right now. "I guess what I'm trying to say is . . . I'd like to court you."

There! It was all laid out now, no hiding behind false pretenses. He held his breath, waiting for an answer.

20

Juliana stared at Josh. Had she heard him right? Was he actually asking to court *her*? Juliana couldn't stop the hammering in her heart, and she took her hand out of Josh's because she couldn't think clearly with him holding it. She took a deep breath and looked at his eager face and eyes full of hope. He wore an expectant expression that spread across his face and furrowed his brows, as if he was holding back something else he'd like to say. A passing couple, who were trying to handle their three active children on the boardwalk, caused him to pull her into the shelter of the porch of the general store.

"Josh, I'm flattered," she stammered. "I—"

"That is, unless you and Mark have an understanding, of course." He let out a whoosh of air.

A giggle escaped her. "No! We do not have anything of the sort. We are merely friends."

"So, is that a yes, then?" He still held her elbow, and she could feel the ripple of muscles in his forearm against her side. Who would have thought a quiet, gentle man like Josh could demonstrate so much anticipation at wanting to know her better? She was more than a bit surprised but secretly delighted.

"I guess it is. Yes, I'd like that very much." She felt her cheeks burn. "But can we continue walking? I want to see about that room at the boardinghouse."

He dropped his hand from her elbow. "I'll walk you to the boardinghouse. The livery is just ahead. So what about after church tomorrow? Maybe we could ride out to the countryside and see all the wildflowers. I promise to have you back before supper so you'll be rested for work on Monday."

Juliana thought a moment before answering. "I did tell Albert I would go to church tomorrow. Maybe we could leave from there. Should I bring my horse?"

"No, I'll drive the wagon, and we can go after the service."

"What about lunch? I don't have a kitchen to fix anything." She chewed her bottom lip, already feeling nervous.

"Don't you worry about a thing. I'll have Andy pack us some sandwiches to munch on. How's that?" His face beamed like a child who had just been given a stick of candy.

"That sounds nice, Josh." She paused as they reached the front of the boardinghouse. "Wish me luck."

"Do you need help with your belongings if you get a room? I can stay a while longer to help."

"That's very sweet of you, but I . . . really own very little."

"All right then. I'll be seeing you at church." He tipped his hat, and once again she saw the purple lump. It didn't seem to be hurting him, but it looked awful.

"See you tomorrow. Take care that no one is following behind you. Another conk on the head, and we might not be talking like this," she teased.

"So you do have a sense of humor. That's good to know,"

he said. He backed down the boardwalk with a broad smile and bumped into a passerby. Juliana laughed as he hurriedly apologized to the man and strode toward the livery. Watching him go, she noticed that for all the strength of his physique, he had a fluid way of carrying himself. Broad shoulders, muscular neck and back, with a broad forehead underneath a thick head of hair . . . Josh was nice to look at, and his voice resonated deep within his chest and intrigued her. The sound of it lingered long after he spoke.

She allowed a pleasant feeling to wash over her. She had a suitor!

Juliana jerked her mind back to the task of looking for a room, then marched up to the front door of the boardinghouse with renewed hope in her heart and a bounce in her step.

A slightly stooped elderly lady in a knitted shawl covering her thin shoulders answered the door. Juliana recognized her as Miss Margaret from the social club. She motioned for Juliana to come into the foyer with a sweep of her bony, blue-veined hand. The foyer had a light lemony smell with its gleaming hardwood floors, and a round table in the center held an array of flowers.

"What can I do for you, little lady?" Miss Margaret's voice held a slight tremble, as did her hands.

"I saw your sign in the window for a room to rent," Juliana said. "Remember me from the Ladies Social Club meeting?"

"Oh, yes, dear. Please come in. You hardly look old enough to live alone, much less rent a room. Are your parents with you?" The older lady peered over her round spectacles, pulling her slipping shawl further up onto her shoulders.

"No, I'm afraid it's just me, ma'am. I'll be eighteen in a few months," Juliana said, then quickly added, "but remember that I work for the newspaper, if you need references."

The older lady squinted. "I see. There's no need for references since you work for Albert Spencer."

"That's right. Do you know him?"

"Well, indeed I do. He's my son." The old lady chuckled. Albert must have favored his father because Juliana saw no resemblance to his mother.

"Come, I'll show you the room that has just been vacated. It's on the second floor, but you're young and shouldn't have any problem doing stairs. I, on the other hand, try to avoid them as much as possible."

Juliana followed Miss Margaret up the beautiful winding staircase and turned to the right of the spacious hallway. The delicate smell of rose water wafted ahead of her. Miss Margaret's keys jangled from a chain at her waist as she picked the proper one to turn the key in the lock, and then she pushed the door open.

Juliana followed her inside and clapped her hands to her chest. Sunlight bathed the room, which was painted in a shade of blue like the Montana sky. The bed was white ironstone, neatly made up in a blue and white spread of toile with matching draperies. Blue Willow plates adorned a plate rack, and two wingback chairs created a small sitting area. "My! What a lovely room. I daresay I can't afford this one. Do you have something a little simpler?"

"What? This is my favorite room, but if it doesn't suit your taste, I'm sure—"

Juliana interrupted, "Oh no, no. It's not that at all. It's exquisite. But I don't think I can afford such a room. Do you have something smaller?"

"I'm afraid not, dear. All the rooms are quite large. I designed them that way when we built this house. As to whether or not you can afford it, why don't you let me be the judge of that?" Her smile was contagious, and Juliana knew she had found a friend. "I'm sure we can come to an amicable rate to fit your pocketbook. Call it a favor for my son."

"I can't let you do that. I wouldn't want to take advantage of my employer."

"He never has to know, but I figured if he hired you, you must be special. You aren't a man, and you're so very young. This is just delicious and surprising." Miss Margaret opened a door to reveal a real closet for her things and extra blankets on a shelf. In the shack she'd shared with her mother, Juliana had only a shelf for her clothes.

"When do you need the room?"

"Today, if we could work something out." Juliana didn't want to get too excited. She had never lived in anything so grand. *Lord, if You're really there, like Josh says you are, please let me work something out with Miss Margaret that I can afford*, she prayed.

"Excellent. My daughters Natalie and Louise live with me and have their own rooms. You met them at the ladies social circle. They're several years older than you. They help me run the place now that my dear husband has passed on. I'd never be able to do this by myself. Right now we have two vacancies, so it's a little quieter around here."

"I'm sorry about your husband. Your daughters were both very kind to me when I attended the meeting. But not everyone was as kind." She was remembering a couple of the ladies who'd acted a little snobby toward her.

"Yes," Miss Margaret said. "That would be Esther, who's never worked a day in her life for anything, and Cynthia, who tries to run everything, although I've heard Marion can be a little controlling too."

When Juliana didn't say anything, Miss Margaret walked toward the door. "I'm old, so I can get away with speaking my mind. Sometimes the women need to be put in their place. Anyway, come along, and we'll go downstairs and find you a key. We have breakfast at 7:30 and dinner at 6:00 sharp if you intend to have your meals here."

"I'd like that, Miss Margaret."

Miss Margaret beamed at her, and Juliana could tell she was pleased to have her as a new boarder. "You're allowed to use the kitchen if you'd like on Saturday."

"I work every weekday, so it would be nice just to be able to brew a cup of tea."

They reached the landing downstairs, and Miss Margaret guided her to a cozy parlor that held a writing desk and found an extra key. They settled on an amount for the room and food that Juliana thought was more than generous. The older lady grasped Juliana's hand and welcomed her into her home. Something told Juliana that her experience here would be more than that of just an ordinary boarder as she walked back to collect her things from the Stockton Hotel.

Juliana's stomach growled at the scent of bacon frying when she passed the hotel's dining room. No time for that now, and no money either, after paying Miss Margaret. She had only a few coins left.

Marion caught her eye and waved. It was as good a time as any to tell Marion she was moving out, so she approached her table.

163

"Goodness. You were out and about early this morning," Marion said, setting down her fork. "Take a seat and have some breakfast."

"I'm not hungry," she lied, remaining standing. "I was in luck. The boardinghouse had an empty room, and I'll be moving my things over there this morning."

"All right, but you know you didn't have to do this. There was no hurry." Marion's face held a frown.

"I know that, but I'd have to leave at some point anyway. I'd just feel better if I went ahead and did it now. The owner happens to be my employer's mother."

"Yes, I know. She's a very nice lady, and her daughters are too. I'm sure you will like living there." Marion's face reflected sadness. "But I'm going to miss having you around."

"I'll only be two blocks away. We can get together most anytime."

"Where will you board Choco? Does she have a place for him?"

"I never thought to ask, but I will this morning. Thank you again, Marion, and please give your father my greatest appreciation."

Marion rose and gave her a brief hug. "I'm really proud of you, you know. You've grown a lot since your mother passed. If you need anything at all, please let me know, okay?"

"I will. You've been a good friend to me." Juliana stepped back to look her friend square in the eye. "I won't forget your kindness. Now go finish your breakfast."

Back in her room, it didn't take more than ten minutes for Juliana to gather her things. The bed was still unmade, but she knew the maid would put fresh sheets on it once she left.

She wondered if Josh had slept well last night in this room. She felt some satisfaction knowing she had given him a place to lay his injured head. As she bent to pull her suitcase from under the bed, something just under the edge of the bed rail caught her eye. It was a leather book. Turning it over, she saw it was not an ordinary book but a Bible. Made of soft black leather aged from use, it had gold writing on the bottom edge. *Josh McBride.* She flipped it opened and saw it was from his mother, Alice McBride, given to him on his seventeenth birthday. He must have been reading and somehow it slid off the bed. She'd see that he got it back tomorrow at church, but for now she tucked it away in her suitcase. She looked around the room and figured she'd make another trip for her box of books.

Nellie paused at the doorway and looked in. "Are ya leaving us, Miss Juliana?"

"Hi, Nellie. Yes, but I'm not going too far. I've rented a room at Mrs. Spencer's boardinghouse."

"I'd be glad to help you with that box of books on the floor there." Nellie stepped into the room.

"Thanks, but you have work to do, and they'll be looking for you. I don't want you getting into trouble on my behalf."

"Naw, they won't be missing me, mum. I'll just take a shorter lunch break." Nellie bent down to lift the box. "I'm strong, see, and you need the help. It won't take more'n ten minutes." She grinned.

"If you're sure, Nellie. That's very sweet of you."

"Think nothing of it. Now you won't have to return for this box. Us working girls have to stick together, right?" She winked at her, and Juliana laughingly agreed.

In less than ten minutes they had carried Juliana's things

upstairs, and Nellie was flabbergasted at the beautiful toile accessories in the room. "Oh, mum, I'd love to sew something that looked like this. I'm good with a needle but don't have a lot of free time with me job." Nellie fingered the coverlet on the bed.

"Then maybe you could teach me what you know sometime. I could always use some lessons."

"This is such a lovely room. You'll have no trouble sleeping in 'ere. I'm sure it's much quieter than the Stockton." She headed toward the door. "Well, I'd best be off now and let you get settled."

"Nellie, wait." Juliana strode over to her, took her last two coins out of her change purse, and put them in Nellie's hand. "Thank you."

"No, I don't want pay." Nellie shook her head. "I did this just to help you out. You'd do the same for me, I know. I can tell."

"Please, I want you to keep it," Juliana insisted. "Besides, you have to clean my room now."

"You're too kind. Thank you. I'll be seeing you 'round town, I'm sure." Nellie left quickly to get back to work, and Juliana turned to unpack her suitcase, thinking about all the nice people she'd come to know recently, in spite of losing her mother. Maybe Marion and Josh had been right. *I guess I should thank You, Lord, for seeing me through this far, for this beautiful room, and for sweet Margaret, who took much less rent than the room was worth. I'm grateful.*

21

"Why didn't you come back last night?" Andy scurried over to Josh with Shebe in tow, who barked in greeting. Josh pulled back on the horses' reins, bringing the rattling wagon of supplies to a halt, and lifted his hat in explanation. Andy let out a loud whistle when he saw the purple lump. "Jumpin' Jehoshaphat! How'd you get that?"

"It seems as though someone is still after the Yogos." Josh climbed out of the wagon, gingerly placing his hat back on his head. He heard the bleating of the sheep, even though the camp, set up at some distance from the herd, continued to move daily. "I'm glad I went ahead and took them to the assayer's." He leaned down to affectionately pat Shebe's head, and she licked his fingers. He didn't mention that he'd left one stone to be fashioned into a ring. He'd feel foolish saying anything because Andy would want to know who it was being made for, and he wasn't ready to share his feelings about a hopeful relationship with Juliana.

"So you think someone is trying to steal the Yogos?" Andy whispered, as though someone could hear their conversation.

"Yep. I wonder how the word got out, don't you?"

"What happened? You sure you're all right? That looks purty nasty to me, I gotta tell ya." Andy shook his head.

"Aw, the doctor said it wasn't too serious, just painful, but he thought I'd better stay in town for the night. Would you believe that the newspaper man found me and took me into the hotel? You'd have loved it, Andy. I had two women fussin' over me. Marion— her father owns the hotel—and Juliana, who gave up her room for me last night. So I slept very nicely." He gave Andy a wink.

"Boy howdy! You seem to have all the luck, Josh." Andy started taking the supplies out of the back of the wagon.

Josh took off his leather gloves and stuffed them in his hip pocket. "Marion is a bit too old for you, I'm afraid, but she's a right fine-looking woman. A bit pushy, but I don't think she means any harm. It's just her way."

"All I can say is, next week it's my turn to go into town for a break. Agreed?"

"Agreed." Josh reached into the wagon for the flour and sugar.

"After that hit on your head, have you thought any more about doing business with Hoover?" Andy paused, leaning against the wagon's side.

"I haven't thought too hard about it. I've had other things on my mind. But how'd you do with me being gone? Everything all right?"

"It's been right fine, Boss. I only had to untangle a ram that decided he'd rather go hiking alone and get stuck in the brambles and briars than stick with his brothers."

His comment made Josh chuckle. Andy saw humor in just about everything. Probably because he had decided early on that he was better off if he could laugh about life instead of sitting around regretting his childhood of abuse from an alcoholic father. Josh knew he was like an older brother to Andy, and it did his heart good.

"I plan on going to church tomorrow. Wanna go?"

Andy scratched his head. "Yeah. I need to hear the Good Book preached. Helps keep me living right. Besides, there's a pretty girl I met last time I attended. Maybe she'll be there tomorrow."

"Good. You'll have to take your own horse, 'cause I'm meeting Juliana after church. Do you think you could help me pack up some dinner?"

Andy gave him a nudge in the ribs. "No kiddin'? Sounds like you did more than pick up supplies while you were in town!"

Josh was busy unharnessing the horses from the wagon but shifted his gaze to Andy's grinning face. "Well, look who's talking. Maybe I'll tell you at supper . . . or maybe I won't, if we don't get some work done around here."

"Mmm, we have stuff to make sandwiches with if I bake some bread this afternoon." Apparently Andy wasn't thinking about the weather but rather about what to prepare for Sunday. "I can make some hard-boiled eggs and whip up some bread dough to rise this afternoon, if you check on the sheep and keep 'em out of mischief."

"Such a deal. Bread making is not my cup of tea," Josh answered.

Leaning against his bedroll next to the campfire after supper, Josh observed the twinkling stars beckoning overhead. He loved the stillness of the night, interrupted with an occasional stirring and baaing of a stray lamb looking for its mother. Tonight was warm enough to sleep outside, so he and Andy threw their bedrolls under the canopy of the inky black sky. He thought about his walk with Juliana earlier that morning and hoped she'd been able to find a room. He could understand why she felt it necessary to move. In a way he was glad, because if he courted her, it'd make it easier than having to run into Marion every time at the hotel. She just might have a way of making him feel guilty.

He looked around at the quiet hills. It'd be so nice to have Juliana's head lying in the crook of his arm just now. They could look up and name the stars and talk about the future. Excited at the thought, Josh breathed deeply to clear his head. He couldn't wait until after church. Before he drifted off to sleep, he prayed for Juliana's heart.

In Lewistown, Juliana had retired for the evening, thoroughly satisfied with her room and with the proprietor and her daughters. She had found a new friend in Nellie, who reminded her of herself. She smiled, thinking that here it felt like a real home with a family. She sat with her feet curled up under her legs in the side chair, in her very own toile-decorated bedroom. She pulled the reading lamp closer and gingerly opened up Josh's Bible. The smell of old paper and ink drifted from its parchment paper, not an unpleasant smell to her because she loved the smell of books. It felt peculiar to be holding something Josh had read, or, for that matter, lived by. Some of the pages had notations next to the verses.

Juliana had never owned a Bible, but her mother had quoted

Scripture from memory. Many of their personal belongings, including their Bible, had been lost on their way to Lewistown, when their wagon had plunged into McDonald Creek and its contents were pulled downstream by the current.

Her eyes latched onto a Scripture underlined in Job 28:11: "He bindeth the floods from overflowing; and the thing that is hid bringeth he forth to light." She wondered why he had this particular verse marked. What did it mean? She flipped through the Psalms, reading and feeling oddly at peace, until her eyes could barely stay open.

The Sabbath dawned bright and beautiful. Juliana dressed in the best blue dress she owned and carried her sunbonnet in her hand when she stepped to the stairway to join the others for breakfast. She wanted to pinch herself, she was so happy at this moment. Things were looking up! One thing was for certain: living here, Juliana would not go to bed hungry. Miss Margaret saw to that.

Breakfast smells enticed her as she entered the dining room to find Natalie and Louise already seated along with their mother. The homey scene of the table set with matching dishes, tablecloth, and napkins caused tears to form in Juliana's eyes. In the table's center was a beautiful rose pitcher and bowl. Such niceties Juliana had never been privileged to enjoy. Her room alone with its small reading area was more than she had ever hoped for.

"Good morning. Don't you look nice." Miss Margaret smiled approvingly at Juliana.

"Thank you, ma'am. It's the only church dress I own."

"It brings out the color of your eyes," Natalie said.

"Thank you, Natalie." Juliana took her seat with the others. She'd liked Natalie from the moment she had met her at the social club. Her sister, Louise, was a little shy and always spoke in a very soft voice.

"Is it all right if I walk to church with you ladies?" Juliana asked as she helped herself to pancakes and syrup.

Louise set her teacup down. "Of course you may. Reverend Carlson will be so happy to see you again. Where have you attended church before coming here?"

So innocently asked. Louise obviously knew nothing of why Juliana squirmed in her seat and made great pretense of slathering the butter on her pancakes before answering. "I wasn't a member anywhere else. My parents moved a lot. Most of the time we worked six days a week, which didn't leave us any free time."

"Oh . . . I wasn't trying to be nosy." Louise poured more coffee for everyone.

"It's okay, really. Albert invited me, and I told him I would come."

"Our brother told us that he'd hired a young girl and that you were doing a terrific job," Natalie said.

Juliana's heart warmed at her comment. "I enjoy working with him, and I was grateful for the chance."

"We're very sorry for the loss of your mother. Have you no family left?" Miss Margaret asked, her eyes softening when she looked at Juliana.

"I'm afraid not." She wasn't going to tell them her father had abandoned them, but she figured the word had gotten around when her mother died and the Stocktons took her in.

"No matter, dear, you'll have us now," Miss Margaret said, patting her shoulder when she stepped to the sideboard for the cream. "I always wanted another daughter."

"You do me an honor, Miss Margaret. I appreciate your genuine hospitality." Juliana meant the words and hoped they conveyed her gratitude. Natalie looked over the rim of her cup at Juliana. "Are you going to be here for lunch?"

"No. I'm meeting a gentleman for lunch, but I'll be back by suppertime."

"Ooh, how divine. Do we know him, if you don't mind my asking?" Natalie said.

Juliana's lips twitched with amusement. "I don't mind. His name is Josh McBride."

"I don't believe we know him," Miss Margaret said.

"He's a sheepherder." She wanted to add that he had the most magnificent amber eyes and rich-sounding voice that caused her heart to flip-flop, but they would think her daft.

"I see," was all Miss Margaret said.

Was that response disapproval? Juliana wasn't sure.

"Sheep are very noisy, and their smell is disgusting," Natalie said, wrinkling her nose as though the very odor had entered the room.

Juliana shrugged. "Oh, I don't know that I'd agree. They have a peculiar musky smell, but they are sweet, gentle creatures, and Josh and his sheepherder, Andy, are really fine people."

"I didn't mean to imply that they weren't," Natalie quickly added. "I assure you, I was only speaking of the sheep. Sheepherding is the fastest growing industry in Montana."

"I'm sure he'll be quite successful then. Let's finish our breakfast and clean up, or we'll all be late for the service," Miss Margaret said. "Juliana, do you know how to drive a team?"

"No, but I'm willing to learn if you'll teach me." She smiled.

"Louise can teach you. She's quite skillful and has a way with horses," Natalie said of her shy sister.

"Indeed?" Juliana threw Louise a warm smile, who blushed at the compliment. Reticent Louise. Who would have thought it? Juliana was beginning to think that life at the boardinghouse would not be dull—not dull at all—and she was looking forward to every moment.

Josh's thick hair was neatly combed under his hat, and he was dressed in a dark woolen coat, a crisp white shirt, and a black string tie. He was uncomfortable in this Sunday getup. The collar felt tight, and the starch from his shirt scratched his thick neck, but he refrained from loosening the tie, wanting to look presentable when Juliana saw him. He wondered if Juliana had already arrived at church. He and Andy were already late getting there, and with all the rushing around this morning, it had put him in a strange dither.

Josh parked the wagon under a spreading cottonwood tree, where their lunch would be in the shade. Lots of wagons, buggies, and horses were parked in the church's yard. Andy had ridden alongside the wagon in great spirits, chattering the entire way, probably with nervous anticipation of seeing the young gal he'd met the last time he'd attended church. Josh told him that he cleaned up good, hoping not to embarrass him, but Andy didn't seem to mind at all. He tied his horse to the back of the wagon and slicked his hair down with his palm.

Josh stood outside the front of the white clapboard church, its bells pealing out across the valley as worshipers made their way inside. He gazed up at the white steeple that seemed to point the way toward heaven. It created a sharp contrast against the brilliant blue sky and the few puffy clouds.

"I think they must be inside," he said. "Let's go on in, the organ's starting up."

The door to the church stood open, and both men strode up the steps to a packed congregation inside. Andy found his friend and scooted in next to her. Josh scanned the crowd crammed like leaves in a tobacco tin for a glimpse of just one person. Why was it so packed? It wasn't even Easter. As he looked a second time, he saw her. Juliana was sitting with two other young ladies and someone he figured to be their mother. He paused, looking down the pew and wondering if he should try to sit next to her. Their eyes caught and held briefly. Juliana shifted in her seat, but he felt a hand touch him from behind on the elbow. It was Marion.

"Josh, what a delight it is to see you. Come sit me with me. There's lots of space," Marion said, tugging on his coat sleeve. Before he could make a move, she latched on to his arm, pulling him toward the pew. He threw Juliana a helpless look, shrugged his shoulders, and sat down next to Marion. Juliana turned toward the altar as Reverend Carlson took his place at the podium.

"I want to welcome all of you this wonderful Sunday morning to our house of worship. And we want to do that right now—worship. Let's turn to page 192, and I'll lead us in this great hymn of faith."

Josh knew Juliana was upset, but what was he supposed to do? The church pews were crowded. Marion opened her hymnal and held it out for them to share. Her smile was bright enough to light up a room. *Don't go getting any ideas about me, Miss Redhead. I only have eyes for one.* From where he was sitting, he could see Juliana's dark curls escaping her bonnet, and her small shoulders set perfectly straight beneath her fetching blue dress. Now he felt bad that he hadn't said no to Marion and forced himself between Juliana and her friend. Especially with Marion smiling at him like this.

Though a few windows were open, he was uncomfortably warm as the singing continued and wished he could slip off his coat. So much for being fresh when he had lunch with Juliana. Through his pants leg, he could feel Marion pressing against him, and he inched farther away.

Reverend Carlson was an effective speaker, and Josh had always enjoyed his sermons, but this morning he was having a bit of a hard time concentrating on what he said. He hadn't been able to locate his Bible, so he couldn't follow along with today's Scripture reading. Marion quickly flipped open her Bible to 1 Thessalonians 5:18, holding it out so they could share, and he held one corner. The sermon topic was about being thankful no matter what happens because it is God's will for those who belong to Christ.

The pastor's voice was like a soothing balm, flowing from him in a rich baritone. "We need to trust when we don't understand. Folks, God never changes, and His love for you never changes. We need to accept life's circumstances with thanksgiving. That's not always easy to do, is it?"

Josh saw Juliana glance over her shoulder to him as the pastor continued to speak, and he wondered what she might be thinking. Was she thinking about her own grief and situation?

At the conclusion, Reverend Carlson's face took on a sympathetic look as he said, "Tell God what your needs are, and don't worry about anything. Whether you're currently living in sunshine or rain, He is there, ready to assist and give you comfort and peace." Closing his Bible, the pastor bowed his head and dismissed them with prayer.

Everyone poured out of the church, greeting one another with a slap on the back or a handshake. Juliana followed Miss Margaret and her daughters out into the yard, and they stood talking with Cynthia and Esther.

"Juliana is my newest boarder, and we are delighted to have her, aren't we, girls?" Miss Margaret said, beaming at her.

Cynthia nodded. "Yes, we've met."

Esther forced a half smile. "Still working for the newspaper?"

Juliana noticed Esther's emphasis on her job. "I certainly am, and I so enjoy working for Miss Margaret's son."

"Small world, isn't it?" Esther said.

Miss Margaret's bony hand grasped Juliana's arm. "Isn't it, though? But I believe Albert knew what he was doing when he hired an intelligent woman to help keep us all informed through newsworthy articles."

Esther looked unconvinced. "Indeed."

"Mother, we should hurry along so Juliana can go on her picnic," Natalie reminded her.

Cynthia raised an eyebrow. "Picnic? With whom?"

As if Juliana couldn't speak for herself, Louise answered, "She's going with Josh McBride."

"Really? Is that the man in question over there, engaged in an intimate conversation with Marion?" Cynthia asked.

"Thanks for reminding me, Louise. Yes, that's Josh, and I don't want to keep him waiting. See you all later."

Leaving the ladies twittering behind gloved hands, Juliana gave a tiny wave of her hand and hurried across the grassy area to where Josh stood talking with Marion next to the wagon.

Clutching Josh's Bible, her heart thudded as she approached him. "Hello," she said, suddenly bashful. Had he asked Marion along? Three was a crowd. Maybe Juliana could make some excuse and go back to the boardinghouse. Suddenly she felt a little sick inside. Whatever was wrong with her?

The two stopped talking and turned to greet her. "I was waiting for you." Josh smiled and took off his hat, revealing a mark clear around his thick head of hair like a permanent hatband. "Are you ready to go?"

Marion raised an eyebrow. "Going? Has someone invited you two to lunch? I was just about to do that. The chef has prepared a succulent goose with pearl onions and peas that would gratify any palate."

Josh reached for Juliana's hand to assist her into the wagon, and his hand felt warm and strong. "Not this time, Marion. We thought we'd take a ride while the weather is nice and have a picnic. But we sure appreciate your invitation."

Juliana almost laughed but held herself in check, because the frown on Marion's face looked pitiful. She felt a pang of sympathy for her friend.

"Uh, okay. Have a nice afternoon. Oh, there's Mark. I must have a word with him." She scurried away with a long face.

"Do you think I should have invited her?" Josh asked.

"That's entirely up to you," she answered, not wanting to

179

appear that she had any rights on him. But in her mind this was *their* date. After all, Marion did get to sit through church with him.

"I didn't want to make her feel totally friendless." He picked up the reins and yelled "giddyap" to the team. They sped down the lane by the church cemetery, nearing Andy and Nellie.

When Juliana saw them she drew in a surprised breath. How sweet! She liked Nellie a lot and had been impressed with Andy when she first met him at the camp. She waved vigorously as they went by the young couple.

Juliana showed Josh his Bible. "I found this at the edge of my bed that night you stayed in my room."

"That's where I left it! I couldn't imagine what I had done with it. I guess I must have accidentally knocked it under the bed frame. Thank you for bringing it. It's very dear to me. It was a gift to me from my mother." He steered the team expertly around stumps and ruts as they went along.

"I knew it must be special to you because I saw places you had underlined or marked."

"You did? You were reading it then?"

"I'll confess I did take a look. I'm not certain I understand some of the verses' meanings, though. Our family Bible was lost in the rushing water of McDonald Creek, so I've not had my own to read." Her voice softened.

"I'm sorry. Would you like to keep mine for a while? I wouldn't mind." Josh glanced sideways at her.

"Oh, I couldn't do that, but you're sweet to offer."

"I can be as sweet as candy, if I'm given half a chance."

Juliana felt her cheeks burn. "You seemed pretty interested in sitting with Marion at church." Now what made her blurt that out?

"Sorry, I really didn't think I had much choice. The church was so crowded today. But the reverend preached a good sermon, don't you think?"

She was hoping for a better explanation since she was his date today, but when none was forthcoming, she just bit her tongue. "Yes, I think I'm beginning to understand that I need to have more faith than I've exercised lately." It was true. Some of the reverend's words had touched her heart. He had been able to make her see that God was always right there. That He'd never left.

Gently sloping hills of thick ash and cottonwood trees peppered the countryside on Josh and Juliana's ride beneath the shadow of the magnificent Judith Mountains. Meadowlarks warbled out their delightful tunes at the coming summer while squirrels scampered about, playing among the huge ponderosa pines. Josh and Juliana watched a soaring eagle high above tip his wings to dive toward his prey in the distant field in a wondrous demonstration of nature.

"That clump of cottonwood trees near the creek looks like a fine place to stop and spread our lunch, don't you think?" Josh asked. Without waiting for an answer, he turned the team toward the small grove. As they stopped, he hopped down from the wagon, reached up to take hold of Juliana's waist, and lifted her down.

They stood only inches apart, and she felt peculiar and wonderful at the same time. His eyes twinkled with amusement, and she noticed he had nice, even teeth, with appealing lips that curved upward. His hands held her sides as his eyes sought hers. Was it hard to breathe from her corset, or was it the sheer nearness of him?

Abruptly, he let go and reached into the back of the wagon for the basket of lunch and a large blanket. Juliana watched as he strolled over to the shade of the cottonwood tree and set the basket down. She realized she was standing there watching like a wooden statue, so she cleared her head of the prior thoughts of his nearness and quickly sprang into action to help spread the blanket on the grass, disturbing the chipmunks.

"Do you mind if I remove this coat? I've been warm ever since we were in the church," Josh said.

"Of course not. It was cooler this morning, but it's quickly warming up, isn't it?" Her tongue stuck to the roof of her mouth when he removed the woolen coat. Seeing the band of muscles across his broad back caused a small catch in her breath. He removed his hat as well, placed it on top of his coat, and ran his fingers through his thick hair.

"Now I feel better! A picnic is supposed to be a fun, comfortable pleasure." His eyes swept over her and seemed to follow her every movement. She expelled a deep sigh. Maybe this wasn't such a good idea. They should have invited Marion along.

Removing her bonnet, she knelt down on the blanket, opened the basket, and clapped her hands together. "Homemade bread. I'm impressed!"

"Don't get too excited. I didn't make it, Andy did. But we do have thick cheese and slices of roast beef, hard-boiled eggs, and dried fruit. I *did* have a hand in drying the fruit myself," he said proudly, taking a seat in a crossed-legged fashion to face her.

Juliana regarded him. "A man of many talents, I see."

"I'd like to think so." He gave her a mischievous grin, but her gaze skittered away.

"There's cold apple cider in the canteen—or at least it was cold when I started out this morning."

She continued to unpack their lunch, finding two napkins at the bottom of the basket, along with blue-speckled enamel drinking cups and plates. "What lovely china we have here," she teased.

"Fit for a princess." Josh laughed. "I'm sorry, I don't own any nice dishes. But my wife will choose those for our home in the near future, I hope."

"Wife?" She blinked at him. "Then surely I must be in the way of your well-thought-out plans." She placed slices of meat on his plate, then unwrapped the fresh bread. She dared not look up because she didn't trust herself to look into those deep amber eyes.

Josh took out a knife to slice the thick, crusty bread. "She may be nearer than you know," he said with a chuckle. He leaned on his side and propped up on his elbow, studying her reaction.

Juliana fixed her gaze on him, but all she saw were his eyes dancing in mischief. Was he teasing her? She wasn't sure she was ready to trust any man. Could she trust him? Or would he be like her father was, or, worse still, like Wes?

"You look so pretty in blue, you know. Your dress matches the color of your eyes, just like a jewel does."

Juliana felt her heart pick up its pace beneath her ribs. "Thank you." She took a bite out of her sandwich. "I didn't know I was so hungry. This is delicious."

"I'm glad you like it," Josh said, munching on his sandwich but never taking his eyes off her. "What did you think of the reverend?"

"I think he's a very good speaker. His sermon seemed to be

written just for me," she admitted. "I haven't been very good at trusting God in the last few months since Mama died."

"You must miss your mother. Not to have any family is lonely."

"Do you still have family, Josh?"

"Oh yes, a very sweet mother named Alice who is sometimes humble to a fault, and my father, Jim. My sister, April, is high-strung but can be a lot of fun," he answered, taking a drink of cider.

"Where do they live?" She was so glad to have him talk about himself for a change and realized she knew very little about his background.

"Steamboat, Colorado. Ever been there?"

"No, I haven't. Do you miss home?"

"Sometimes I do." His face became serious, and his voice was soft. "I'll take you there one day. It's different from Montana, and very beautiful."

"Then why did you leave if your family was there and you liked it so well?"

He paused before answering. "My father and I had words about how to run the ranch and how much more land and water rights he wanted to take from other struggling ranchers. Nothing is ever enough for him. And . . ."

She studied his eyes. "And what? Is there something else?"

"There was a lady I was very much interested in at the time, but she loved someone else and broke it off with me." He sat up and put down his sandwich.

"I'm sorry, Josh." He had been hurt. She was sure of that just from watching his face. She found herself wanting to touch his clenched jaw and comfort him, which surprised her.

"It was all for the best. Now I can see that, otherwise I wouldn't have met you. I believe God had a better plan."

"You mean you think He wanted you to meet me?" That was too incredible to comprehend to Juliana. "You said yourself I was a lot younger than you, so I'm mystified as to why you find me all that interesting."

He scooted over closer to her, and she resisted moving away, which was what she ought to do but somehow couldn't. She could feel his energy and strength as he picked up her hand and rubbed her palm gently back and forth with his thumb.

"I'm drawn to you in a way I'm afraid I don't totally understand." He hesitated before speaking again, looking steadily into her eyes. "I felt this magnetic pull on my soul when I saw you the first time. Then I couldn't get you out of my head, so I made up excuses to keep coming back into town, hoping to catch a glimpse of you," he said huskily. He continued to stroke her hand.

Juliana took a deep breath and let it out slowly. "I'm not sure what to say." Her eyes searched his for a clue.

"You don't need to say anything right now. Just listen to me. From the beginning your eyes have pierced me right here," he said, placing her hand over his heart. She could feel his pulse beating through the fabric of his shirt. His hands were nice and warm, not soft but strong, and in this proximity, she noticed he had a perfectly shaped nose that would be the envy of most women.

Josh reached up and lifted a lock of hair the breeze had caught and placed it behind her ear. Just a simple act, but the sweetness of it touched Juliana immeasurably. She wondered what his lips would feel like today, and she almost leaned in close enough for him to kiss her, but she thought he might think she was being too forward.

What in the clouds above was wrong with her? Had she just lost all reserve? He should be the one to make the first move. His scent was an odd mixture, a little like the outdoors, sunshine, soap, and a dash of perspiration. A strange mixture, but not altogether unpleasant to her. The look in his amber eyes drew her in as they grew serious.

As Josh leaned toward her even closer, her heart pounded in her ears until she thought she'd go deaf. Her lips parted in anticipation, and she leaned into him.

Just as Josh was about to touch his lips to hers, Juliana let out a yelp. "Ouch! Oh no!"

"What is it? What's wrong, did I offend you?" Josh drew back sharply.

Juliana scrambled up, swatting her legs and feet with her hands. Josh looked down. Her feet and legs were covered by a host of ants crawling over her as if marching to war. "Help me! They're stinging me!" she screamed, batting at her legs. "They're in my shoes!"

"Take off your shoes and stockings!" Josh shouted, jumping up and dragging her off the blanket.

Juliana looked at him as if he were from another planet. "What? I can't do that!" She danced about, stomped her feet to shake the ants loose, and continued to bat at her legs.

"Juliana, listen to me—take off your shoes and stockings! Now! I'll turn my back, but be quick or you'll be covered in a flash!" His voice boomed irritably as he turned his back to her.

Juliana yanked off her shoes, reached under her dress, and quickly peeled off her stockings. She was covered with ants, and they were now crawling up into her bodice. "I don't know what to do! Oh, goodness! They're crawling farther up!" Her body was starting to feel like it was on fire.

Turning back around, Josh scooped her up so fast that she didn't know what was happening and ran headlong toward the rushing stream.

Josh slid waist deep into the water, nearly falling over the slick rocks at the creek's edge, and deposited Juliana none too gently. He plunged her under by her shoulders, then brought her quickly back up.

"I knew there was a reason to picnic by the stream!" He roared with laughter as he held Juliana in the swift current. She looked madder than one of his rams caught in a thicket.

His eyes widened as they swept over her form. Her dripping wet hair was plastered to her sopping dress, which revealed her womanly curves. He felt guilty seeing her like this but couldn't deny the pleasure it gave him.

"I don't know how to swim, you fool!" she hollered, spitting out water and wiping her nose with the back of her hand.

"I'm sorry," he answered, still tickled. "It was the fastest way to get the ants off you and cool down the burning. Don't you feel better now?" He helped her up the creek bank, but she pushed him away. He chuckled, shielding his mouth with his fist. "Would you rather I left you for them to have for lunch?"

Juliana marched past him, dragging her wet, heavy skirts in each hand. She struggled up the creek's bank, mud clinging to her garments. He followed her and watched as she stood with her back against a scraggly pine. She crossed her arms against her bosom and blocked out his stare.

"Now what am I supposed to do about these wet clothes? I can't go back to the boardinghouse looking like this," she fumed.

"You're shivering. Let me get my coat." Josh went to get his coat for her, then hurried back. Her pert nose was stuck up in the air, and her jaw was set in a hard line, but he ignored her tantrum to slide the coat over her shaking shoulders. "There! All better now?" He paused. Taking the lapels of the coat in his hand, he pulled her close to his face, then lifted her chin with his fingertips. "I'm sorry. I didn't notice the ant bed when we spread the blanket out. Guess I was too eager to have lunch. At least we drowned the buggers!" But Juliana simply looked back at him and was quiet.

He looked into her flashing blue eyes and leaned in to touch his lips to hers, lightly at first, then with more fervor as he placed his hand on her back. Josh was pleasantly surprised at their softness but more so their tenderness. A deep, sweet longing was filled in that tender kiss, and he pulled away with a deep sigh, then he brushed her eyelashes with a couple of light kisses, still holding her close. He wanted to hold her like this until the stars twinkled in the evening sky. The rest of the world didn't matter. He had been waiting for *her*.

She leaned against him but kept her face tilted toward his. She closed her eyes dreamily, and her lips formed a half smile of contentment until a dragonfly buzzed around her head, and they slowly pulled apart. In that moment, their hearts committed to what they had already known weeks ago in their heads.

The thundering sound of horses' hooves broke the peaceful afternoon silence and the intimate moment of the courting couple. Josh jerked his head around, watching as a pair on horseback rode furiously toward them. Juliana put her arms through the sleeves of Josh's coat and pulled it together, hiding her wet dress as best as she could.

"Looks like something's wrong," Josh whispered under his breath.

Juliana lifted her hand to shield it from the sun, squinting to see who it was. "I think it's Andy and Nellie."

As the pair approached, Josh walked toward them as Andy reined in, his horse's sides heaving. Josh took hold of the horse's bridle to steady him. "Boss, we've got trouble," Andy spit out, clearly agitated. His breathing was ragged, and his hat was missing. "Just beyond our camp, I'm not sure, but it might be a prairie fire coming. There's smoke. Lots of it. Me and Nellie rounded up as many of the sheep as we could and drove them to the other side of the ravine in case it comes this way. I left Shebe with them."

Josh moved quickly, rushing to the buckboard and unharness-ing the horses. "Can you ride bareback, Juliana?"

"I guess I could."

He lifted her up to the horse's broad back before mounting the other one. "What about the wagon?" she asked.

"No time for that now. You ride back into town where it's safe."

"Are you crazy? I'm coming with you." She looked him square in the eye for a brief moment. She knew from his expression that he was thinking it was a waste of time to argue with her. Worry creased his brow, and he slammed his hat on.

Josh yelled orders as his horse danced around in a half circle, waiting for direction. "Andy, you get back to the sheep and keep pushing them out as far as you can. I'll head to camp and try to save the sheepherders' wagon and supplies. Nellie, you'd better go on back to town."

"No, Josh, I'm going with Andy."

"Fool women," Josh muttered under his breath.

"Let's go! There's no time to lose!" Andy said. Giving his horse a swift kick in the side, he galloped off with Nellie. Josh and Juli-ana went the opposite direction. Any thoughts of a lazy Sunday afternoon were shattered.

Upon reaching the campsite, they could see a red glow on the horizon along the western slope. It was a frightening sight to behold, and it was moving fast. Juliana had never seen anything like it and sat stunned, looking at its approaching blaze. They would never be able to stop this disaster, and her heart was full of fear now. She hoped Josh's half-built home lay beyond the fire's fury, and she prayed it had somehow miraculously escaped its onslaught.

Josh practically threw himself off his horse when they reached the campsite. "Juliana, we've got to hitch the horses to the sheepherders' wagon, and I'll need your help. Grab the harness," he barked. Beads of sweat broke out over his furrowed brow. He jerked the nervous horses to the front of the wagon to maintain some control to keep them calm. They seemed to sense some impending danger.

Juliana watched Josh tighten the leather straps over his horse's back and tried to copy what he did, meeting him in the middle where the harnesses came together. She hoped the fire would die out before it reached the ravine, sparing the sheep, but what if it didn't? *Lord, help us, please.* She sneaked a glance at Josh, whose face was sober, his square jaw clenched and his face lined with worry. His pants were wet up to his waist, but he didn't seem to notice.

The task completed, he assisted her into the expensive Candlish wagon she'd toured when she visited the campsite, and she suddenly realized she was barefoot. Her face flamed red just thinking what Andy and Nellie must have thought. Maybe they hadn't had time to notice.

Josh slapped the reins across the horses' back, and they sprang forward, leaving the campsite in a furious fashion. Juliana clung to the side of the hard wooden seat to keep from falling, feeling miserable and chilly in her damp dress despite Josh's coat. She hadn't sat this high above ground since she'd crossed the plains in a covered wagon as a child.

The peculiar smell of smoke burdened the afternoon breeze, and Juliana wondered again if the ranch had escaped the fire. In the distance they saw flames lick the dry tree limbs, sending fire shooting up into the pine trees. Wildlife scattered in sheer terror. Juliana felt a pang of sorrow for them and uttered another small prayer.

Despite the crackling heat behind them, she could hear the constant bleating of the sheep from across the ravine, where Andy and Nellie had frantically tried to move the frightened herd in a desperate attempt to save them. Shebe barked, running this way and that and snapping at the sheep's heels in an attempt to keep the animals together.

When they had driven as many of the frenzied sheep as they could to safety and moved the wagon as far as they could away from the fast-moving fire, the pitiful bunch sat slumped together, exhausted and stunned. They watched the raging rhythm of the strong wind and hot air as it took a dramatic shift in direction and pushed the fire southward and away from them. Shebe limped up to her master, tongue hanging out from exhaustion and thirst.

The smell of smoke and smoldering ash was sharp in Juliana's nostrils. In their line of vision, scores of charred woolies littered the once beautiful landscape.

"I've never seen anything like it," Andy said, his large eyes staring in shock.

"What do you think caused the fire?" Nellie asked, her round face smudged from the soot and smoke. Juliana knew all of them must look rather frightful. And she was full of an emotion that was hard to explain—horror, yes, but also a sensation of how fast life could change.

"It could have been from a lightning strike in the forest or nature's natural burn," Josh said. He wiped his brow with his handkerchief, then tucked it into his back pocket. "Or worse—it could have been set on purpose."

"Let's hope not. I can't imagine anyone doing something so wicked." Juliana stared at the disaster. "Thank goodness it didn't happen at night while you two were sleeping."

Josh stood, hands on his hips. "Juliana, why don't you and Nellie ride back to where we left the buckboard and go on back into town. We'll come get the buckboard later. There's nothing more you can do here. Andy and I will have to dig a large hole deep enough to bury the burned sheep." His face looked numb and sad. Juliana thought that if he hadn't been a man, he would have cried, and he might have anyway if she and Nellie hadn't been present.

"Sounds like a good idea." Nellie grabbed Juliana's arm. "Come on, let's go find your shoes." She stared down at Juliana's bare feet with a curious look. Juliana's feet were dirty with red welts on them, but that seemed insignificant compared to what had just happened.

"We must all be thankful we survived," Nellie said.

"If the wind hadn't shifted like it did, we wouldn't be standing here to talk about it," Andy said, nodding his head.

Juliana let Nellie guide her back to her horse, but she looked back over her shoulder at Josh. She wanted to tell him how wonderful his kisses and the picnic had been, but instead could only say, "I'm sorry." Then she walked over to him and slipped off the coat. "Here. You'll need this tonight."

Josh took his coat from her without even looking and said nothing. He was staring into the distance, and Juliana could barely stand to see the sorrow etched on his face. She turned to go, stopping long enough to pat Shebe's head. "Good girl, Shebe. You're a hard-working dog, and I'm sure you've saved many sheep today."

The odor of smoke clung to Shebe's thick fur. She sniffed and nuzzled Juliana's hand, her brown eyes shining up at her, but she never left the side of her master.

A lone figure camped out under the evening stars, aware of the pungent smell of charred forest that lingered heavily on the night air. He'd barely escaped the fire and was horrified at what he'd done by accident. He foolishly thought he would locate the Yogos in the sheepherder's house and be back in town by nightfall, but instead he found nothing. Frustrated, he had stalked out of the house and mounted his horse, flicking his cigarette aside. Like spontaneous combustion in the dry brush, it ignited, and a fire quickly began to spread. God help him! What had he done?

Worn out, dejected, and exasperated, Josh instructed Andy to stay with the herd while he rode back to see what was left of the ranch. He knew what to expect, but maybe, just maybe, God had spared him that grief.

When he couldn't make out a roofline from his usual spot, he instantly knew his home had not survived. With a heavy heart, he slowed his horse to a walk and faced the wreckage of what used to be his ranch. It had been gutted by the fire. Burning embers of blackened timber glowed against the backdrop of the brick fireplace he'd proudly laid himself.

A lump caught in his throat, and his eyes burned with tears. He hadn't even finished all of it yet! *Why, God? Why did this have to happen? I put every cent I had into this ranch and the sheep. Now I have nothing!*

There was no point in even dismounting. Nothing was left to salvage. Josh turned his horse back to camp, his mind a fog. His plans had been so different. He had secretly hoped to complete his home while courting Juliana, drive the herd to Billings, then hopefully ask her to marry him.

Now all his plans would have to change. He owned very little and would never ask his father for a dime. Never! A loan at the bank was out of the question. He'd already borrowed to buy the property. He couldn't afford a wife, much less to rebuild the ranch. His dreams of giving Juliana a better life had just dissolved into ash like the burning timber.

Andy had moved the camp and herd further eastward beyond the ravages of the fire. He'd already set up a campfire and had thrown together something for supper by the time Josh returned.

"Boss?" Andy looked at Josh with sympathy. "I can tell from the look on your face that the news is not good. I'm just as sorry as I can be." Andy stood by the fire, his arms folded across his chest and a weary look on his face.

"No, it's not good. I just don't believe it. Everything wiped out in a flash. Everything I've worked so hard for." He slapped his dusty hat against his leg in anger.

"Well, we survived, and the ladies too, along with about twenty-eight hundred head of the woolies. It could have been all of 'em. I'm feelin' pretty lucky about now. Here, sit yourself down. I threw together some soup, and there's some leftover bread."

"I'm not hungry. But I'll take some coffee." Josh took the bridle off his horse and fed him some oats. Shebe trailed Josh with every step he took until he stopped and stroked her head and face.

Andy poured Josh a steaming cup of coffee. "Tomorrow everything will look a little better, Boss."

Josh was usually the one to give encouragement about such things, but tonight he didn't have one ounce of it to give, and he wasn't looking forward to tomorrow.

Nellie and Juliana had managed to gather the remnants of the picnic and hitch the wagon to their horses. They said very little on the way back to Lewistown. From the bustling excitement as they drove into town, it appeared the news of the fire had quickly reached the townsfolk from neighboring ranches. A few people looked curiously at them as they made their way to the boardinghouse.

For her first time to drive a team and wagon, Juliana had done well. She stopped the wagon in front of the boardinghouse, and the front door flew open, with Miss Margaret and her daughters nearly tumbling over each other in their rush down the steps to reach her and Nellie.

"My goodness, are you two all right?" Miss Margaret hobbled to Juliana's side as quickly as her cane would allow and took hold of Juliana's arm, appraising the worn-out women.

"We're okay. Nellie and I are just really tired and could use some water," Juliana answered.

Natalie assisted them inside with Miss Margaret's help, while Louise raced to get them water to drink.

"You poor dears!" Miss Margaret led them to the parlor. "Have a seat." She was fussing over them like they were her family.

Louise brought water, and the two gratefully drank it. "Nothing has ever tasted so good!" Nellie remarked after emptying her glass.

Natalie shook her head in sympathy. "Please, tell us what happened. How did you get caught up in the goings-on of a fire?"

"It came out of nowhere, it seems." Juliana pushed her hair off her face. Her dress was dirty, and she knew from the looks the ladies gave her and Nellie that they were a little the worse for wear. "Josh lost some sheep, but he and his sheepherder, Andy, are fine." She stared down at her hands, which were blistered from holding the reins without the protection of gloves.

"How terrible. I wonder if it was just a wildfire that popped up. We haven't had much rain, and things are dry around here," Miss Margaret said. She sat on the edge of her settee with so much concern in her lined face that Juliana felt as if she was the one who needed a hug.

"That'd be hard to know for certain, unless someone actually saw it happen," Nellie said.

"You're right—we probably will never know." Louise's calm voice was like a soothing balm for Juliana's heart.

"I say let's run a hot bath for these two gals and rustle up some supper." Miss Margaret stood up and started giving directions to her daughter.

"I must be going home. Me mum will be scared out of her wits wondering where I got off to. But thank you so much for thinking of me." Nellie gave her new friend a quick hug.

"Thanks, Nellie, for all your help. I know Josh appreciates it. I'll see you soon." Juliana stood to walk her to the door.

"It was no trouble at all. Your Josh fellow looked like a mighty sad man. I'm hoping Andy's cheerful nature will be able to perk him up after a few days." She gave her thanks to Miss Margaret and her daughters for their kindness, and slipped out the front door.

After a warm bath and a bowl of thick chicken soup with crusty bread and milk, Juliana bade them all good night. She was so tired, and tomorrow was a workday. Before she closed her bedroom door, she turned to Miss Margaret. "If I can get Albert to let me return the buckboard to Josh, I'd like to pack him and Andy lunch. Besides, I could write a story firsthand."

"Sounds like a good idea to me. In fact, you just march into work and ask my son for a couple hours off in the morning. If he gives you any trouble, just let me know. The girls and I will make up a hearty lunch for your young man and his friend. Now, don't you worry any."

"Miss Margaret, you're just too good to me."

"Off to bed with you. You look exhausted."

In truth, Juliana could barely stand up and couldn't wait to sink her head into her soft pillow.

Downstairs in the kitchen, Miss Margaret told Natalie and Louise about her plan to put together enough staples of food to last for a couple of days for Josh and Andy, besides making their lunches. There was no argument from them, and they started taking out of the pantry jars of pears, applesauce, and beans they'd canned themselves from last summer's garden. In the morning they would make up sandwiches and other necessary items.

"So you think Albert won't mind Juliana taking time off in the morning to drive the wagon back?" Natalie broke the silence as they worked quietly.

"Humph. Albert may be a hard worker, but he always has compassion for folks who need it. I reckon Juliana learned right quick-like how to drive that team." Miss Margaret chuckled. "She's tough, and she's got spunk in her, that's for sure. From what I hear from Sally and Albert, she's had it hard in her young life."

Louise put her arm around her mother's shoulders. "You're just the one to make her feel good about herself."

Miss Margaret beamed at her daughter. "I sure hope so. It's only been a few weeks since she lost her mother, and she hasn't seen her father in a decade. I don't think she trusts too many people."

"Bless her heart," Natalie said as she stacked the cleaned dishes from dinner.

"Yes, may God bless her really good," Miss Margaret agreed.

A thick cloud of depression covered Josh like a mantle when he surveyed the acres of charred grass. He realized how quickly his circumstances had changed, along with his hopes and dreams, but most of all he was thinking of all the work and countless hours that had gone into building his house. The only good thing was that he hadn't really furnished it yet.

As he walked around the ruins, a hard knot began to form in the center of his chest. He and Andy had buried the sheep in one gigantic hole, and he was worn out physically and mentally. His usual cheerful spirit was sinking just below sea level.

He slipped off Pete and let him wander about. He knew ol' Pete wouldn't stray very far from him. Sitting down on a large boulder near the clearing's edge, Josh surveyed the land, trying to think things through. If he did rebuild, where? The first place he'd picked had been the perfect spot. But the new place would have to be farther away from this awful-looking, scorched landscape, because he couldn't stand to look at it.

The taste of bitterness crept into his heart, and he clenched his teeth. Grasses would quickly return, but the trees would take years. He sighed and put his head in his hands, looking down at the space between his feet.

He heard the jingle of horses and buggy coming up the road. Lifting his head, he watched Marion drive a fine, matching pair of bays and a shiny black buggy over to where Pete stood. She wasted no time but scrambled down and walked over to where he sat.

"Josh . . . I have no words to express how sorry I am for what happened yesterday. What can I do, how can I help?" She gave his arm an affectionate pat.

For a moment he thought she was going to burst into tears. Grateful that she didn't, he lifted his gaze to stare out at the rubble that was his home. "There's nothing you can do," he declared thickly. "Nothing at all."

"At least you and Andy didn't lose your lives. You can start over, build another house." Marion knelt down next to him, placing a hand on his shoulder.

"No, I can't. There's no money left, and I had a loan for my land. The house *was* my collateral."

"I can help—"

"What's the use? I lost part of my herd, most of the grazing land is burned to a crisp . . ." Josh slowly exhaled.

Marion shrugged. "Josh, there's always hope, and there's always help. I'm not without means. I could advance you the money until you sell the wool, or whatever it is you planned to do. All is not lost."

He knew she meant it from the tone of her voice and concern in her face. "I can't let you do that. What would people think?"

"That we're partners?"

He froze and arched an eyebrow at her. "Partners?"

"Well . . . only if someone asks. I could care less about raising sheep," she said.

He hesitated, thinking about her offer. It would be ready cash, and he had no one else he could turn to. He didn't want to go back to Colorado and face his father with his failure. "Why would you want to do this for me?" It was an honest question.

"Because you're in need, and I'd like to help because we're friends. Right?" She leaned closer, looking up at him.

He stiffened. She was so close that he could smell rose water from the movement of her hair lifting on the morning breeze. Should he take her offer? Goodness knows, he didn't have much left, just a few sapphires for safekeeping. He wasn't sure how he was going to pay Andy his wages.

"Just say yes, Josh, and we can get to work on this," she pleaded.

"Okay. We'll talk about it. But it needs to be written up and legal," he said. He reached for her hand in a firm handshake that she returned. "Pardner!" His spirits lifted a little, and Marion gave him a wide smile. She leaned against his shoulder, giving him a hug as his head touched hers briefly in gratitude.

26

The brilliant sun was already high in the azure sky by the time Juliana made her way toward Josh's camp. Albert had assured her that her morning off would be time well spent. Upon her return she would work on the lead story about the fire for the newspaper. Albert said a couple of other farmers had suffered from the fire as well.

She'd slept soundly from sheer exhaustion but hurried through the morning. She loaded the wagon with Natalie and Louise's help, then hitched Choco to the back for her return trip. She couldn't get the vision of Josh's drawn face out of her mind. She wished she could do something somehow. Was it just a few weeks ago she had stood in his kitchen discussing plans on where to place his stove? It seemed like years.

She sighed deeply. Every time she got discouraged, she'd try to remember what the reverend said about how God is there even when we walk through the bad times. She didn't want to dwell on sadness. She'd done that long enough, and it was time to look forward to what the future held . . . maybe a future with Josh? Why else would he ask to court her?

Juliana's heart skipped a beat. She would help him through this valley he was in right now. After all, he'd helped her in her time of need and made her start thinking about God again.

Andy removed his floppy hat and greeted Juliana with less than his normal cheery hello when she drove up. "If it's Josh you're looking for, he's out at his ranch—or should I say what's left of the ranch." He walked over and assisted her down.

"He is? I wanted to return his wagon. I've also brought along a few supplies you might be needing, and a hearty lunch that Miss Margaret and her girls were kind enough to prepare for you and Josh." She turned, lifting a basket from the back. "If you'll get those other boxes there, I'd appreciate it."

"Wow. That's wonderful! It'll be nice not to eat my own cooking for a change," Andy said with a wink. "I'll put these things away. Why don't I take some of the lunch, and then you take the rest and go have lunch with Josh? Maybe that would cheer him up."

"Okay, but I can't stay long. I have to write a story about the fire for today's paper. Did you get any rest?"

"Somewhat. I think we're both in shock. We buried sheep, and all that digging plumb wore me out. Did Nellie get back all right?" His face lit up when he said her name.

"She did. She is a sweet girl and a hard worker, Andy. I can tell."

"I have to agree with you. She's a lot like you," he said, glancing in her direction as he grabbed some supplies.

"Really?" She sneaked a peek at Andy. "I'll take that as a compliment." She reached inside the basket, took part of the lunch out, and handed it to him. "I'd better get going now. Are you sure Josh is still out at the ranch?"

"That's where he was heading. He has some plans to work out if he's going to rebuild his house."

"Why wouldn't he?" Juliana raised an eyebrow.

Andy shrugged his lean shoulders. "You'll have to ask him. I don't know what he's thinking right now."

Juliana mounted Choco and looked down at Andy. "See you later, Andy."

He looked up at her. "Please thank Mrs. Spencer and her daughters. That was mighty kind of them, and thanks for returning our wagon."

"I'll tell them, and you're welcome." She gave her horse a light kick and cantered off in the direction of Josh's place.

Juliana slowed Choco when she drew closer to the area where she thought Josh's ranch lay. Everything looked different now, and she had to get her bearings. She was unprepared for the scene before her as she approached the clearing where his house once stood, and she barely noticed the burned-out barn and house. Marion was leaning against Josh, and their heads were touching. A flash of hurt spurted through her body, and she thought her heart would stop beating. Marion was her friend! Why was she doing this? Worse yet, why was Josh holding her?

They pulled apart as soon as Josh spotted her. His face reddened. From guilt? She wasn't sure, but she pursed her lips into a tight line when Josh stood up. Marion flushed and straightened her dress.

"Juliana. I'm surprised to see you this morning." Josh cleared his throat.

I'll just bet you are. Are you trying to act as though the two of us are only friends?

"I brought the wagon back with some supplies for your and a lunch." She handed him the basket without getting off her horse.

He reached up to take it from her, and their fingers brushed. Juliana flinched. Josh frowned, but she said nothing and nodded toward Marion.

"Well, hi, Juliana." Marion smiled. "How thoughtful of you to bring lunch."

Juliana stiffened and glanced at Marion. "Actually, it was Margaret Spencer who sent it since I was bringing Josh's wagon back." Juliana could barely look at either of them, especially those amber eyes of Josh's. "I left the wagon with Andy."

"That was very thoughtful of Mrs. Spencer. Aren't you going to get down and join us?" Josh asked, peeking inside the basket. He smacked his lips and squinted at Juliana.

She felt herself waiver momentarily when his eyes held hers. His warm amber eyes looked perplexed. She felt she had no reason to stay, really. He seemed to be doing quite well without her. "No, I must be getting back to work. I told Albert I wouldn't be long. Enjoy the lunch." She spun her horse around without waiting for a response, sending dusty ash flying.

Juliana rode Choco harder than she meant to, fuming on the way back to town. She thought Josh was a man of his word. Was he no different from most of the men she'd met or heard about? And her friend Marion! She certainly wasted no time to be alone with Josh.

Inside her head, a million thoughts were bouncing around. Had he been toying with her? She felt like she had just been duped. She should have never let it go this far. She knew better. She would get back to town, concentrate on writing the article, and put Josh out of her mind. She had her job and her new friends at the boardinghouse. She didn't need him.

She turned her attention to the beautiful, sun-kissed meadow that lay in the direction of Lewistown, a stark contrast to the burned grasslands behind her. The craggy mountain peaks lent a picturesque backdrop that never ceased to inspire her. She slowed her horse, leading him to the edge of the creek where just the day before, she and Josh had enjoyed a lovely picnic and had their first real kiss. Her response had been embarrassingly swift, she realized now. She felt her face grow hot at the thought of him pressing against her in her soggy dress. No lady should allow herself to be kissed that way. Right? If her mama could see her now, what advice would she give her?

Juliana slid off the horse's back and stood beside the creek to allow Choco to drink after the hard gallop. Rushing water foamed as it bubbled over the huge rocks in the sparkling creek bed. She loved the beautiful sound it created as it washed the rocks clean and smooth.

Juliana sat down on a fallen tree trunk, leaned back against a large rock, and watched the water in its endless flow downstream, until the sight of it began to calm her mind and create a balm over her soul. The creek was a strange thing, only a couple of miles away from yesterday's fire but still too far away to douse it. It brought to mind something she'd read in Josh's Bible. Was it from the book of Mark? That if she believed in the Lord, she would never thirst? Maybe she was just beginning to see what that meant.

She bowed her head and said a brief prayer that God would fill every corner of her heart with the promise that she would never again thirst. She wanted that. What had the reverend said? That man may fail us, but God never would, and He was the same yesterday, today, and tomorrow. Or something like that. She may have thought she *really* needed Josh, but the truth was she needed God more, in order to understand what the truth was. She thanked Him that lives were spared and that Josh hadn't lost his entire herd.

She didn't want to be angry at Josh or Marion. What good would that serve? With a deep sigh, she rose and patted Choco's thick neck and pulled herself back into the saddle. Her heart felt calmer now. Though she knew she loved Josh, she would step back and see where the Lord would lead. Maybe with a clearer mind, she'd be able to write about the fire a little more objectively.

Lunch had been eaten rather quickly after Juliana left. Josh could tell Marion was trying her best to keep the conversation light, but Josh wasn't feeling very hungry. He knew Juliana didn't understand what she had seen, and he wanted to tear out after her to explain, but that would have made him look even guiltier. He wasn't guilty of anything. Was he? He hoped Marion didn't take his reaction to her kindness as anything more than it was— comfort. Only comfort and perhaps hope.

"Marion," Josh said rather abruptly, standing up. "I need to get on back to work." He started to gather the remains of their lunch.

Sighing loudly, Marion picked up the leftover sandwiches and handed them to Josh. "I understand. You have a lot to do and consider. When you're ready to buy the materials to start building your home, let me know. My mother left me a small inheritance, and I can have my attorney draw up a legal document you'll be satisfied with. You can consider it an advance until you're able to see your way clear. No hurry."

"I'll give it some thought, I promise." Josh nodded.

She gave his arm a squeeze, and he turned to help her into her buggy. "See you in town soon, I hope." She lightly tapped the reins across the horses' backs, and they moved forward.

Josh stood watching as she turned the buggy easily in the direction of town. She was a good horsewoman, and he thought his sister, April, would agree. Marion was a really nice lady, that was sure, but she didn't touch his heart the way Juliana had. Even Crystal hadn't done that. He'd have to make it a point to talk to Juliana, but right now he'd better ride back to camp or Andy would think he wasn't returning at all.

Josh's back was aching from all that digging. Shoot! He might not be able to beat the other men off Juliana. With a heavy heart, he rode his mount in the direction of the sheep camp.

Shebe left the flock and ran as fast as her four legs could carry her to greet Josh when he returned. Dismounting Pete, Josh leaned over and ruffled the thick hair around Shebe's neck. She sniffed his palm, looking for her usual jerky treat.

"Sorry about that, my ol' friend. My pockets are empty today." *And my heart too*, he thought.

Andy sprinted up to take Pete's reins. "Don't let her fool you none. I gave her plenty of treats already. Did Juliana find you without any trouble?"

"She did."

"Good. The Spencers packed us a mighty hearty lunch, didn't they?" Andy guided Pete to where a rope was strung between two trees. He flipped the reins around the rope. "Want me to unsaddle your horse?" Andy said with his hands on his hips.

Josh shuffled over to pour a cup of coffee before answering. "Thanks, Andy. I first thought I might ride into Lewistown this afternoon, but I think I'll wait until tomorrow." He stood, staring into his cup. "I'll rub Pete down in a few minutes."

"Josh, is something bothering you? Something happen at the

ranch?" Andy's eyebrows shot up, and he pushed his hat further back on his head.

"You could say that." He took a swig of the hot brew and continued. "This coffee is old. Why don't you make a fresh pot?" Josh flung the liquid out of his cup. "I had two visitors. Marion came to offer a cash advance to get the house built again." Josh took a seat on the camp stool and crossed his leg over his knee. "She said there would be no hurry to pay it back."

"Hey now, that's good news, don't you think? That could settle all your problems."

"Well, hold on, Andy. I'm in no hurry to rebuild the house yet. I don't have a family," he said, staring out at the sheep. "Thank God we still have land that the flock can graze on."

"True, but the Stocktons are some of the wealthiest people in town. Marion will never miss the money." Andy leaned down to add more wood to the fire, then threw out the old coffee. He stepped over to the wagon and scooped up fresh coffee, then filled the pot with water from the barrel strapped on the wagon's back panel.

"I don't want to take her money, but I'm grateful for her offer. It'll cost a pretty penny to replace one of our prized rams we lost in the fire."

"I don't mind working for my keep, Josh. I know you'll pay my wages when you sell this year's wool, so don't worry on that score. I like my job. Besides, I'm the only one who'll put up with you day and night!" Andy laughed.

Josh chuckled. "You're almost as good as a wife! And a dog-gone good cook too." Josh was glad Andy felt so comfortable working with him.

Andy shrugged. "I do my best to please. Nellie seems to agree with you."

"Aw, I see how it is now. That gal is gonna take you away from me, I'm sure of it."

"Could be. But until then, I'm all yours."

"Then what's for dinner?" Josh clapped him on the shoulder.

"Are you changing the subject? Seems to me you're the one who'll be hitched to that sweet young Juliana soon." Andy's face held a grin a mile wide. "I saw how she looked when she was talking to you."

"Is that a fact? Well, she was none too happy with me today."

"Whaddya mean?" Andy placed the coffeepot over the burning fire, then paused to look back at Josh.

"I think she saw something this morning between me and Marion and took it the wrong way."

"Uh-oh. You're in hot water now. Did Juliana get mad?"

"What do you think? She was as friendly to me as an icy winter morning."

Andy rolled his eyes. "If she means what I think she does to you, then you'd better get it squared away with her. My grandpa used to say that a woman's heart is like a campfire—if you don't tend to it, you'll lose it." Andy continued stoking the fire under the coffeepot until it blazed hot.

Josh rose, strolled over to Pete, and started removing his saddle. "That's just what I intend to do. Stoke the fire."

Before the dusky twilight settled over the mountain peaks, Josh heard Andy ringing the dinner bell. He still didn't have much of an appetite. Along with Shebe's help, he had spent the rest of the afternoon trying to keep track of the baby lambs, forcing them to stay with the flock. He knew that after the fire, predators would be more prevalent in search of food. Considering how quickly the fire had swept through without warning, he guessed he'd been fortunate. The dumb sheep carried on more or less like nothing had occurred. He figured he wasn't the only one who had suffered loss from the fire. He'd find out who else had when he went back to town.

While he traipsed back toward camp with Shebe next to him, his thoughts were centered on Juliana. It was best to go see her and talk to her, but he was glad a little time had elapsed so she could cool down, and he could ruminate over what he should say. It may not matter to her in the first place, although Josh thought he saw a streak of jealousy flash across her face this morning. Or was that wishful thinking? If it was jealousy, then it made him feel certain she cared for him like he did for her. Their kiss at the creek had been more than a kiss to Josh. When he'd held her in his arms, she'd filled the vacant spot and the longing in his heart, and he felt like he'd finally come home.

"Whaddya say, Shebe? It's dinnertime, and we'd best get back to camp or risk upsetting Andy. You know how he is when it comes to his cooking."

Shebe yapped a sharp reply with knowing in her large brown eyes.

On Tuesday morning, Josh could see that Juliana and Albert were having a morning break with a woman he guessed to be

Albert's wife when he looked through the newspaper's glass window. Perfect. He pushed the door to the office, and it flew open so hard that the bell jangled furiously from its chain. They all turned at the sound of the noise as Josh strode into the room.

"What in tarnation . . . ?" Albert said.

"Sorry for that. I didn't mean to push so hard," Josh muttered. He glanced at the muffins. Normally he would have enjoyed one, but not this morning.

Albert smiled. "Don't worry about that. The hinges are loose, and I just haven't taken the time to work on it. How's the head, Josh?"

Josh took off his hat and held it in his hands. "See for yourself. The swelling's gone down, and I no longer have a headache." He pointed to his head. He looked at Juliana and said hello, but she only nodded and walked back to her desk, every bit the business-woman.

"Allow me to introduce my wife to you. Sally, this is a new friend of mine, Josh McBride. The one I told you about who was clobbered on the head a few nights ago."

"Oh, dear me. Nice to meet you, Josh. I'm so sorry someone decided to take advantage of you. Really! What's this world coming to?" Sally was pleasingly plump, and her chest heaved as she spoke. She had graying hair weaved throughout her brown tresses, which were pulled neatly to the back of her neck. She reached out her hand to take his. "So nice to meet you."

"And you," he said.

"We heard about the fire, Josh. Really sorry about that. Juliana wrote a fine article about it in yesterday's paper." Albert reached over to his desk and handed Josh a copy. "You may have that copy, if you want it."

Josh put his hat back on and reached for the newspaper. "Much obliged, Albert. I'm in a bit of a hurry this morning and really came to see if I could have a word with Juliana." Josh glanced over at Juliana, who had sat down at her desk and was now moving papers around in a futile attempt to look busy.

"Oh? What about?" Juliana raised an eyebrow with a puzzled look on her face. The face Josh wanted to kiss.

Josh shifted his weight. "Well, I, uh . . ."

Albert reached for his wife's hand. "Come on, Sally, I'll walk you back home."

"What's your hurry? Here, Josh, have a muffin." But seeing that Albert wasn't going to answer her and Josh passed on the muffin, Sally picked up her basket, placed the leftover muffins inside, and gave a quick wave to Juliana. She took Albert's arm, and he winked at Josh, leaving the two alone.

The air hung heavy and thick with silence. Josh swallowed. This was not easy for him, and he didn't have much practice where relationships with females were concerned.

Juliana continued filing papers, not looking at him, until Josh blurted out, "Will you please just stop that for one minute?" He hadn't meant to raise his voice, but he'd been just a little on edge the last couple of days.

"What? I'm working. That's what I do here every day." She threw a stack of papers that were in her hands onto her desk and stood with her arms akimbo. "You don't need to raise your voice. I have perfectly good hearing."

Josh stumbled over a trash can to get close to her, and he clasped her hand, not letting go. "Juliana, I'm sorry. It wasn't what you thought!"

"Whatever are you talking about?" She blinked.

"Marion. I have no desire for Marion." His breathing stepped up a notch, and he noticed she hadn't pulled her hand away. He laid his copy of the newspaper on the edge of her desk.

"It surely didn't look that way to me. Anyway, what you do is none of my business." Her blue eyes snapped.

He took a step closer and could smell the lavender soap and femininity that he loved about her, and he breathed it in. "You have to believe me. Marion was there to offer some ready cash as a friend. That's all. Just to get me started back on the house and to hold things together for a while."

"Is that right? What I saw was two heads bending together— closer than friends." Juliana thrust her chin up at him and took a small step back, but he wouldn't let go of her hand.

"I'll admit she was trying to comfort me, but not like you think." Josh shifted his weight from one hip to the other.

"Then why did you have your head against her pretty one, tell me that."

Goodness, but she was even appealing when she was riled up. "Because I felt like it. I was sad, so she leaned over and patted my arm and told me she was sorry. Same thing any friend would do." He was getting exasperated.

"I see."

"No, you don't see." Josh pulled Juliana to him and held her within the circle of his arms. He was only a couple of inches taller than her, and they seem to be fitted for one another. "If you think I'm going to stand here and explain my every move, you're wrong."

She struggled against him, but he held her tight, feeling the outline of her legs against his. His hands stroked the small of her back in a light up and down motion, then touched her waist and pulled her even closer. His pulse leaped. Desire flashed over him, and he was surprised at the intensity but kept himself in control. When his head leaned against hers, his hat fell to the floor.

"Josh—don't do this. We should talk." But as she said it, she looked up at him, and she took a deep breath, her eyelids fluttering. Her blue eyes were liquid pools of desire. She tilted her head upward to meet his kiss.

He brought his face to hers, barely brushing her brow with a light kiss. His breathing was ragged as he whispered hoarsely, "You're my Jewel." Still holding her tightly, he lowered his head and kissed her sweet, pouting mouth. He was surprised once again at the softness of her lips.

A soft moan escaped her throat. A jolt coursed through him as she trembled slightly in his arms, and he held his breath. He marveled at the fact that she could respond to him this way. He could kiss her dozens of times a day and never tire of the sweetness. Finally, he pulled back.

"Juliana, I never would have asked to court you if I hadn't meant it." His voice was raspy as he moved a straying lock of hair from her face. Its texture was silky between his fingers. He lifted both her hands and kissed her slender fingers.

Juliana sighed deeply, straightened her shoulders, and pulled her hands free. "I want to believe you. But I've seen how Marion is around you. You seemed to really enjoy the attention she gave you when we all had dinner together. Laughing and smiling at her every word. And that night someone hit you on the head, it was very evident that she was after you."

"Doesn't mean a thing. She was good company, that's all."

She hesitated, then slowly took a few steps away and turned. "But don't you see . . . we can't mistake passion for love. If you find her company delightful and her money enticing, then what do *we* have?"

Josh stiffened and clamped his jaw.

"I don't want to find myself alone like my mother. You may tire of me soon when I'm no longer entertaining, and I can't compete with Marion's wealth."

"You're making no sense at all, woman." Josh picked up his newspaper. "I love you for who you are, not what you have!" His voice was tight, and his face was burning now from anger. Stiff shouldered, he waited for her response. Nothing.

Josh reached down, picked up his hat off the floor, and placed it none too gently on his head. "Maybe when you get a little older and you get it through that thick head of yours that not all men are alike, *maybe* then you can learn to trust. I'm tired of reminding you!"

Josh stormed out the door, his boots pounding loudly on the boardwalk. He had already lost his house and a prized ram, and half of his land had burned to a crisp. Now it looked like he'd lost the woman he wanted to share his life with, and he'd gotten a good dressing-down from her as well. He knew she had felt the passion as much as he did, or she wouldn't have mentioned it. But if she couldn't trust him, no amount of passion would be enough.

Josh had been walking so fast that he almost missed a wiry older man who called out to him.

"Josh McBride!" The older gentleman put his arm out. "Whoa there, fella. You almost walked right over me."

"I'm very sorry, Mr. Smith," Josh said.

"I just wanted to tell you that the ring has been set and will be ready next week for you to pick up. I think you'll be very pleased." Smith moved his head up and down for emphasis.

"Thanks, but doesn't look like I'll need a ring anytime too soon." Josh tipped his hat and kept walking, leaving Smith rubbing his bearded chin as Josh melded into the flow of people.

28

Josh strode down an entire block, hot under the collar that one woman could turn him inside out this way, making him want to be near her and lose his temper all at the same time. What should he do? What *must* he do? He would tell her he didn't mean to walk out that way, ask her if they could talk again, and ask her to give him another chance to explain. Then he would hold her again, gently this time. The ring he'd had Smith fashion for him would fit only one hand—his Jewel's.

He spun around and sprinted back to the newspaper's office. By now he had worked up a sweat and was breathing hard, so he paused once he drew close. Through the letters on the glass window, Josh was surprised to see Juliana smiling up at Mark, who stood near the stove, pouring a cup of coffee. She said something that made him laugh, and Josh could hear her silvery laugh in return. Josh saw Mark fish something out of his coat pocket and hand it to her. She looked very pleased in response.

Josh swallowed hard. How could she look so happy so quickly? Didn't they just have a fight? His hands made fists as he struggled with his emotions, so he stuffed them in his pockets. He couldn't stand here another minute and watch the handsome doctor filling his Jewel's ear with heaven knows what. No point in hanging around here. He turned and plodded down the boardwalk to Smithy's, where he'd left Pete to be shod.

From the corner of her eye, Juliana saw Josh gazing through the front window and was about to excuse herself to go speak to him when he turned and walked away. There was something sad in the way his shoulders were hunched, and she found herself wanting to run after him.

Juliana laid the notes Mark gave her about X-rays on her desk. She wished Mark hadn't popped in when he did.

"You were saying . . ." Juliana turned her attention back to Mark.

"I wanted to let you know that little Jane has suffered a setback," he said.

"Oh no. Is it her head?"

Mark cleared his throat. "I'm afraid not. Her concussion is completely healed, but she seems to have lost interest in walking or regaining her strength."

Juliana gasped. "How terrible for that little girl, and her mother."

"Yes, it is. Cynthia is a widow, you know. Her husband was killed in a mining accident several years ago. It seems she is struggling financially and in need of a job now. I knew you would want to know and perhaps even go see her."

"I'll drop in and pay her a visit, maybe this afternoon. I can go see her during my lunch break." Juliana had a soft spot for children and couldn't bear to think the little girl might not be able to walk again. Jane had seemed to be doing so well the last time she and Marion paid her a visit.

"Well, I must be on my way. I just wanted to stop in and give you some of the facts about X-rays since you seemed interested." Mark's bright smile showed off his nice, even teeth.

"I appreciate that so much. I'll most likely be able to get the article written for the newspaper in a day or two." Juliana ushered him to the door and quickly said good-bye, eager to be alone with her thoughts.

Fighting her feelings between finding Josh and just letting their discussion lie for now wasn't too difficult because Juliana knew work came first, especially with Albert gone. But try as she might to read the notes Mark had jotted down about X-rays, thoughts of Josh's demanding kiss clouded her thinking. She felt her face heat up as she remembered her response to him. Was this the same woman who didn't want to belong to any man? But she loved the possessiveness of his hands pressing on her back. His strong arms were well formed and muscular. She was attracted to his strength in a strange sort of way.

Juliana was so confused that she closed her eyes and rubbed her forehead, acknowledging that she did indeed have very strong feelings for Josh. His very presence had seemed to fill the room when he'd strode into the office, the same way it had that first day she'd met him. Josh was a man of character, commanding attention merely by his energy and strength. Though he seemed quiet at first, today Juliana knew he was also a man to be reckoned with when he was riled. She was secretly pleased that he seemed to think he was in love with her. But she had to admit to herself they needed more than a physical attraction. What did she have to offer the relationship? Certainly not money. She had no family left that she knew of. She owned no possessions save Choco. Josh was a much stronger Christian than she was too. So what was it he *did* like about her?

The bell jangled above the door, and Miss Margaret and Albert came in, chatting pleasantly. Juliana forced herself to turn her attention back to the present. After a brief moment and a quick hug from his mother, Albert donned his printer's apron and headed to his printing press, leaving the two ladies alone.

"Good morning, Miss Margaret."

"Hello, my dear. Are you doing well? I missed you at breakfast this morning. I slept a tiny bit later than was normal for me today." Miss Margaret's cheery voice did little to lift Juliana's spirits, and the older lady eyed her keenly. Miss Margaret even smelled old, like cedar and the liniment she rubbed over her joints. Juliana thought her dress of cream foulard with tiny rosebud print and delicate lace collar, though old, was fresh and neatly pressed.

"Are you feeling well?"

"Yes, my goodness, yes. Just a bit of rheumatism and old age creeping in, I'm afraid," she replied, sitting down in the chair next to the desk. "I'd like to run an ad in the paper. Albert said you could help me with that. My girls are finding it harder and harder to run the boardinghouse without a little help."

Juliana pulled out a clean piece of paper and pencil, trying to put on a cheery smile. "I certainly can. Now, what is it you wish to say?"

"Oh, let's see . . . something like, 'Good kitchen help needed. Must be willing to do other odd jobs.'" Miss Margaret paused. Juliana was toying with her pencil and looking out the window, waiting for Miss Margaret to decide what she wanted to say, but her mind was centered on Josh.

"Uh, are you with me, dear? You're not taking this down." Miss Margaret leaned forward in her chair.

"I'm sorry, Miss Margaret," Juliana sighed, closing off thoughts of Josh. "Wait just a minute." Juliana laid down her pencil. "I just heard of someone today looking for a job. Mrs. Hood. Cynthia Hood."

"Really? My goodness! I thought that when her husband was killed he left her with a pile of money. Why, Cynthia used to be part of the 'society' around here." Miss Margaret shook her head. "Her husband was part owner of a thriving mine, but sometimes circumstances can suddenly change our lives. So unfortunate . . ."

Juliana saw Miss Margaret's gray eyes grow misty and wondered if she was thinking about her own husband. "I know nothing about her personally, other than what I was told."

"Mmm . . . money doesn't last forever, I say. If a man won't work, neither let him eat. That's straight from the Good Book and can apply to a woman as well, and I say it's excellent advice." The older lady appeared thoughtful for a moment. "I wonder if she'd be interested in the job. Reckon she can cook?"

Juliana grinned at her comment. "If you're willing to wait until tonight for your answer, I will ask her myself, because I'm planning on stopping in to see Jane. I want to check on her progress."

"That will work out fine." The old lady rose rather stiffly, and Juliana assisted her. "See you at supper?"

"Oh yes. It's the highlight of my day, Miss Margaret."

Miss Margaret's eyes narrowed as she regarded Juliana. "Something on your mind, Juliana?"

Juliana chewed her bottom lip. "No, not really." Did the older lady ever miss anything?

Miss Margaret tilted her head. "We can talk later then."

She seemed to be suggesting that there was something bothering Juliana. Could be that Miss Margaret was someone she could trust.

Before Josh left the blacksmith's, he'd picked up a bit of interesting news. Smithy said he'd heard talk that a man who was thought to have robbed the bank might be the same one who'd mugged Josh, according to an eyewitness account. Sheriff Wilson said the person wanted his name withheld and was not seeking the reward for fear of his own life.

So someone *had* seen Josh mugged but hadn't wanted to get involved. Josh scratched his head and wondered if the same man had been the one to ransack his camp. Maybe his Yogos were worth more than he thought they were. Could those incidents be related? He thought it was time to pay Sheriff Wilson a visit before heading back home, perhaps tell him about the camp incident.

Josh paid Smithy and was walking Pete out of the barn when he saw Mark. Great. He was the last person Josh wanted to talk to right now, so he pretended he hadn't seen him, but Mark spied him.

"Josh, hello there," Mark called out to him. "I just heard you were one of the ones affected by the fire. I'm really sorry. Is there any way I can help? Anything you need?"

Sure is. Leave Juliana alone. But Josh didn't say what his heart was shouting. "I appreciate your offer." Josh busied himself with tightening the stirrups before pulling himself astride Pete. "There's not much one can do but wait for the grass to recover. At least I have most of my herd."

"I'm truly sorry." Mark paused and shuffled his feet as if he had something else to add. "Look, I've been meaning to talk to you. I see how it is with you and Juliana, and while I really admire her and like her, I just want to say, well . . ."

"Well, what?" Josh wanted to be on his way.

"Just that I'm taking myself out of the picture. I get the feeling it's mutual with how she feels about you too." Mark passed his hat from one hand to the other, not meeting Josh's gaze.

Josh shifted in the saddle. He was more than a little surprised that Mark would be so open with him like this. "I'm not so sure you're right about that. I'm not near as confident about her as you seem to be."

"It's just the way I see it. I knew it the night we all had dinner together at the hotel. Well, either way, I wanted you to know my intentions, and I'll stay out of the way." Mark put his hat back on and yanked his vest down, smoothing the front. "I respect you and hope we can remain mutual friends. What do you think?"

Josh shot a hard look at Mark. "Are you sure you want to give up on courting Juliana?"

"I'm positive, Josh." The doctor's dark brows furrowed into a serious line above his large eyes.

"Well then, let's shake on it," Josh said, and reached down to take Mark's outstretched hand.

"Take good care of her, Josh, and treat her tenderly. She's young." Mark hesitated as though he had something further to say, but he just said, "Be seeing you around." He turned on his heel and headed toward his office.

Josh nodded solemnly, watching Mark until he turned the corner. Something he'd dreaded had turned out a whole lot different than he'd expected. Still, where Juliana was concerned, he didn't feel too much hope. And then there was Marion. He hadn't made up his mind about her offer. Something about it made him uneasy.

He guided his horse down the street in the direction of the sheriff's office, his mind deep in thought.

The sheriff was propped up in a chair, leaning against the wall on the front porch, his hat covering his face. Asleep, no doubt. Josh secured Pete at the hitching rail and walked up the steps. The sound of their squeaking boards woke Sheriff Wilson out of his nap.

"Howdy, Josh." Sheriff Wilson dropped the front legs of the chair to the floor. "What can I do fer ya?"

"Mornin', Sheriff Wilson." Josh took the chair next to him, watching the road out front as farmers and miners went about their normal workday. "I heard some of the talk about the bank robbery and thought I'd see if I could get some more info."

"Out for that reward, are ya?" Sheriff Wilson looked Josh square in the eye.

"Nope, but I *could* use the money about now. I might have seen the man in question." Josh knew that would grab the sheriff's interest in a flat second. "But if you need your beauty rest more, then I'll just be moseyin' along."

Sheriff Wilson jerked around in his wooden chair to face him, his eyes crinkled at the corners. "Doggone it! Now you know you've got my attention. Do tell. What's going on?"

"I had a little incident at my camp a few nights ago. I thought you'd be interested in knowing about it." Josh went on to give a brief description of the man who'd rummaged through his camp and told how someone had knocked him out.

"You don't say? What were they looking for, gold?"

"No, I think they were looking for sapphires." Josh wasn't even certain his speculation was right. He needed to go see Hoover, but he filed that thought away for the time being.

Sheriff Wilson squinted from the morning sun when he looked up at Josh. "From your description, they could be the same person. My informant told me his name was Davin. But I have no proof that what he's telling me is the truth."

"I'd say if the man who told you wasn't looking for the reward, then it's probably true. Why else would he tell you this?"

"Beats the devil outta me." Sheriff Wilson scratched his graying head, and his badge twinkled as the sun struck it.

"I guess you're not about to tell me who gave you this information?"

"You guessed right, pardner. I can't do that. But I'll check out what you told me."

Josh shook Sheriff Wilson's rough hand and tromped down the steps to his horse. He had one more stop to make. His clothes had been burned in the fire, so to start with, he'd have to buy at least a change of clothes.

Josh pulled a sugar cube out of his pocket and gave it to Pete, patting his thick neck. "One more stop, fella, and then we'll go home, I promise." Pete snorted, shaking his mane.

29

Two elderly men playing a serious game of checkers sat in rocking chairs and bent over a checkerboard placed on top of a flour barrel. Their bony, veined hands shook as they made their moves. They were so intent on their game that they didn't even glance up as Josh took the steps two at a time, making the boards of the porch groan in protest.

Josh loved the smell of the general store. It made him think of the times as a child that he was allowed to go to town with his mama. His younger sister, April, always tagged along, whining for this and that as soon as they passed through the front door. Mama couldn't resist April's pleading and always wound up buying them sticks of candy, paper dolls for April or ribbons for her hair, and a slingshot or something similar for Josh. It seemed just the other day that he was a child, and he missed his sister, though there were times when she could make him want to pull his hair out. Still, maybe he should write and ask her to come to Montana for a visit.

The memories were evidence to him of how fast life was passing him by. He wanted his own children to spoil a little. But not as much as his sister was spoiled, for sure.

Earl was busy waiting on customers but waved to Josh when he walked in. Josh nodded, indicating that he would look around. He walked past rows of canned staples and glass cases that held a variety of hard candy. He wrinkled his nose as he strolled past an area where the smell of liniment, tobacco, turpentine, and rubbing alcohol was almost overpowering. There were shelves of nails, screws, twine, rope, and farming implements hanging on large hooks against the wall. Earl carried the basics, Josh knew, and anything that wasn't a staple had to be ordered out of the Sears and Roebuck catalog.

His eyes lingered on a table of ladies' powder, hairpins, and other feminine paraphernalia. He fingered the lawny fabric of a lacy, embroidered nightgown and marveled at its softness. He visualized Juliana wearing it, her dark hair tumbling about her shoulders as she prepared for bed. Josh shook himself mentally. Perhaps someday he'd be buying things like that, but not now.

One narrow shelf held a row of books and Bibles. Josh picked up a small, leather-bound Bible, just right for a lady's hands. He remembered that Juliana didn't own one. Maybe this could be a peace offering. He tucked it under his arm and continued his perusing as if he had all the time in the world. He needed to get finished here and get back home, because the purpose in coming was to buy another set of clothes. His clothes—as well as nearly everything else he possessed—had been lost in the fire. *I'll give back the years that the locusts have eaten*, a voice said in his head.

Josh sighed and walked over to the men's area of the store, which displayed shirts, suspenders, vests, hats, and a variety of leather boots. He picked up a russet-colored chambray shirt, a pair of denim waist

232

overalls, and a couple of pairs of socks. When he looked up, standing across the table from him was none other than Wes.

"Boy howdy. Fancy meeting you here, sheepherder." Wes hooked his thumbs in his hip pockets and rocked back on his heels.

Josh clamped his jaw tight. He didn't miss the fine, tooled leather belt that held up Wes's britches and the perfectly rolled brim of his Stetson hat. He may not have decent manners, but it was obvious he liked good-quality belts and first-class hats. From where he stood behind the table, Josh had no doubt that Wes's boots would speak of the same focus on detail and quality.

Josh harrumphed. "Last time I looked, the sign outside the store said 'Open to the public.'"

"For a fact it is." Wes held a lopsided grin. "I heard you got hit with the prairie fire."

"What if I did?" Josh didn't feel like spending his time yakking with a cowboy just looking for someone to poke fun at.

Wes swaggered around to the end of the table to stand in front of Josh. "Contrary to what you may think, I wouldn't wish that on my worst enemy."

Josh's eyes fell to Wes's boots out of pure curiosity. Just as he thought. He could spot a pair of Justin boots in a crowd. Fine, supple leather boots with silver Mexican spurs. Josh should know. He used to wear only the best Western wear that money could buy in Colorado, before he became a sheepherder. He groaned inwardly. His fine boots had burned in the fire.

Josh stared at Wes. "Do I detect a tone of sympathy?"

Wes's smile betrayed his sardonic mood. "Call it whatever you like."

"What do you want, Wes? I'm busy." Josh sized up the tall, lanky cowboy.

"Just wondering how that gal Juliana was. Figured you'd know, after the scene the last time we were here."

"She's fine," Josh said curtly. "Why do you want to know? She's *not* interested in you."

"For a fact she's not. I tried to wrangle a kiss outta her. Didn't she tell you?"

"About what?" Josh was getting curious now.

"The struggle for a kiss." Wes shifted his weight onto his other boot heel.

"When did you do that?" Josh laid the clothes back down on the table and folded his arms across his chest, the Bible still tucked under his arm.

Wes snickered. "I didn't. Didn't I just tell you I *tried*? I was miffed that she wouldn't go on a date when I asked her twice, so I caught her one day when she was out riding. I wasn't trying to scare her, I just didn't like being snubbed. I pressed her too hard for a kiss, I reckon, and we fell. I felt bad about that—"

Josh was furious. "You did what?" He felt his neck growing hot as he clenched and unclenched his fists. He was trying to maintain calm this time, but what he wanted to do was slug Wes again.

"Don't get so danged hot under the collar. It's clear she won't have anything to do with me. I think she has her sights set on you, but why a poor sheepherder, I don't know." Wes scratched the hair on his jaw.

"Wes, I'm warning you. Leave Juliana alone."

"I'm not *that* thickheaded. I know when I'm not wanted."

"Then why don't you learn some manners about how to treat a lady?" Josh shook his head.

Wes rolled his eyes. "My pa taught me everything about how to get attention from a woman. That's all I know."

"And look where it got you." Why was Wes telling him all this? He looked scruffy, and his face showed two days' growth of hair. Josh didn't smell any alcohol on him, but his hair and clothes looked like they could stand a good scrubbing in the trough out front. Josh would have loved to pitch him in there after what he'd just told him.

"I'm talking about something altogether different. Respect. You need to earn respect, Wes. It isn't given to you."

"I'm not *all* bad, and I'm willing to learn a few things if it'll help my situation." Wes pulled his shoulders back. "Especially if it'll help me win the heart of a pretty woman." He had a ridiculous grin on his face.

Josh reached for the Bible he had tucked under his armpit. "You could start with this." He shoved it at Wes.

"The Bible! Come on now." He looked at Josh like he had just handed him a stick of dynamite. "You've got to be kiddin'!"

"Yes, Wes. This book. Everything you need for life is right here, if you'll take time to read it. You can read, can't you?"

"Of course I can read. But are you telling me it has stuff in there on how to treat a lady?" Wes's eyes grew large with interest.

"I wouldn't lie. It will instruct you on how to treat your fellow man too." Josh moved away and tucked the Bible back under his arm, then turned to pick up the bundle of clothes.

"How to treat your fellow man, huh? Well, it might be just a little too late for that."

"Now, what's that supposed to mean?" Josh asked.

"It's just that I had to tell the sheriff about a fellow man, and it's not settin' well with me," Wes said, pushing back his hat.

Josh was all ears now. Could it be that Wes would tell him something about the robbery?

"It wasn't somethin' I wanted to do, but somethin' I had to do." Wes paused and took a deep breath. "I know I'm not the perfect gentleman, but I wouldn't hurt nobody intentionally."

Josh was starting to rethink what he knew about Wes, which wasn't much. Suddenly a thought hit him like a lightning bolt. He glanced over at Earl and noticed he was still waiting on one of his customers. "Wes, would you like to go grab a cup of coffee at the café?" Josh nodded in Earl's direction. "Looks like Earl's a little too busy at the moment to help me out with my list of purchases."

The look on Wes's face said it all. "Are you meaning me, Wes Owen?" His brows knit together, and he placed his hands on his hips.

Josh looked around the store. "Is there another Wes you know of?" He knew Wes was taken completely off guard that anyone could possibly want to get to know him, much less share a cup of coffee. Josh wasn't sure why he'd even asked. Had he plumb lost his mind since the fire?

Wes shifted his weight on his boot heels, seemingly flabbergasted. He shrugged. "Uh, I reckon. Yeah, I mean, okay. Let's go grab a cup."

Only a handful of patrons were seated in Maggie's Café. Josh and Wes took a seat by the window. The smell of brewing coffee and the morning's breakfast meats wafted throughout the room. They ordered coffee and nothing else, and after an awkward moment of silence, Josh nodded for Wes to take a look outside the window. "That's a fine horse at the hitchin' post there," he said, looking at the chestnut horse with a black mane and tail. He must have been about eighteen hands high.

"You got that right, mister!" Wes said.

"Is he yours?"

"Naw, but I bred him."

Josh quickly looked back at Wes. "You don't say?"

"I did, for a fact." Wes smiled with pride. "Looks like you have a good eye for horseflesh, Josh."

"I was raised around horses, so I know a little about them. My sister, April, is quite the horsewoman, and even the horses seemed to know it. So, do you raise horses?" Josh took the cup of coffee the waiter poured, handed it to Wes, and then took the second cup.

"That's how I make my living. Are you in the market for a horse?" Wes took a gulp of the steaming black liquid.

"No, I'm not. Just asking the question, that's all. I couldn't help but notice your hand-tooled belt and boots. Where's your place?"

"I have a small old house and a couple acres about five miles northwest of town along Big Spring Creek. My pa left it to me. It was the one good thing he did." Wes eyed Josh with a level gaze. "You and Juliana officially courting?"

Wes's question took Josh off guard. "Well, yes and no."

"So, there might be a chance for me yet?" Wes grinned.

"No. What I meant was, we were, but we had a little disagreement. I'm sure we'll work it out."

Wes's face fell. "I guess I'm doomed to live alone."

Josh blew on the cup of coffee in his hands before taking a sip. "I hardly know you, Wes, but I think there's somebody out there for you. God has a plan for each of us, of that I'm sure. The problem is that most of us take things into our own hands instead of seeing what He has planned for us."

"Get outta here. You don't really believe that stuff about God and all that, do you?" His eyebrows arched, his eyes squinting in doubt.

Josh thought for a moment. The way he'd been questioning and railing against God because of the unfortunate fire and turn of events made him feel inadequate to be telling Wes what he should do. And here this morning, God had given Josh an opportunity to tell Wes about Him. Now he felt like a fool for being angry about what had happened. Instead of being disillusioned, he should have remained faithful in his heart, knowing God would see him through anything.

"Yes, I do, but that doesn't mean I'm perfect or that I don't struggle with some things," Josh finally answered. "You know, you did the right thing in talking to the sheriff if you had any clue about who the bank robber was, or who hit me on the head."

"I don't know." Wes looked away. "The man is not all bad either. He pulled me away from Juliana when I was trying to plant a kiss on her and we fell. Davin was looking out for her, but I swear I wasn't trying to hurt her—"

Shock registered on Wes's face, and Josh knew he had just let the man's name slip. *Davin* . . . Where had he heard that name before?

"I'll just have to take your word for it," Josh said, swallowing the last drop of coffee.

Wes stood abruptly, pulling out a bill to pay for the coffee, but Josh pushed back his chair and shoved the money back toward him. "I invited you. The coffee's on me."

Wes seemed surprised but tucked the bill back into his pocket. "Well, thanks for the coffee."

"Don't forget what I said. The Good Book has something in there for everyone," Josh said as they walked out into the bright sunshine.

"I'll take that under consideration, but don't count on it."

Wes walked off, and Josh turned back to cross the street to the general store once again. His heart felt lighter somehow—until he remembered where he'd first heard the name Davin.

Tall blue lupines swayed in the midday breeze along the weed-covered path leading up to Cynthia's front door. Juliana had eaten a quick sandwich Miss Margaret had made for her so she'd have a minute to run over and check on Jane. She reached up and rang the doorbell, hearing the chime in the foyer behind a thick door badly in need of a good coat of paint. The door steps sagged, and one board had bowed up on one end, its nail pushing upward. The outside of the house seemed totally opposite of Cynthia's air of privilege she carried around her shoulders like a mantle. Well, it was apparent that the house was in need of repair. Juliana knew there was a short distance from being wealthy to being poor. Just look at her mother and how she'd lived her final years.

The hinges on the door squeaked as it swung open, and Cynthia's solemn face appeared. "Juliana, what a surprise. Please come in." She stepped aside, allowing Juliana to enter the foyer.

"Cynthia, I'm on my lunch break, and I thought I'd stop in and see how Jane is doing." Juliana stood looking about the interior that must have been elegant once, but now peeling wallpaper exposed the wall underneath, and the hardwood floor lacked its former luster. An old, musky smell clung to the house's interior.

"She'll be delighted to have a visitor. She's in her room. I'm afraid I can't coax her to sit in the parlor. She says she likes it better upstairs, away from everyone. I must warn you, she isn't walking yet, though Doctor Mark has assured me the use of her legs should come back in time."

Juliana paused at the bottom of the stairs. "Yes, I'm sure he's right. She took a very bad blow to her head and neck."

"Follow me," Cynthia said, her back straight and stiff as a rod. She turned at the top of the stairs to the first door on the right. "Jane, my dear. We have company. Juliana has stopped by to see you."

Jane sat in her bed, her pale face forming a half smile when she saw Juliana. "Miss Juliana, I'm so glad you came." Jane spoke in a low tone, as if someone was in the room sleeping.

Juliana walked over to the bed, lifted Jane's hand, and patted it. "It's good to see you too, Jane."

"Can I get you anything to drink, Juliana? I was just about to bring a tray up to Jane."

"Nothing for me, thanks."

Cynthia paused, looking at her daughter without a bit of expression on her face. "Well then, I'll just run down and get your lunch, Jane. I won't be but a moment."

Juliana pulled up a chair next to the bed. "So tell me, Jane, can you move your legs at all?"

Jane looked wistfully out the window. "No, I can't. I have a little tingling in my legs, but that's all. I don't have energy to even pick up my book to read." Juliana watched as a tear slid down the young girl's pale cheek. She leaned over and wiped it away, feeling an ache in her chest for the little girl's suffering.

Jane turned and looked at her with sad eyes. "I fear I'll never walk again."

"Well, sweetie, if you continue to sit in this bed and don't at least exercise your legs, you may be quite right. You *will* become too weak to do anything. But we can't let that happen. Does your mother do any special exercises with you involving your legs?" Juliana was doing her best to sound upbeat, but she was worried at the lack of expression, maybe even hopelessness, reflected in the little girl's eyes, and the monotone of her voice.

"She does."

"It'll just take time, but you *must* do it several times a day, you know. You need to go outdoors and get some sunshine. Do you have a wheelchair?"

"What? Me in a wheelchair? Not hardly," Jane snapped. "I'll sit here in this bed and rot before I'll sit in that contraption." Jane pointed her finger in the direction of her bedroom corner. A used wicker-backed wheelchair sat waiting for its occupant with a lap robe draped over its arm.

Juliana was taken aback at the anger in the crestfallen young face. What could she say that would be helpful? "I'm sure Doctor Mark and your mother are doing everything they can to help you. Have you seen Marilee?"

Jane shrugged her shoulders. "She's been by once since the accident. She doesn't have time for a cripple," she said bitterly.

"I'm sure that's not the case—"

"Here we go." Cynthia entered the bedroom with a lunch tray for her daughter and placed it in front of her.

"I told you, Mama. I'm not hungry." Jane cast an irritated look at her mother and pushed the tray aside.

Cynthia glanced briefly at Juliana with a pleading look. Juliana understood her frustration. "Why don't I read to you for about fifteen minutes until your appetite returns? Then I'll get on back to work. Okay?"

Cynthia threw Juliana a grateful smile, her large eyes blinking back tears as she left the room.

"Mmm, all right. There's a couple of books on my dresser. Take your pick." Jane snuggled against her pillow.

Before Juliana left, she was finally able to get a genuine smile out of Jane. She gave Jane a brief hug, promising to come again. Downstairs, she found Cynthia pacing in the foyer. When Cynthia saw her, she touched her on the arm.

"Thank you so much for brightening her day. I'm not sure what to do with her. Doctor Mark says he can't find any reason she shouldn't be walking."

"She seems somewhat depressed. She needs to be around people. It's the best medicine for the ailing. See if you can get Marilee to visit more often. Jane feels like Marilee no longer cares about her now."

"I'll do what I can."

"By the way, I wanted to ask you—Margaret Spencer is looking for someone to help out with running the boardinghouse. Mark told me you might be looking for a job. Is that so?"

Cynthia sighed and looked down at her clasped hands. "Unfortunately, it looks like I'll have to go to work. Since my husband died a few years back, things are getting a bit tight," she said, her lips pursing into a thin line.

This didn't sound like the Cynthia Juliana had first met at the Ladies Social Club. "Why don't you stop in to talk to her and see what she has to offer?" Juliana hurried on to keep Cynthia from feeling uncomfortable talking about her finances. "I believe she'd be interested in talking to you."

"I'll go speak with her about it. Thanks for taking an interest in Jane and me." She opened the front door, and Juliana stepped outside.

"Let me know if there's any way I can help," Juliana said. "I'll be back again, but I must be off now. See you soon." She hurried down the walkway toward the newspaper office, happy that the days were getting warmer. As she passed the hotel, she saw Marion on her way out.

"Well, hello there, friend." Marion paused on the boardwalk.

Juliana almost decided not to speak but instead mumbled hello and gave Marion a curt nod, then left her standing stock-still with an odd look on her face. Juliana was in no mood to talk to her today.

Miss Margaret sat in her favorite chair after dinner with her daughters and Juliana. Louise was playing a tune on the piano for their enjoyment. Juliana had always wanted to learn the piano, but that would have required her to actually own one. Her mother played for her when she was small, but the piano was one of the things left behind when her father decided they'd move to Montana. It wasn't long after being settled in Lewistown that he left for Colorado in search of gold, and he'd left with a promise to return.

Enough thinking about the past. It only made her heart grieve. She looked over at Miss Margaret, who gave Juliana an endearing look. How could she have been so lucky to live with this family? They had been wonderful to her, and every night after work she looked forward to their chats during dinner. She even stayed around to help Natalie and Louise clean up the dishes.

When Louise finished her tune, she sat down near her mother and picked up her needlework.

"Thank you for entertaining us," Juliana said. "I envy your playing."

Louise shot her a smile. "You'll get sick of it when the holidays roll around."

"Oh, I doubt that."

Natalie flopped down on the settee with Juliana. "We'll be a whole lot busier too. We usually add several new boarders to our mix in colder weather. Some of the miners share a room for a couple of months because living in a tent during the harsh winter can be brutal."

"The more the merrier!" Miss Margaret looked at them from over the top of her wire spectacles. "Having a lot to do keeps one young, I say—"

"Yes, I know—idle hands are the devil's workshop," Natalie finished for her.

Juliana snickered, then covered her mouth with her hand. Miss

Margaret grinned at her daughter. "I guess I've said that one too many times."

The doorbell chimed, and Louise hopped up to answer it. "Good evening, Helen. Please come in."

"Is Juliana around?"

"Yes, ma'am, she's in the parlor with Mama and Natalie."

Helen swept into the parlor with her usual take-charge authority. "Wonderful. You're all here."

Miss Margaret rose to her feet, steadying herself with her cane. "Do sit down, Helen." She waved her hand in the direction of the chair across from her. "Whatever are you doing out at this late hour?"

"It's not late, Miss Margaret, and it's a perfect spring evening. I have finalized all the plans for the fund-raiser the Ladies Social Club will host. It will be an art auction." She clapped her hands with enthusiasm. "It'll be such fun. I already have several artists willing to donate their work for charity."

Juliana saw the excitement reflected in Helen's face. Her enthusiasm spilled onto the others.

"Could you make sure we announce it in the paper, Juliana?" Helen asked. "Perhaps, since it's for charity, Albert would donate the ad. What do you think?"

"I'll ask him first thing in the morning," Juliana said. "Where will the art show be held?"

"I suggest the church, but first we have to clear that with Reverend Carlson."

Miss Margaret took her seat. "The fellowship hall at the church would be a perfect place to hang the art, and I can't imagine why Albert wouldn't donate a space in the paper. I'll see to that."

245

Helen beamed. "That's what I thought."

"I can talk to the reverend tomorrow. I'm sure he'll agree. I helped fund the addition for that room." Miss Margaret laughed. "Of course, I was looking for a place to have church holiday plays, socials, and wedding receptions for my daughters."

Natalie and Louise seemed uncomfortable at the mention of the word *wedding*, Juliana thought.

"Mother, one has to be engaged to have your plans carried out. Neither of us has a beau," Natalie blurted out.

"Girls, it doesn't matter. You will soon, and I'm just looking forward to your futures," Miss Margaret answered.

Her daughters just laughed. Juliana thought it was wonderful that Louise and Natalie were so loved. She wished she'd had a sister or brother. While she was stunned at how Miss Margaret always spoke her mind, never mincing her words, Juliana admired the old lady.

Juliana turned to Helen. "I saw Jane today. She's lonely and misses Marilee."

Helen's look was thoughtful for a moment. "Marilee told me Jane was not in a good mood and not fun to be around."

"True," Juliana said, "but she really needs her friends right now to pull her out of the doldrums."

"I'll try to encourage Marilee to go see her again." Helen rose to leave. "I must be going now. I don't want to keep Miss Margaret up late."

"I never said *I* wanted to go to bed. I just said *you* were out late," the older lady quipped, and the others laughed. Miss Margaret got up to walk Helen to the front door, and Helen waved to the girls and hurried down the sidewalk into the moonlit night.

Springtime breezes shifted quickly to warmer days, and with them came swollen streams from mountain snow melts. Fledgling meadowlarks left their nests, and playful grizzly cubs tumbled under their mother's watchful eye among rapidly growing wheatgrass. Chipmunks and black squirrels scampered below the towering ponderosa pines and hillsides. Josh noticed tufts of fur clinging to branches and nearby rocks, and he knew it was a sign that a molting gray wolf was in the vicinity. For this reason he had great concern for his sheep. He knew Shebe was a good sheepdog and would defend the lambs with her life, as she had last year. Still, she couldn't be everywhere. It had occurred to him more than once that he really should acquire another sheepdog, especially since the fire.

A sudden breeze carried the smell of rain and Andy's simmering chili, and Josh's stomach growled. They always had supper by dusk, which suited him fine. He reclined against a tree and looked over the flock. Their gentle movement and bleating, which was irritating to some, brought comfort to his soul. He'd already written a breeder about purchasing another ram while he was in Lewistown.

Josh looked over toward the campfire, watching Andy stir the pot. He was glad his and Andy's paths had crossed that day he'd arrived in Montana at the stage station. Andy had been fresh out of cash and a job. It had been Andy's custom to go from ranch to ranch each season as a horse wrangler. He never revealed much of his past life to Josh, but Josh knew Andy had a little wanderlust in his spirit, because he'd left home at sixteen and might leave again whenever that urge struck. Presently, it seemed Nellie was the reason he was still here.

Anyway, he was grateful for Andy's friendship and eagerness to please. If it hadn't been for him or Shebe, they never would have saved the dumb flock of sheep, who squealed with fright during the fire. *Not without Juliana and Nellie's help too*, his conscience reminded him.

Droplets of rain fell just as Andy called out, "Chili's up!" Josh hurried over to the campsite.

Andy stood with a wooden ladle in one hand and the cast-iron pot of chili in the other. "I thought I smelled rain. Make a run for the wagon. I've got cornbread in the oven."

"I'm right behind you," Josh said as he entered the camp and rain pelted his hat.

They scrambled inside the wagon to the cozy smell of cornbread warming in the oven, and Josh lit the kerosene lantern. Andy placed the heavy pot on the stove's cooktop.

Shebe ran up the steps and poked her head in the doorway, which they'd left fastened back to one side. "Come on in, girl," Andy said to the sniffing dog. "We got just enough room for you."

Josh pulled out bowls and saucers for the cornbread. "Hand me Shebe's bowl and I'll cool a little chili for her, Andy."

"Before I met you, I wouldn't waste my chili on no dog! But Shebe here is different and special, ain't that right?" Andy said, looking down at Shebe. She responded with her usual bark and wagged her tail. "I know, you want some of that cornbread too. Bossy little thing." But despite his teasing and protest, he proceeded to cut her a slice to cool on the saucer.

Josh chuckled. "She is that. But she deserves to be treated special, don't you think? Still, I'm thinking about looking for another sheepdog to help out. Plus it'll be good companionship for Shebe."

Andy paused from ladling chili into their bowls and looked at Josh. "I think that's a good idea. Know anyone who raises sheepdogs?"

"When I found Shebe, I was lucky. But now I don't know if I can locate the man I bought her from. I can always ask around town."

"Or you could run an ad in the paper Juliana works for. Give you an excuse to see her," Andy teased.

Josh only sighed and dug into the thick chili, smacking his lips. "This is so good to have on a drizzly day. I've said it before and I'll say it again. If you were a woman, I'd marry you."

Andy laughed. "Thanks, Boss. I enjoy cooking. If I had a real home, I could whip up some of the best dinners you ever had, instead of making do outside without all the essentials."

"Where did you learn to cook like this, Andy?"

"I had no mother to teach me anything, but once I left home, I tried to learn whatever I could from being on the trail and on different ranches through the years. I guess it paid off. I like taking something and turning it into a delicious dish that makes people happy. Like a challenge, I suppose. Besides, I don't usually like anybody's cooking but my own."

"Does that mean you'll be the cook when you and Nellie get married?" Josh finished off his cornbread, then handed Shebe the bowl he'd cooled.

Andy's face flushed. "If we do, I hope we can be a partnership."

"And that's the way it should be, Andy."

Shebe stopped eating abruptly, lifting her head with her ears up. Josh asked, "What is it, girl? You hear something?" But she went back to eating after a moment.

"Reckon there's something out there?" Andy uncrossed his legs and walked over to the open doorway. "I don't see anything."

"I think there might be a wolf hanging around here. I saw evidence of hair tufts today when I was out riding around the perimeter. They molt in the spring, so don't be surprised to find one sneaking around the flock. We'll need to be extra careful now and keep our eyes open. The sheep are just too dumb to run most times."

"I've never seen wolves up close, though I've heard 'em howling. Have you?"

Josh stood and looked out at the drizzling rain. "I have. The gray wolf is not to be messed with. He's quite large. I say we keep our guns close by."

By now Shebe had finished eating and wanted out of the wagon. Josh let her out and turned to help Andy clean up. "We'd better finish here and go check on the herd. If the rain stops, we'll keep the fire going tonight."

Juliana listened to the patter of rain outside her window and snuggled further down into the covers of her bed. Though the sound of the rain should have lulled her to sleep, she stayed wide awake. They'd been very busy at the paper, and she was looking forward to some free time. She had written an article about the new information on X-rays, and she was delighted that several citizens had commented to her and Albert about how much they enjoyed reading about people braving new frontiers in medicine. Besides coming up with interesting ads for customers about their various products or services, she felt she had proven her worth to Albert.

There was always plenty to do at the newspaper. Juliana ran errands for Albert and ordered paper, ink, and supplies, and he asked for her opinion on his editorials all the time now.

He and Sally had become so protective of her that she felt she had been adopted by them. Sometimes they would dine with the other Spencers at the boardinghouse, and Juliana felt that those were particularly fun evenings watching the entire family interact and laugh with each other. It was something she had never experienced, and it was obvious to her what she had missed. She prayed that one day she would have that kind of family—caring, loving, and devoted to one another.

Cynthia Hood had come to work for Miss Margaret, and it appeared that though she was still reserved around everyone, the job was working out nicely for her, and a bit of light had returned to her hazel eyes. Juliana now dropped in on Jane as often as she could.

But the real reason she lay awake was Josh. It had been a few weeks since their meeting. She wasn't sure how to remedy the situation but desperately missed him and his mild sense of humor. So she'd talked to Miss Margaret after supper one night.

"It appears to me that you're denying yourself the one you love just because of your experience with your father. I urge you to pray about this and listen to your heart," Miss Margaret had said. "Don't waste time on worrying about Marion and what she thinks about Josh. It doesn't matter. What does matter is that he's told you he loves you. He's a good man, and you say you love him."

Juliana protested that she was so much younger than Josh—not that it mattered to her, but she wanted him to treat her as an equal.

"You'll be turning eighteen in May and will be considered an adult and a woman. Have you any evidence that he hasn't treated you as an equal?" Miss Margaret asked her. Juliana couldn't think of one single thing.

Perhaps she should ride out to see him and Andy, and maybe take Nellie along. She'd wait and see if the rain would end, and if so, she'd go on Saturday.

Josh hadn't been to church the last few weeks. She prayed for him to find a way out of his troubles, though she could understand them, and she had seen the pain in his eyes. It just took time to work through things. She should know. Just look at her own difficulties.

Oh, how she longed to talk with her mother! She was grateful for Miss Margaret, and she believed God had had a hand in sending Miss Margaret her way, just as He had in her working for Albert. But she missed her mother's gentle ways, even as she saw God working in her life. Miss Margaret and Josh had been instrumental in that understanding, and yes, in the beginning, even Marion. But Marion was another matter that needed settling, one she didn't relish.

Finally Juliana drifted off to sleep. She slept fitfully, dreaming that Josh was in trouble and she was trying to reach him. In the dream she vaguely remembered that it was nighttime, and Shebe seemed to be in distress. Before the dream ended, she snapped awake with tears streaming down her face.

Juliana shuddered, feeling cold, and she snuggled back down under her blanket, pulling it tightly up to her chin. Relieved that the dream wasn't real, she tried to shut her eyes, but it took awhile for her to go back to sleep.

The rain had finally stopped, and since the weather was warmer, Josh and Andy now slept outdoors. The campfire burned low as both men slept.

Josh turned over in his bedroll. Something had awakened him, and he sat up, rubbed his eyes, and listened. He could see Shebe standing near the back of the flock, outlined by the moonlight and barking into the shadows.

Instantly, Josh was on his feet, still fully clothed and holding his Winchester close. It had to be the gray wolf, although from where he was, he couldn't make it out.

He gave Andy a swift jab with his boot, startling him awake. "Shebe sees something, and it might be the wolf," he whispered.

Andy hopped up and followed Josh, who was quietly creeping to the edge of the clearing where Shebe stood still, watching. The wolf was just as Josh thought—a big gray, nearly five feet long, and he guessed weighing sixty pounds. The wolf's fur bristled, and his lips pulled back, displaying his incisors. Josh could see by the moonlight that his tail stuck straight out and his eyes narrowed. The wolf crouched, ready to seize a lamb who stood in total fear, unable to move or even bleat out a pitiful warning.

Shebe's ears were laid back, her teeth were bared, and she growled, threatening to pounce in her fight to protect. Josh held his arm out, signaling Andy to halt. "Hold on. I'll get him."

Suddenly pandemonium broke loose. The wolf jumped on the lamb, but Shebe attacked the wolf with such fierceness that he turned to fight her off. The two of them spun around with gnashing teeth and loud growls, making it hard for Josh to take aim in the dark. He didn't want to hit Shebe by mistake, but then the wolf backed away from Shebe and lunged at Josh, taking him by complete surprise. Shebe propelled herself to cover him, and he lost his grasp on his gun when she wedged herself between him and the wolf, causing Josh to fall to the ground.

The wolf yelped in pain as Andy's shot hit its target. Andy stood over the wolf and finally lowered his gun. Josh had the wind knocked out of him momentarily, and Shebe lay panting next to him with a dark red stain on her thigh.

Andy hurried over to assist Josh, but he pulled himself up onto his knees and bent down over his beloved Shebe. Her breathing was shallow, and Josh quickly lifted her limp body and carried her to the wagon without as much as a backward glance at the instigator of the deadly fight.

The gash in Shebe's thigh was deep but fixable as long as they could control the bleeding. Together Josh and Andy disinfected and dressed the area with ointment, then used sewing thread to stitch the wound closed. Josh wrapped it in one of Andy's clean dishrags. He looked into Shebe's sad, pleading eyes that seemed to say "help me," and his heart melted. Shebe was like family, and as he sat next to her, he hoped Andy couldn't see his eyes welling up with tears. *Please make her be okay, Lord*, he prayed. *She's such a good and faithful dog. Heal her wound. We need her. I need her. I love her.*

Josh sat next to Shebe throughout the night and into midmorning, waiting for her to make a turn for the better. A few hours later, she was stirring. That was a good sign, and Josh's heart lifted. He stroked her face to soothe her and keep her calm.

When Andy returned from morning chores, Shebe's eyes were open slits, but they were at least open, and her breathing was stronger. "Josh, I think she's gonna make it, now that she's awake," Andy said.

At the sounds of his voice, Shebe tried to sit up, but Josh restrained her. She was still too weak and didn't put up much of a fuss, laying her head back wearily on the makeshift bed of quilts.

"I think you may be right." Josh wiped his face with his handkerchief. "I need to get some fresh air," he said, making his way down the wagon steps.

"I just put a pot of fresh coffee on, and there's some leftover biscuits whenever you're ready for a bite. You haven't eaten since yesterday." Andy indicated the covered pan next to the coffeepot over the campfire.

"Maybe in a minute. I need to stretch my legs right now." He turned around and directed his gaze to Andy. "In case I didn't tell you, thanks for watching my back."

"Anytime, Boss. Anytime."

By bedtime, Shebe had hobbled several times to the edge of the woods. Andy carried her bedding and placed it between his and Josh's bedrolls for the evening. "I think that beef broth gave Shebe some strength, don't you?" Andy asked, giving Shebe an affectionate pat on her head. She was lying stretched out with her head resting on her front paws.

"I believe you're right. She has perked up a lot. I just hope that leg and thigh heal nicely."

"Why don't you take her to see Doc Mark, just to make sure no infection sets in and that she doesn't get rabies?" Andy said.

"Good thinking, Andy. We'll need to watch out for any signs of redness, if we can see any through that thick coat of hair she has."

They sat around the fire talking about the wolf and the past few weeks' events. "Have you made up your mind about going into the mining business?" Andy asked.

Josh tilted his head and looked at Andy. "I have. It just doesn't seem like the thing to do. It's too uncertain, and it takes money to invest to even start mining. I want to see if Hoover is interested in buying my section of the land where I found the Yogos. Then hopefully I wouldn't need to borrow from the bank again or from Marion. I could restock what sheep we've lost and at some point start on the house again."

"Sounds like a good plan." Andy nodded.

"Would you be willing to stay on? I'd like to keep you, Andy.

You could be my cook at the ranch house, and I could find another sheepherder to take your place. I'll buy you the best stove out there."

"Are you serious? Nothing could make me happier. I like it here and hope to marry Nellie." Even in the campfire light Josh could see the animation on Andy's face at this new proposition.

"I'll extend that offer to Nellie as well if you two wed. We'll build a bigger house so there's room for everyone."

"What about your wife, Boss? She may not like that arrangement. She may want to do her own cooking."

"Juliana? She can't cook, and I'm not sure she wants to learn." Josh chuckled, trying to envision Juliana in the kitchen.

"So you *do* plan on asking her to marry you." It was more of a statement than a question.

Josh sighed and yawned. "If I can convince her."

"Why don't you get some sleep, and I'll take first watch." Hopping up, Andy lifted his rifle.

Josh felt dead on his feet after nursing Shebe, and a little shut-eye wouldn't hurt him any. "You've twisted my arm. I can hardly keep my eyes open. I think I'll just crawl into my bedroll and catch a catnap."

31

Juliana did her laundry first thing on Saturday morning so later she would be free to go riding and visit Josh. When she carried her basket of clothes out to the backyard, she looked at the remnants of Miss Margaret's vegetable and flower garden, now withered and dry after the winter. Soon Miss Margaret would plant for a spring garden. That woman never ceased to amaze her. She seemed to know a little bit about how to do everything. Juliana had become quite fond of Miss Margaret and her daughters.

Today Juliana was in a wonderful mood and could hardly finish her chore fast enough. She hung her clothes on the clothesline and stood back, watching them flap in the breeze. She loved the smell the outdoors gave her clothes.

"Yoo-hoo! Are you back there?" Nellie called out as she came through the white picket garden gate. "I was on my way to work and thought I'd drop by."

"I'm here, Nellie." Juliana walked toward her with her empty laundry basket. "I was going to walk over to your house when I got finished to see if you'd be interested in riding with me out to

Josh's place as soon as you're through with work today. I want to go see him."

"I'd like that. Then I can see Andy too. I know they've been busy since the fire. He rode over last week to see me and told me they'd been going through the rubble of the house, trying to clear up the mess. Everything was lost." A flicker of sadness crossed Nellie's face.

"Yes, I know . . . Will you be free later?"

"Yes. I work half days on Saturdays, but I don't have a horse."

Juliana thought for a moment. "I'm sure we can borrow the wagon from the boardinghouse, but I'll have to ask first."

They walked in the back kitchen door and saw Miss Margaret going over her dinner menu. "I don't want to disturb you, Miss Margaret, but would it be all right if I borrowed the wagon and team this morning?"

Miss Margaret looked up with a twinkle in her eye. "Where are you going?"

"Nellie and I are going to ride out to Josh's place and see how things are going. I haven't seen him in a few weeks, and I'm kind of concerned."

"Well, in that case, yes, you may." She turned to Nellie, who stood quietly with her hands behind her back. "How are you today?"

Nellie bobbed on one knee. "Fine, thank you, mum."

Miss Margaret giggled. "Dear me, you don't have to curtsy, Nellie."

"Sorry, mum. I guess it's my English upbringing." She smiled at the old lady.

"Just come back when you're through working, Nellie." Juliana gave Miss Margaret a brief hug. "Thank you, and I'll see you at supper." Juliana took off for the barn, and Nellie went to work at the hotel, promising to return as soon as her shift ended.

Before long they were heading away from town, and the morning couldn't be finer.

"Have you seen Josh's house since it burned down?" Nellie asked.

"Yes, but only for a few minutes." Juliana glanced at her friend's wrinkled brow. "It seemed he was a bit distracted when I returned with his wagon and lunch the next day."

"What do you mean? Cleaning up the place? I can surely understand that—"

"No, that's not what I mean. Marion got there first." Juliana could feel her jealousy rearing its head. "Their heads were close together, touching."

Nellie gasped. "You don't say? But I thought he was courting *you*."

Juliana snorted. "So did I. I think Marion is after him."

"What did you say? What did he say?" Nellie talked fast, watching Juliana.

"Nothing much was said right then. He came to town later and apologized."

"That's good, Juliana. Is everything okay now?"

Juliana pulled back on the reins and slowed the horses as they neared Josh's place. "No, it isn't." She sighed. "I told him we needed more than just passion, and I was worried I couldn't compete with Marion."

"Marion?" Nellie harrumphed. "She can't hold a candle to you. Besides, Josh is in love with you. It's obvious by the way he looks at you."

"You can see that?" Juliana was stunned.

Nellie giggled. "Of course. Is Josh a good kisser?"

Juliana squirmed in her seat. "Uh . . . his kisses were wonderful, but of course I don't have anything to compare to. Wes tried to kiss me once, but I didn't let him. He tried hard, and we got into a tangle and fell. He picked on the wrong girl."

"For goodness' sake!" Nellie looked shocked. "I know Wes. He thinks all the girls are just dying for his attention. How did you stop him?"

"When we tumbled to the ground, a miner friend of his happened along and told him to leave me alone."

Nellie shook her curly head. "You know, men are so different. Not that we don't have desires, but theirs seem to be instantaneous." She laughed. "Andy and I will wait until we're married to become intimate, but it's not easy. He makes me go all mush inside."

"I know that feeling," Juliana agreed, remembering Josh's arms pulling her close and the taste of his kisses. "Has Andy asked you to marry him then?"

"Yes, and we've talked about it. We haven't set a date, but I believe we will soon."

"I'm very happy for you, Nellie." Juliana let her thoughts wander back to Josh. What would it be like being married to him, waking up every day looking into the face of someone who made her heart sing? She admitted that she wanted to be Josh's wife, but what if he decided to be a miner? Juliana didn't want the worry that came along with that job. There was nothing wrong with sheepherding, no matter what cattle ranchers said. Sheepherding was fast becoming the biggest part of Montana's economy, and she had faith that Josh would do well if he stuck with it.

As they neared Josh's campsite, an earsplitting boom splintered the stillness of the morning, spooking the horses into an all-out gallop. Juliana struggled to control them, her own heart pounding from the sudden noise, and Nellie hung on to the wagon seat with white knuckles. They bounced and tumbled about wildly, hitting deep ruts in the road, as the harnesses jingled and the horses' hooves pounded. They were close to their destination before Juliana could get the horses somewhat under control, and she flew a few hundred yards past the campsite. Already skittish from the sound of the blast, a white cloud of sheep scrambled out of the way of the oncoming wagon.

Finally the wagon stopped, rocking back and forth. The horses stomped and tossed their heads, but Juliana managed to keep control of the reins. Thank goodness she'd put on gloves this morning, or her hands would be ripped to shreds.

Juliana looked at Nellie and gasped for breath. "What was that noise?"

Nellie's eyes were enormous. "I don't know, but I'm not hankering to take that ride again."

Josh and Andy sprinted to where the wagon stopped. Andy held the horses' harnesses and talked to them as Josh checked on the ladies. "Are you two okay?" he asked.

Juliana was so happy to see his face that her heart did a somersault. "We're fine. What was that noise—what happened?"

"I think it may have been an explosion at the Broadwater mine, but it didn't sound like an ordinary blast. We're about to run over there to see since it's close by. Care to come along? If it wasn't routine blasting, they might need some help."

"Of course. We'll follow you. Are you okay with that, Nellie?"

Nellie nodded, and they followed the men on their horses in the direction of the mine.

On the short ride, Josh was thinking how lovely Juliana looked as she flew into camp, her cheeks flushed, her hair tousled by the wind, and her blue eyes filled with fear. He'd avoided her since their confrontation, but seeing her now, he wondered how he could have let this go on for a few weeks. He desired her as his wife even more than ever, and he had missed that petulant look she gave him when he pressed her for kisses, knowing that she surely wanted them as much as he. It gave him a good feeling that she had come to see him.

He had noticed that Juliana, though fiercely independent, was always willing to help others, and she had readily agreed to go with them to the mine. This was something he really liked about her. He hoped they could talk and work out their problems. Could it be she really cared deeply for him? He worried about the age difference. Though he found her to be wise and mature beyond her years, what if she thought the age gap too wide?

Chaos met them at the mine, and through thick, heavy smoke, it was apparent to Josh that something terrible had occurred. Something not planned. People were running, some yelling out to others in fear. The ground was littered with rocky debris and bodies. Two men were bent over a miner who appeared to be dead. Several of the miners seemed unable to hear because of the loud blast. Josh and his friends hurried forward to aid the wounded.

Josh rushed past the men's tents and picked his way through muck and smoke and over ore carts to find someone in charge. He saw a man barking orders to others around him. "Sir, please, what can we do to help?"

"And who are you?" The man jerked around to look at Josh but continued striding through the wounded. Josh knew there was no time to waste.

"I'm Josh, and this is Andy. I live nearby and heard the blast. Looks like you have some seriously injured men."

"That we do—it was a terrible accident. Is that your wagon?" He nodded to where Juliana had parked the wagon. Josh and Andy followed him through the crowd of men who were pulling others out from the scattered debris.

"It's my friend's, but you have permission to use it."

"We could use it to put the injured in to be looked at. We already have one wagon loaded with three seriously injured men. We'll transport them to Great Falls by train when it arrives." The man bent down to place his arms under a miner's shoulder. "Help me lift this man—he's badly hurt."

"Let me do that for you," Andy said, reaching down to help.

By the looks of his injuries, Josh figured the man would not see the end of the day.

"I appreciate it," the man said over his shoulder. He walked about, checking to see how many were killed or hurt.

Juliana and Nellie were already in the midst of the injured, seeing the extent of their wounds. The odor of blood and death, mixed with the smell of smoldering powder from the blast, was nauseating, and the cries and moans from the injured were alarming.

Richard, the foreman, handed them a first-aid kit for emergency use. Juliana pulled up her skirt and ripped her petticoat into ribbons to use as a tourniquet for one man's leg, winding it as tightly as she could. She watched two men lift a dead miner and carry him away. Nellie cradled a man who had suffered an awful injury to his head and one side of his face.

Both women were heedless of the blood and grime that covered their clothes as they went about offering what help they could. Richard returned with a clipboard and pencil, then proceeded to record every man's name and whether he was injured or dead.

An injured man cried out to Juliana. It appeared he had suffered extensive injury, and he was blood-soaked from his chest to his abdomen. "Please," the man gasped, his head sagging forward vainly in his struggle to move, "could you . . . help . . . me?"

Through the grime and blood, Juliana recognized him as the miner who had interrupted Wes's advances. *Small world—now I can help him in his time of need.* She bent down, placed her arms under his, and tugged, but she wasn't strong enough to move him.

"Juliana . . . thank . . . God," he gasped. "Please . . . I need to talk . . . to you."

"Shh, this is not the time for talking. Wait here, and I'll get help." Juliana turned, but Josh was already there by her side and immediately lifted the man with his strong, muscular arms. The miner didn't let go of Juliana's hand as Josh carried him to their wagon.

Josh felt so sorry for the man. It was obvious to him that he wouldn't make it, as a few others hadn't already. He'd found out they thought a man named Frank was thawing the powder, got too close with his candle, and ignited about thirty sticks of the gunpowder, causing the explosion. That set off a box of dynamite, and he was thrown twenty feet from the magazine. The miners had just finished their meal and were heading back into the mine, and they walked right past the magazine when it exploded with deadly force.

Josh laid the man in the wagon as gently as he could, and the man started shivering.

"Don't leave me, Juliana . . . please . . ."

Josh was mystified. How did the miner know her name?

"I won't leave, I promise." She turned to Josh. "In the kit over there with Nellie, there are some bandages and some laudanum. He's going to need something for pain. Please hurry and bring it to me." She scrambled to the front of the wagon, found an old quilt that was used as a coverlet during cold days, and quickly covered the man.

Richard hurried over as another miner, with Andy's help, carried another injured man and placed him on the wagon bed. Richard looked at the miner holding tightly to Juliana's hand. "I didn't get his name." He turned to the other miner. "Do you know him, Douglas?"

"Yes, sir, I do. His name is Davin Brady."

Juliana froze. Shock flashed throughout her entire body. Had she heard him right? Had he said Davin Brady? That just couldn't be! She tried to pull her hand from the man's, but he continued to clasp it as hard as his waning strength would allow.

"Excuse me, did you say Davin Brady?" she asked Douglas, not sure she wanted to hear the answer.

"Yes, ma'am. He's only worked for us a short time. Nice guy. He came from the gold fields in Colorado, as I recall." Douglas paused a moment, looking at Davin with sadness. He shook his head sadly and said, "Poor fellow," then followed his foreman.

Juliana looked at Josh, whose eyes were full of sympathy, then back to the man again. Her heart constricted as if someone had just reached inside her chest and given it a hard squeeze. *Oh, no, please, Lord. This can't be happening. This can't be my father!*

32

Juliana swallowed hard and glared at the man lying in the wagon. Her father. Not exactly the way she'd hoped she'd find him again. She felt Josh watching her closely, but she couldn't meet his gaze. She didn't know whether to run or stay. *Stay*, she heard in her heart. *Stay*.

She bent close to the man's face, now covered with dirt and powder residue from the blast. As she looked closer, she wondered why she hadn't seen the resemblance that day in the woods.

"Are you really Davin Brady?" she whispered.

He nodded.

"How do you know who I am?"

"I've watched you from afar." His breathing was ragged. "I didn't know that Grace, your mother . . . had . . . passed on."

Juliana struggled, a million thoughts assaulting her. "Why did you wait eight years to return? Didn't you care about us?" She felt helpless as she watched Josh try to staunch the flow of blood from her father's abdomen. Josh looked at her and shook his head. Juliana understood what he was trying to convey.

"I had . . . nothing to offer you and your mother. I was"—he jerked in pain—"flat broke. After all those years, I couldn't come back to you like that. I just kept trying to hit pay dirt . . . I'm sorry. Please forgive a dying father . . . beautiful little Juliana," he pleaded between winces of pain.

"But eight years is a long time . . ." She finally pulled her hand from his.

"I wronged you and your mother. I . . . know that. I'm not worth forgiving."

Juliana didn't say anything but stared as his dark brown eyes pleaded with her. He lifted his hand, motioning for Josh to come near. "I'm sorry for hitting you on the head . . . I was after the sapphires so I wouldn't be empty-handed when I saw my daughter."

Josh's eyes glinted, and Juliana wished she knew what he was thinking.

Her father continued. "There's more . . . I was the one who robbed the bank that day. The money is hidden underneath a tree near the railroad . . . You'll find every dollar . . . I just couldn't bring myself to spend it . . ."

"But why did you steal it?" Juliana felt like screaming at him.

"Pride . . . I guess. I didn't want you to see me with nothing. I wanted to give you so much. When I struck gold, I'd gamble it away, thinking I could double my money every time, but time got away from me more than once . . . and I lost everything."

"I don't know what to say." Juliana felt tears coursing down her cheeks. "All I wanted was a family."

Her father glanced at Josh. "I need to confess again. I accidentally started the fire that day with a cigarette." He stopped again and closed his eyes. Juliana and Josh locked eyes for a moment, and she felt nauseated. *This is my father confessing to these terrible things. What kind of man has he become? What will Josh think of my family now? Oh, Lord . . .*

For a moment Juliana thought he was gone, then she thought he was trying to muster strength to talk. She heard the sound of a train in the background, and everything seemed to move in slow motion around her. She was faintly aware that someone was attending to the other miner lying in the wagon. But she felt numb.

"Just hold on, Mr. Brady. The train is going to transport you to Great Falls, where you and the others will get proper care," Josh said, trying to comfort him.

"No." He rallied. "I won't make it . . . Just tell me I'm forgiven, please . . . I know you two are sweethearts . . . and I don't want you to start out with this between you . . . these terrible things I've done."

Juliana thought he certainly knew more about her than she did him. "You should be asking God to forgive you, not me," she said.

Josh patted the man's shoulder. "It's okay. Your confession is enough."

Davin gazed at Juliana, tears falling. "I've made peace with my Maker. In my pocket . . . in my pocket I wrote exactly where I hid the money I stole."

"It's okay," she croaked, grasping his hands with her trembling ones.

"I love you, Juliana. I always did . . . I'm sorry . . . so sorry." His eyes never left her face but then became fixed. Josh put his fingers over her father's eyes and pulled his lids down.

Juliana's shoulders started to shake, and tears came hard from somewhere deep inside her soul. She reached out and touched his face tenderly, whispering, "I'm sorry too."

Josh moved to her side, enveloped her in his arms, and rocked her back and forth like a child, stroking her head. It felt like a long time that he held her while she sobbed, and her nose was stuffy and red. Josh handed her his handkerchief, and she sniffed and blew into it loudly. She let Josh scoop her up out of the wagon while someone covered her father's body. Nellie and Andy had been standing quietly in the background, and she knew they'd heard her father's confession. Nellie ran to her as soon as Juliana's feet touched the ground and put her arms around her shoulders. Andy and Josh walked off to find the foreman.

"I'm so very sorry for you, Juliana. What a shock you've had!" Nellie's eyes were shining with tears.

Juliana could do little more than murmur, "Yes," and wipe her eyes. She looked around at all the pandemonium and thought, *What a tragedy!* How swiftly the Maker had called the miners home—in a heartbeat. It made her wonder if her mother would see her father now . . . She wept again for the lives lost this morning.

She lifted her head and saw Josh, Andy, and the foreman coming toward her, all with sad expressions lining their faces. Nellie held her hand.

"I'm very sorry, Miss Brady. I wanted to speak with you about what to do with the body. Josh here said you might want to take him back to Lewistown. Whatever you want to do," Richard said softly.

"Thank you. Maybe that would be best. Can I count on you, Josh or Andy, to help me with that?"

"You don't even have to ask," Josh said.

"Well then, it's settled. I have others to attend to. Once again, I'm sorry for your loss, Miss Brady." The foreman left, making his way to the train that would carry the injured away.

Juliana let Josh guide her back to the wagon. "I'll ride with you and Nellie. Andy's going back to camp." Josh turned to Andy. "I'll be back later on. Make sure Shebe doesn't overdo."

Juliana's brain registered something about Shebe, but she just couldn't process it now. She would remember to ask Josh later.

"All right, Boss. Not to worry. I'll take good care of her." Andy gave Nellie a brief hug and took Juliana's hand. "Sorry for what you're going through. I really am. I hope to see you soon." He tipped his hat, then left.

Josh watched Juliana on the ride back to Lewistown. Only the wheels and sound of the horses broke the quiet stillness of the warm spring day. Sadness fell over the three of them like a dark cloak. He looked over at Juliana, whose slight shoulders sagged, and his heart twisted in his chest. He felt helpless to soothe her heartache.

Juliana looked straight ahead, blinking back tears and twisting the handkerchief in her hands. What private battle must be going through her mind? What an awful way to see her father, and more importantly, to find out the things he'd done. Josh didn't trust himself to even say the appropriate words to

Juliana. Instead, he reached over and held her hand in his. He hoped Miss Margaret would be able to take her under her wing and comfort her.

Josh glanced back over his shoulder at Nellie, who gave him a feeble smile. She was such a sweet person, and he understood what it was Andy liked about her. He was grateful for her friendship with Juliana.

Grateful. How could he *not* be grateful after many misfortunes? He'd barely escaped the fire, and the blow to his head could have killed him. What if the mine had belonged to him? He sent up a brief prayer for the families of the seven men who had perished. He was beginning to get a clearer picture of reasons not to go into mining. What would he gain? Money? Probably. But at what risks? He had seen all he wanted to see about mining today, about how it affected lives.

He made up his mind. He would sell his claim to Hoover, if he was interested. Being a sheepherder suited Josh, and apparently it suited Juliana. When the time was right, he would tell her his decision. But for now, his focus was on her broken heart.

"Land sakes!" Miss Margaret declared when the wagon rolled into the front yard while she sat in her favorite rocker. She dropped her needlepoint in the chair and hurried down the porch steps as fast as she could, leaning on her cane. "What are you doing here, Josh?" Then her eyes flitted to Juliana's bloodstained dress.

Juliana clapped her hand to her mouth, stifling a sob, and collapsed into Miss Margaret's arms. "Oh, Miss Margaret . . ." She choked on her words.

Miss Margaret held her tightly and looked at Josh in surprise, questions showing in her gray eyes.

He gestured to the back of the wagon as Nellie hopped down to assist Juliana. "There's been a terrible mining accident, Miss Margaret. We need to get Juliana inside. Then we can tell you what happened."

"Of course! Nellie, please go find Natalie and Louise, and tell them to come to the parlor immediately." Miss Margaret kept her arm around Juliana and walked her to the house, with Josh close behind.

"Yes, mum. I'll find them." Nellie scurried up the broad steps leading to the porch.

Juliana let them take over and numbly did what they told her to do. Miss Margaret had her lie back on the settee. She loosened the collar at Juliana's throat, then tucked a pillow under her feet. Juliana didn't care what they made her do, she would not feel any better. *First my mother, and now my father.* It was too much to bear.

Josh motioned for Miss Margaret to meet him in the foyer, and she left the room, shutting the door. Momentarily she returned and reached down, stroking Juliana's forehead. "Oh, you poor dear. I'm so sorry to hear this news of your father, Juliana. Josh told me what happened." This brought a fresh round of tears, and Juliana buried her face in her hands.

The door flew open, and Miss Margaret's daughters and Nellie hurried in. Natalie knelt next to Juliana, and Louise reached down and grabbed Juliana's hand. They murmured words of sympathy, trying to console their friend who was in a disheveled state.

"I'm okay." Juliana shivered. "No, I lied. I'm not okay. I'm very sad. Please stay with me awhile," she pleaded.

Natalie handed her a fresh handkerchief. "We want you to know we will be right here by your side." Louise sat on the edge of the settee, patting Juliana's hand.

Nellie leaned over, whispering, "I'm truly sorry for your heartache. I'm going home for now. You know where to find me if you need me. You're in good hands."

Juliana pressed her hand. "Thank you," she whispered. Even in her grief, Juliana sensed their concern was genuine. "Where's Josh?" she asked, scanning the room.

"He's taken your father to the undertaker's to start the arrangements for you, if that's all right," Miss Margaret answered.

"Yes. I'm so grateful to have Josh." She blew her nose into the fine linen hanky Miss Margaret handed her. "I'm still in disbelief. Life isn't supposed to be this way, Miss Margaret."

"I know, dear. It's hard to lose someone we love."

"I'm not sure I loved him. I didn't really know him. I hadn't seen him since I was ten years old." She fingered the lace workings on the handkerchief.

"But you've had God's love in your heart for him as his daughter and little girl since you were born. That's why you were so affected now, despite what he's done. You've just lost something you hoped to have again, and that hurts. Your pain is very real. You'll get through this, we'll see to it."

Louise grabbed her arms and pulled. "Come, my dear friend, let's get you upstairs, cleaned up, and into comfortable clothes, and you can rest better in your bed. Natalie will make us some tea, won't you, dear?"

"Certainly. You get freshened up, and I'll bring it right up."

Miss Margaret moved aside as Louise led Juliana upstairs. "I'll be up directly, dear."

Juliana paused on the landing, "You'll let me know when Josh returns?"

"As fast as a jackrabbit hops!"

It would be a long afternoon to face without Josh, Juliana thought. She needed his strength and his arms around her holding her tight like he had earlier.

Josh returned within the hour, and when Juliana came back downstairs, her hair was brushed and pulled back, and she wore a clean dress. "The service will be tomorrow afternoon. You need to let Reverend Carlson know what you'd like him to say at the gravesite. We assumed that since few knew your father, you would want a simple service. Is that right?" She looked exhausted and somber, but lovelier than ever to Josh.

"Yes, you're right. No one here knew my father." She paused. "Not even me, but I do want him to have a proper burial. My mother would want him to be buried next to her."

He took her small hand in his larger one. "I'm very sorry you had to hear those confessions, but you must respect your father for that at least." Josh waited for her reaction, but she merely turned and stared out the window. He sensed that deep in her heart the "okay" she'd said to Davin was forgiveness, but he also sensed the struggle she was having. "He did love you, after all."

Juliana whirled around. "Then why, Josh, *why* did he have to stay away? He knew we needed him. How could he do that to us? How? Tell me!"

He pulled her to him, and she laid her head on his shoulder. "Jewel," he whispered, "I really don't have the answer to your questions. We may never know more than what he told you, but one thing he said registered with me. He'd made peace with his Maker. You *will* see him again, just as you'll see your mother." Josh stroked her dark hair and inhaled the sweet lavender soap smell.

"I pray you're right," she said. She pulled back to look at him, her eyes brimming with tears.

"I have something for you to take to the service tomorrow." Josh rose, picked up a package he had placed on the piano earlier, and handed it to her.

"Josh, what's this?" Juliana untied the string around the brown paper wrapping and drew in her breath. "My very own Bible! Josh, you shouldn't have," she said with genuine surprise. She leaned over to touch his face, drawing her hand down to his cheek, then briefly touched her lips to his. "Thank you," she said softly as big tears rolled down her cheeks.

Josh wanted to kiss the tears from her eyes but instead gently wiped them aside with his thumb. His hands shook. Her unexpected kiss had sent a jolt of lightning through him. "Nothing's too good for my Jewel." He wanted to tell her he would spend his life trying to give her everything her heart desired if she would only be his wife, but he knew this was not the time to talk about that. Not when she was hurting so much. "I hope you don't mind. I've marked a few verses for you that are some of my favorites. Maybe someday we can have your name engraved on the front."

Juliana opened it to the dedication page that read, *To Jewel, with love, Josh McBride*. "I will cherish this, Josh." Juliana clasped the Bible to her chest. "I've never had my own Bible. I can't thank you enough." Juliana's eyes burned with affection, and she leaned over to hug him again.

Miss Margaret walked in, and they pulled apart. "I hope you're feeling somewhat better, Juliana. I've prepared a light supper for us all, with Natalie and Louise's help. Cynthia is off today. I'm sure you haven't eaten a thing all day."

"Oh, Miss Margaret, I can't impose," Josh said with a serious look. "I'll just be heading back home now, but I'll see you both tomorrow."

"Don't be silly, Josh. You'll eat and *then* you can leave. Right, Juliana?"

"Right." Juliana hooked her arm through his and looked at him through red-rimmed eyes.

"How can I argue with two pretty ladies?" Josh asked.

Miss Margaret tapped her cane on the hardwood floor and scoffed at him. "Exactly my point!" She led the way to the dining room.

Josh left after promising he'd be at the funeral. They agreed that Juliana would go with Miss Margaret, and he and Andy would meet them at the gravesite. Juliana stood on the front porch, watching him leave. When Josh turned in his saddle to wave, she knew she could not live without this powerful but sensitive man in her life.

"Juliana." Miss Margaret came and stood with her on the porch. "We need to go complete the details of the funeral. I have a suit of my late husband's, if you think that would be appropriate for your father to be buried in."

Juliana swallowed the lump in her throat. "Thank you. Yes, that would be perfect and so thoughtful of you. Are you sure you don't mind?"

"I'm sure. I'll go fetch it. Then we'll go together and finish with the funeral arrangements. I've sent Louise over to inform Albert of the situation. He and Sally would want to know. They've grown very fond of you. I'm sure he'll want a story about this terrible tragedy."

Juliana's heart froze. Would he tell everything he knew about her father? How awful that would be. "This is one article I *cannot* write, Miss Margaret."

"I understand, dear. Leave it to Albert. While he would never want to hurt you, the truth must come out, however embarrassing. Still, I'm sure he will be discreet in his story," Miss Margaret assured her. "You just hold your head up high." Miss Margaret gave her a swift embrace.

Juliana was so glad she had moved out of the hotel. Was Miss Margaret yet another gift from God, proving He would watch over her? Maybe so. "I hope you're right," she said, returning Miss Margaret's hug. "Before we leave, remind me to show you the Bible Josh gave me."

The complete quiet that night weighed heavily on Juliana, and she tossed and turned. Between crying and visions of her own father dying in her arms, sleep was out of the question. She cried for what could have been, and she cried for her mother.

She got up and padded in bare feet over to her window that looked out on Main Street. The street was deserted and bathed in pale light from the moon, which peeked timorously from behind slow-moving clouds threatening a late spring rain. She hoped it wouldn't rain. It would be sad enough without a rainy funeral.

This all seemed a dreadful dream that she would soon awaken from. There were so many unanswered questions. Perhaps Josh was right—she would never have all the answers.

A light tap sounded on her bedroom door, startling her. "It's me, dear." Miss Margaret's voice was low. "May I come in?"

Juliana opened the door. Miss Margaret and Louise stood in

their robes next to a tea cart that held a tea cozy over a china pot and a teacup. "How did you know I was still up?"

"I figured as much. I could hear you stirring around. Sleep is hard to come by with so much on your mind, dear. I brought you some chamomile tea. You can go on to bed now, Louise. I want to talk to Juliana. Thanks for your assistance with the tea cart."

"I hope you can sleep, Juliana. Good night." Louise stifled a yawn, then scooted toward her bedroom.

Juliana opened the door for Miss Margaret to pass through. Miss Margaret rolled the tea cart into the room and uncovered a beautiful Blue Willow teapot from its cozy. The familiar scent of liniment that she used on her joints lingered on the air when she walked past Juliana.

Miss Margaret poured the tea, then held the cup out to her. "This will help you sleep."

"Thank you. You shouldn't have gone to so much trouble. You're so sweet to me, and so are Natalie and Louise. Why, Natalie even loaned me a black dress for tomorrow, while Louise ran a bath for me tonight. I'm feeling so pampered."

"Well, then we are accomplishing what we set out to do. This is the time when we should help out a wounded sister in Christ who's feeling overwhelmed. It's our privilege to comfort you, just as we benefited in our time of need. Now, drink up."

Juliana and Miss Margaret sat on her bed, and she sipped her tea under Margaret's watchful eye. "Miss Margaret, what do you know about heaven?"

Miss Margaret rubbed her arthritic hands together. "I know there is one. Scripture reminds us in 2 Corinthians that when Christians are absent from the body, we are present with the Lord.

That gives us hope that we will see our loved ones in heaven, if they were believers."

"Would you please show me where that is in my Bible?" Juliana asked. She lifted her Bible from her bedside table and handed it to Miss Margaret.

"Certainly," Miss Margaret said, taking the book and flipping it open to the passage. "Ah, here it is. I'll place your ribbon marker right there. Was your father a believer?"

"Yes, he was, though he got sidetracked from the truth or he wouldn't have committed such crimes. We attended church as a family before he left for the gold fields." Juliana didn't mean to sound so angry. "He told me and Josh that he had made peace with his Maker."

"Then that means he asked for forgiveness, and you have to take him at his word. But what about you? Did he ask for yours?"

Hot tears fell again, and it was hard for Juliana to see. "He did, and I finally just said, 'It's okay,' but now that sounds feeble. I wished I could have said the actual words, 'I forgive you,' but I just couldn't do it." She hiccupped.

Miss Margaret handed her a fresh handkerchief from the bedside table. "Don't fret, Juliana. Your father knew the hurt he'd caused you, and he understood. It took a lot for him to make such a confession. But in time, you must truly seek to forgive genuinely in your heart in order to heal."

Juliana blew her raw nose. "I'll try, I promise," she said, her breathing ragged.

"That's my girl. Now, I'll leave you to finish your tea. It will help you sleep so you'll be rested. Since tomorrow is Sunday, I think it would be all right if you just slept a little late, if you can.

I'll be here, and Natalie and Louise will go to church. That way I can get things ready for after the service. I'm sure you will have people come by to pay their respects."

Juliana touched Miss Margaret's hand. "I don't know what I'd do without your constant support. You're such a blessing to me."

The old lady's gray eyes twinkled with a tear or two, and she patted Juliana's face. "'Weeping may endure for a night, but joy cometh in the morning.'"

Juliana followed her to the door. "Is that one of your quotes, Miss Margaret, or is that from Scripture too? It's so beautiful."

"Psalm 30:5. Good night, dear one."

Juliana marveled at Miss Margaret's wisdom and kindness. She listened to the tapping of Miss Margaret's cane down the hallway until the sound faded away.

Morning dawned with gray, low-hanging clouds, obliterating the mountain peaks, so there was no sun to wake Juliana. She trudged to the window, pulling aside the drapes. The gray day matched her mood, and on the street below, people dressed in their Sunday clothes were walking the few blocks back from church. That meant she'd slept late. The church bells pealed, tolling the hour. Where was the joy Miss Margaret had talked about?

Last night she had flipped through the soft leather Bible, and two of the passages Josh had marked were in the book of John: "I am the good shepherd, and know my sheep," and, "My sheep hear my voice, and I know them, and they follow me." Such an appropriate passage for a sheepherder to identify with, but she knew he'd underlined it for her benefit too. God would have to work a miracle in her heart for it to mend. When her brain couldn't think anymore, she had finally slept.

Now, as she descended the stairs, delicious smells wafted upward, and though she couldn't believe it, her stomach growled. Miss Margaret met her at the bottom of the stairs, crooking her arm around Juliana's. "Did you eventually sleep?"

"Yes, ma'am, I did. Not well, though." Juliana knew from her reflection in the mirror that her eyes were swollen and had circles under them. How could a person look so tired from simply crying?

Miss Margaret pulled her to the kitchen. "Pour yourself some tea or coffee, and I'll just finish the pound cake I'm putting together. You'll look and feel better once you have a little to eat."

The hot coffee tasted delicious, and Juliana nibbled on some toast and bacon, watching Miss Margaret blend flour, sugar, and butter together.

"Can you cook, Juliana?" Miss Margaret asked, folding beaten eggs into the mixture.

Juliana shook her head. "A little, but I've only cooked simple things." She thought back to life with her mother when money was limited to the necessities of nutrition. So much had changed, she mused. One thing was certain and clear to her now after these last several months—life was about change, constant change.

Miss Margaret poured the batter into a long loaf pan and slid it into the oven, then turned to her and grinned. "Well, from the size of Josh's muscles, you'll have to learn a whole lot more to be able to feed him!"

Juliana almost smiled. "Miss Margaret, we're only just now courting, you know."

"If what I saw yesterday was any indication of his feelings, I'd say you're closer to engagement than you think. He's a fine man, you know." Miss Margaret wiped her hands on her apron.

Juliana felt her face grow pink. "Yes, I do know. Is there anything I can help you do before we go to the"—her voice quivered—"the cemetery?"

Miss Margaret looked at her watch pinned to her apron. "Goodness! The time is flying. I need to get changed. Everything's ready, but if you'll just watch the pound cake, that would help."

"I'll sit right here and watch," she said, taking a sip of her coffee. Miss Margaret hesitated. Juliana nudged her back. "Shoo, now. Go change your dress. I won't let the cake burn."

By the time they were ready to leave, the rain was coming down hard. "It looks like we won't be walking to the church cemetery. We'll have to take the buggy to keep from drowning," Miss Margaret told the girls. She groaned. "Where's a man when you need one? Natalie, you and Louise go hitch the team to the buggy and bring it around front. We'll wait for you on the porch." She pulled a black umbrella from the metal stand next to the door.

Natalie rolled her eyes, but Louise shoved her down the hallway to the back door toward the barn.

"At least the carriage has a cover. Perhaps the rain will slack up on our way," Miss Margaret mused.

Soon the carriage came into view. With a heavy heart, Juliana took the offered umbrella from Miss Margaret and popped it open. Soon this would all be over. She wanted to put this whole nightmare behind her. She clutched the Bible to her chest and assisted Miss Margaret down the sidewalk to the waiting carriage.

Though the afternoon was warm, the dampness sent a chill

through Juliana. Her nerves were on edge as Louise guided the horses through the muddy streets of Lewistown. Would the townsfolk blame her because of her father? In the background, she could hear Natalie chattering on about the art fund-raiser that would be held soon, but Juliana paid no mind to most of what she said.

Abruptly, the carriage came to a halt, jolting Juliana back to the present.

"Oh no, looks like we're stuck in a mud hole!" Louise said, peering over the side of the carriage where the wheel was sunk into the muck.

"We can walk the rest of the way," Juliana said.

"No, you'll have half the mud in the county on the hem of your dress," Louise grumbled.

"It wouldn't be the first time," Juliana responded, standing up. "We can get out and push, and you can pull on the horses' harnesses."

"Mother, you just sit right there, no need for you get out to help. I'm sure that between me and Juliana we can pull the wheel out," Natalie said.

It was still raining, but not nearly as hard as earlier, which was a good thing. Natalie went to the rear of the carriage while Juliana took position near the front wheel, sinking into mud up to her ankles. When everyone was in place, Natalie yelled, "Louise, you pull as Juliana and I push!"

They heaved, pushed, and groaned, but nothing happened. They tried again, and they not only got tired, but without umbrellas they were a sorry-looking bunch, with wet, matted hair and soggy hems dragging in the mud. The horses simply refused to move.

"You ladies need some help here?" Wes traipsed through the

mud over to the carriage. His tall, lanky body didn't seem strong enough to move a bale of hay, from what Juliana could tell.

Juliana shot him a hard look. "We don't need your help."

"Oh yes we do, Wes." Natalie blinked, frowning. "We can't make the horses budge."

Wes stepped up to where Louise was holding the harness. Reaching up, he patted one of the horse's necks and whispered something in his ear. He talked soothingly, but Juliana couldn't make out what he was saying.

He turned back to the winded ladies. "Okay, on the count of three, I want you to give a slight push," he ordered, grasping the harness. "One, two, three." The ladies pushed against the wheels while Wes yanked on the harness, and unexpectedly the horses sprang forward, jerking the wheel from its muddy grip.

Miss Margaret looked on from her seat and clapped. "You did it."

"Thank you. It's apparent you have a way with horses," Louise said.

Wes tipped his hat. "Anytime a lady is in distress, I'm more than happy to offer my expertise."

"Yes, and even if the lady is not in distress," Juliana muttered under her breath.

Wes swaggered over to assist Louise and Natalie back into the carriage. "I can't thank you enough for your help," Miss Margaret said.

Wes stood in the rain, water dripping off his hat brim. "You're welcome. Are you ladies off to that funeral?"

"Yes, we are. I guess our black dresses give us away," Natalie said. "Did you know the man?"

"I did, briefly." Wes offered nothing else.

"Are you attending then?" Louise asked.

"Nope." Wes seemed not to mind the rain. "I'm not much on funerals and weddings."

"Well, he was Juliana's father," Miss Margaret said, touching Juliana on the hand. "It's a sad day for her. We must be going."

Wes directed his gaze over at Juliana, who was now sitting next to Miss Margaret and trying to pat her hair back into place. He nodded. "My condolences, ma'am. I didn't know Davin had a daughter."

"And I didn't know I still had a father, so we're even. Can we please go on now?" Juliana pleaded with Louise. Wes stood back as the carriage rolled on down Main Street.

Juliana watched as he sprinted through the rain to where his horse stood tethered. What did he know about her father?

Natalie looked at Juliana. "Wes is really not all that bad, Juliana. He just pretends to be."

"I don't care for him," Juliana retorted. Natalie's face mirrored surprise at her outburst, and she glanced at her mother. Juliana continued, "I don't see too many redeemable qualities, except for the way he handled your horses."

"I know very little about him, except he raises horses and has a small scrap of land his father left him. I've heard he can be a bit temperamental." Miss Margaret looked at Juliana. "But everyone can be redeemed."

Juliana felt reprimanded. Mortified, she pursed her lips into a tight line and didn't say another word.

34

The small group stood in the afternoon drizzle protected with umbrellas, forming a semicircle near the grave. Juliana insisted that Miss Margaret sit in the carriage out of the rain because of her rheumatism.

Reverend Carlson met them at the cemetery. Holding Juliana's hand, he offered his sympathy again. "I know you're grieving, Juliana. Give yourself time to do that. This is so soon after your mother's passing. We don't understand the reasons why, but God promises to walk us through the valleys of our lives, if we allow Him." He walked with her to where the fresh grave was dug next to her mother's.

Just like that, the one she'd longed to see for years was snatched out of her life as quickly as he'd entered. Like the flicker of a candle snuffed out.

The gaping hole in the ground made her shudder. Only darkness there. A pine box placed on ropes sat on the ground, and rain splashed off its top in a steady beat, while the smell of fresh, wet dirt assailed her nostrils. When Juliana glanced at her mother's grave next to it, her throat closed, and she was unable to speak. Tears sprang once again to her eyes.

Josh walked up with Andy and Nellie and leaned in to hold her arm protectively. Juliana could only stare at the wide expanse of his tanned hand. She felt weary. There were few who had braved the rain for the funeral. Albert and Sally were there, but neither Marion nor her father showed up. Looking around, Juliana decided it didn't matter. The ones who were important to her were here. They were her new family now.

The reverend talked of life after death and the confirmation of God's Word that believers would be reunited someday. After reading select Scriptures to that effect, he ended with a brief prayer. It was nice but short, in view of the weather. When he closed his Bible, he nodded at Josh, Albert, and Andy, and they moved forward. The four of them picked up the ropes, lifted the casket, and lowered it into the grave.

Deep, gripping pain slammed into Juliana's chest while she watched Andy and Josh shovel the dirt to cover the hole. *At least they're next to each other now, and together in heaven*, Juliana thought, but she felt little comfort in her grief. Her eyes burned, and while she shed no more tears, there was a knot in the back of her throat. Nellie held her hand as they watched the men finish.

When they started back to the carriage, Josh strode over and pulled Juliana to him, mindless of the others, and she clung to him under the shelter of her umbrella. No words were necessary. Juliana felt protected with his strong arms around her, and her heart slowed to a steady beat that gave way to a bit of peace.

Josh gently pulled her away from him. "You need to get out of this rain. I'll stop by the boardinghouse before I leave," he said in a husky voice.

Juliana mumbled, "Okay," then dazedly climbed back into the carriage.

Josh was glad the rain was starting to diminish when he got back in the saddle. It had been a soggy and dreary day. Watching Juliana made his heart ache. She was so young to have lost both parents already. He counted himself lucky that his parents were still healthy and alive, though it had been awhile since he'd seen them. Suddenly he really missed them, especially his mother. She had been a guiding force in his life.

He looked over at Andy and Nellie nestled close in the buckboard, sharing an umbrella as they bounced along the wet streets. They were so happy, young, and seemingly without a care, looking forward to life together. He fiercely wanted that. He didn't want to wait much longer to have a family and someone to come home to, to share his dreams. Time was quickly going by. He hoped he could share his life with Juliana. He felt an urgency like never before to tell her of his intentions. But he couldn't rush her now.

At the boardinghouse, Louise opened the door and ushered Josh, Nellie, and Andy to the parlor, where Juliana sat straight as a broom handle on the settee, staring at her clasped hands in her lap. She looked up when they walked in. "Thank you all for coming today," Juliana said. "It meant a lot to me to have you there. Albert and Sally are in the dining room having a bite to eat. You're all welcome to join them."

Miss Margaret hurried in from the kitchen and urged them to have some of the refreshments laid out in the dining room. "There's some sliced ham, rolls, green beans, and a lemon pound cake. Please make yourself at home."

"Please follow me," Natalie said, gesturing to the dining room.

Andy and Nellie followed her to enjoy the spread that Miss Margaret and her daughters had prepared. Sally took Albert's hand and walked behind them to the dining room.

"Are you coming, Josh?" Louise asked.

"Maybe in a moment," he answered, then took a seat next to Juliana.

The doorbell rang, and Louise hurried out of the room. Juliana heard Marion and her father, Howard, talking with Louise. "Please come in," Louise said. "Juliana's in the parlor."

"Thank you," Marion said. "I'm not sure if she'll want to see me."

"I'm sure she will. Come this way."

Juliana looked up and stood with Josh to greet them. Marion flashed a look at Josh, then turned back to Juliana.

Marion's father was the first to speak. "We're very sorry for your loss." Juliana could only nod, noticing that Marion hung back uneasily. She took a step toward Marion, and her gesture seemed to break the awkwardness that they both seemed to feel.

Marion pulled Juliana to her and whispered, "I'm very sorry."

Juliana took a small step back and studied her friend's eyes. "Me too," she said.

Marion gave her a knowing look that said she knew all Juliana was thinking. She acknowledged Josh with a nod and tugged at her father's elbow. "Father, I'd like you to meet Josh McBride. You've heard me and Juliana talk about him."

Mr. Stockton stuck his hand out to Josh. "Good to meet you, regardless of the circumstances."

"I've heard nothing but good things about you, Mr. Stockton, and I've enjoyed a meal or two at your hotel. Let's go have some coffee, shall we? Miss Margaret here would be offended if we didn't try her pound cake."

Miss Margaret tapped her cane on the hardwood floor. "I most certainly would, so why don't you just follow me."

The two men strolled to the dining room, talking about sheepherding with Miss Margaret and leaving Juliana and Marion alone to talk.

Juliana led Marion over to the window. "Look, the sky is finally starting to clear."

"Yes, it is. I'm sorry I didn't make it to the burial. But I'm here now."

"You are, and I appreciate that, Marion. I—"

"No," Marion interrupted. "Let me go first. I'm sorry, I wasn't being a very good friend when I was trying to get Josh's attention." Her face was etched with regret. "I admit that I tried. It's perfectly clear that it's you he cares about." Marion touched Juliana's shoulder.

"Okay, Marion. Let's not talk about it anymore right now."

"You're right. I just wanted to clear the air. I've missed you. I'd like to remain friends."

"I've missed you too, and I'd like nothing better than to stay friends as well." Juliana meant what she said, but suddenly she was weary and swayed slightly.

Marion took her arm. "Are you okay?"

"I think so. Maybe if I just sit down . . ."

Marion led her to the nearest chair. "Have you eaten today? I'll bet not."

Juliana thought Marion was back to her natural way of taking charge. "I had a piece of toast and bacon this morning."

"That isn't sufficient. Sit there, and I'll bring you a plate." But as she said it, Josh came in carrying a plate in either hand.

"I'm not sure I can eat anything," Juliana protested with a shrug of her shoulders.

"We'll just see about that." Josh gave her a tender look that went straight to Juliana's heart. She looked at his hands that were so strong, yet remembered how tender his touch was on her face yesterday, and felt her insides flutter.

"I think I'll go have some refreshment." Marion regarded them with a forced smile and left them alone.

Setting down the plates and taking her hand, Josh turned to Juliana. "I think I'd like another cup of coffee. Want to come with me?" he asked.

"I'll think I'd like to just sit here, if you don't mind."

He stood and said, "Okay, I'll be right back."

When Josh entered the dining room, he watched as Louise poured coffee. Natalie cut generous slices of pound cake and placed them on delicate china plates. "Marion, here, take this plate while I get you a fork," Natalie said, handing her a plate.

"It's delicious, Marion. Just like your mother used to make," her father commented, wiping his upper lip with a napkin as he polished off the slice of cake.

Andy walked back to the table for another piece. "It's really good, and I fancy myself a dang good cook. I'll have to ask Miss Margaret for her recipe."

Nellie touched him on the arm. "Mind your manners and leave some for the rest," she teased.

"There's plenty," Louise said, glancing at Marion. "Would you care for coffee to go along with that? There's also ham for sandwiches. I fear Mother thought there'd be more people dropping by." She indicated the table laden with food with a sweep of her hand.

Andy and Nellie exchanged looks. "I hope people won't harbor bad feelings against Juliana for what's happened. She's having a hard enough time without the town turning against her," Nellie said.

"We'll do everything we can to prevent that from happening," Albert said, piling ham on his plate. The others expressed their agreement with a simple nod of their heads.

Josh cleared his throat. "I think things will turn around once the townsfolk find out Davin Brady never spent the money from the bank. He kept it buried because his conscience got the better of him, but he couldn't figure a way out after the fact. He told me and Juliana that there was a piece of paper in his pocket explaining where he'd hid the money. I located the spot this morning and have already turned the money back over to Sheriff Wilson." Josh left out the fact that Davin tried to steal his sapphires and accidentally started the fire. What would be the point of that now? The damage was already done, and nothing could change that.

"Thank God," Albert said. "I didn't know about that. For some reason, I got the idea Wes had something do with the robbery. I'm not even sure why. Maybe because he's always down on his luck financially and shooting off his mouth. I'm glad I haven't finished writing the story yet. I don't want anything I say to reflect badly on Juliana. She is like a daughter to Sally and me, right, dear?" Sally nodded enthusiastically, her mouth full of cake, and he continued. "Maybe I can make part of the story a human interest one somehow."

"I hope you can," Louise said, filling her brother's coffee cup. "People are always harsh judges when it comes to things like this."

"I think we'd better get back to the hotel, Marion." Mr. Stockton set his cup and plate down. "Thank you, ladies, for doing this for Juliana."

"Yes, I'm sure Juliana is grateful." Marion set her plate down to follow her father, but as she passed Josh, she nudged him out of earshot of the others. "I'll try to just be your friend and nothing more, Josh. I can see how you feel about Juliana. She is quite young. But the loan of money is still being offered, regardless," she whispered.

Josh regarded her with curiosity. What did she just tell him? That she would try to be just friends? Somewhere along the way, he must have given her the wrong impression. A friend was all she would ever be. "I'll not be needing it, Marion. I've got another plan I'm working on right now, but your willingness to do that is not taken lightly, and I want you to know that." Josh shifted on his feet.

She flashed him a dull look. "As you wish. Despite what others may think, I really care about what happens to Juliana, and I was friends with her before you or Nellie and the others came along. But if things don't work out, I'll always be here to lend a hand for you," Marion said. She pulled her shoulders back and started toward the door, her skirts brushing against him.

Josh reached out and touched her elbow, and Marion turned around to gaze at him questioningly. "Just in case you had the wrong idea about you and me, put that out of your mind. I'll be your friend because of Juliana, but nothing more." Josh's tone was low but firm. "Things *will* work out for Juliana and me, I'm sure of it."

She yanked her arm free from him, blinking her eyes, then tossed her head and strutted out the door.

Josh stood unmoving for a moment, staring at her back, then just shook his head and turned back to his chattering friends for another piece of Miss Margaret's famous pound cake. He'd never understand women.

Mark was with Juliana in the parlor when Marion walked in. "Mark, I didn't even know you were here," she said.

He half turned from his chair beside Juliana, his dark eyes shining. "Oh, hi. I was running a little behind. I had to look in on a patient of mine. As always, it's nice to see you again."

Marion gave Mark a weak smile and walked over to Juliana. "I just wanted to tell you I'm leaving now, Juliana."

Juliana thought Marion's face was flushed, and she was curious. "Is everything all right?" she asked, watching her friend closely.

Marion bristled. "Of course it is. Just thought we'd better get out of your hair and let you rest."

"I'll be fine, Marion. Your father said to tell you he'll be waiting for you outside. Thank you again for coming." Juliana rose.

"Please let me know if there is anything I can do for you." Marion waved her hand in the air. "Just drop in anytime."

"I will."

"Let me see you out," Miss Margaret said.

"Miss Margaret, you don't need to. I can find my way. Thanks for taking such good care of Juliana."

Mark rose. "I must be going myself. I'll walk out with you." He bowed slightly. "Excuse me, ladies."

Juliana was relieved when the house was quiet once again. Her head throbbed. Natalie and Louise wouldn't let her help with the cleanup, so she wearily climbed the stairs to her room. Albert told her before he'd left to come to work late on Monday, if she felt like coming at all. Juliana knew the best thing for her was to work, though right now her feet felt like they were lifting heavy railroad ties with each step she took up the staircase.

35

May in Montana couldn't have been any nicer, with cool mornings that grew steadily warmer throughout the day, and the sun's dazzling rays causing a variety of wildflowers to pop in abundant color. Josh enjoyed the faint bleating of his lambs, pausing with Pete along the small rise that overlooked the meadow where the sheep and Andy were. He enjoyed the morning call of the sparrows and a passing cloud or two that floated across the wide expanse of creamy blue sky.

It amazed him how the burned grass had been covered with short green blades in a just a few weeks. It was also a constant reminder of all that had happened. But God was faithful—from the rising of the sun, to the moon hanging in delicate balance in the night sky, to new life springing up and animals foraging where there had been nothing. Life had settled back into the constant routine business of sheepherding, and there was a rhythm to his life once again. Continuity. He liked it.

Josh and Andy would move the flock as needed for greener pasture. Shebe had mended quickly, with a slight limp that didn't seem to slow her down. Evenings were spent planning and sketching out Josh's new home. He wanted it to be larger than the one that had burned. He hoped to fill it with a large family and make it big enough to include Andy, regardless of when he married Nellie. He would build a separate wing for Andy, who was like a brother to him and was a hard worker. They worked so well together that they could almost read each other's minds.

Josh couldn't wait to show his plans to Juliana. He wanted her input on the layout. He wanted her advice on everything— from the style to the furnishing to what color shirt he should wear. That's how involved he wanted her in his life. By golly, if she wanted the kitchen painted yellow, she could have it! Everything about her intrigued him, and he couldn't wait to hold her close again.

He felt warmth radiate out of his heart and flow through his entire body when his mind dwelled on Juliana. The thought of her made Josh smile, and he remembered her sweet kisses. The memory shooting through him was powerful.

After the terrible mining accident, he knew without a doubt that he would never want to have anything to do with mining. That awful scene of death had cured him of any thoughts of going into business with Hoover.

Mining and money held little attraction to him now. Josh chided himself for any time he'd doubted the future. He remembered what his mother always told him: "God won't take away the trials of life but will walk you through them." Now, if Josh could just remember that.

He'd met with Hoover and his partners and sold his two claims. He'd wound up with a very tidy sum that was now tucked away at the Fergus County Bank in Lewistown. Enough to build a new house and order the prized Saxon Merino ram for breeding purposes. He'd kept the sapphires he'd first discovered, and they too were in a safe, along with the beautiful ring he planned to give to Juliana soon.

Through the fire and then the mining accident, he'd learned firsthand some hard lessons about putting possessions and wealth above the more important things in life. Several young men, most of them single, had died in the explosion.

Ever since he'd left Colorado, Josh had spent a lot of time trying to become wealthy and show his father he could make it without him. Maybe that was not the best of motivations. The mining venture might have yielded the kind of wealth men only dream of, but he knew if he'd gone that route, he would have had to give up Juliana and sheepherding. But Josh was focused now. Thinking about his decision, and then Juliana, made his heart sing. No amount of money was enough to lure him away from a life with Juliana.

Andy waved his arms at him from below, indicating he needed something. Josh had best run on down and see what was going on.

Juliana kept the article Albert had written about the mining explosion, and she read it again this morning. She forced herself to remember that it had actually happened and that moments later, she had been there. All a stroke of luck—or was this the divine intervention Miss Margaret talked about?

Montana Powder Explosion Tolls Out Death—Seven Dead, Many Injured

April 1896

The town of Neihart, Montana, mourns the loss of seven miners, all single except one, killed in a deadly powder explosion at the Broadwater mine. It appears the accident occurred when a magazine filled with thirty sticks exploded and set off a box of dynamite.

The seriously injured were transported by train to Great Falls for treatment. This is the third disaster within two weeks in the state.

Juliana folded the paper in half and laid it on her desk, sighing. She felt like she'd been walking through a dream. Juliana had tried not to wear a long face, but it was hard when a few people in town would actually move to the opposite side of the street when they saw her coming. She avoided them as well. She had no excuses for what had happened. If it hadn't been for her new friends and Josh, she didn't know what state of mind she would be in right now. Miss Margaret, bless her heart, was so encouraging, telling her to never give up, that God had a plan for her to be happy in life. She had told her more than once that her heavenly Father would be her father now.

Thankfully, Mac at the bank had survived the bullet to his shoulder, and the bank's money had been returned. But forgiveness was not easy for some people, especially for her, because she felt she was the one who'd been mistreated.

The Bible Josh had given her couldn't have come at a better time. She could feel God softening her heart with every Scripture she read before going to bed. The fact that Josh had wanted her to have her own copy made her feel very special. She could hardly wait to see him this weekend at the art fund-raiser. She missed his arms around her and the wonderful sound of his voice that melted her heart and stayed with her throughout the day. There had always been something about its tone that spoke to her heart.

Maybe the art event would give the town some good news to dwell on. Lewistown was flourishing, and a few new shops had opened on Main Street. Albert had even hinted that he was going to hire more help at the newspaper because he didn't want to work her to death. He'd surprised her with a brand-new Underwood typewriter when she'd returned to work. He was protective of her, and she appreciated that. He wanted to know the details about Josh and what his intentions were. No doubt she would ask Albert to give her away at her wedding, if indeed Josh ever got around to asking her. This brought a smile to her lips, and her pulse quickened. God had returned to her the years the locusts had eaten.

Juliana glanced at her clock. She'd told Natalie and Louise that she'd help them prepare the ground for a vegetable garden before she left to help Helen set up for the fund-raiser this afternoon. She hurried down the staircase and flew out the back door into the garden, where she found the women already hard at work.

"Hello, sleepyhead," Natalie teased. She yanked away dead vines and corn stalks left from last year's garden and placed them in a pile.

"Why didn't you wake me?" Juliana asked. "Show me what to do."

Louise straightened from her bent position with the hoe she was using to yank away the dead growth. "We knew you needed your rest, especially before helping Helen with the art show. Mama only plants a small garden anyway."

Juliana watched Natalie at her task. "But there's plenty of time. Besides, I love to be outside, and I want to help get Miss Margaret's ground prepared for her gardens. I know it's hard for her to get up and down with her arthritic knees. Besides, I feel like family eating here all the time, so I may as well help out. That way I won't feel too bad when I have second helpings." She laughed.

Louise turned to Juliana. "For now, if you just want to carry that dead brush to that pile over there to be burned later, that will be a big help. Here's a pair of gloves to protect your hands," she said, pulling them from her lightweight coat pocket. "We are frightfully behind on this project because of the early snow last year."

Juliana slipped the gloves on and set about dragging the vines and dried cornstalks to the designated pile. "I think the art show is going to be fun. I wonder how much money the Ladies Social Club will earn toward building another school."

Natalie giggled. "Is it the art show, or the fact that you'll see Josh that's making your cheeks rosy?"

Juliana made a funny face at her and placed her hands on her hips. "Mmm . . . could be a little of both, but I'll never tell."

Louise sighed and shot a wistful glance at Natalie. "We should be so lucky . . ."

"We're going to have to work on that, girls. There just *have* to be a few eligible men in this town." Juliana continued clearing the little patch that would soon become a new garden.

"That's debatable," Louise said, lifting a brow. "The ones who are available don't even know we're alive."

"Speak for yourself," Natalie said, shaking the dirt off her gloves. "I'm just picky."

Juliana frowned. "I don't understand it—you're both pretty as a picture. What's wrong with the men? Can't they see that?" She knew Louise was extremely shy, but Juliana thought that underneath her cool exterior was a simmering fire. As to Natalie, she was so outgoing that Juliana couldn't understand why she wasn't snatched up.

Louise harrumphed. "That's a good question. When you get it figured out, please let us know."

"I'll put my thinking cap on." Juliana giggled.

"Oh dear. It's bad enough that we have Mama scouting for us," Louise said, catching Natalie's eye. Her sister joined her in laughter.

After working in companionable chatter for about an hour, Juliana paused, straightening to rub her aching back. They'd accomplished a lot today, and later it would be time to make the rows for planting.

"We've done enough for one morning." Natalie pointed with her hoe handle toward the pile. "I say we leave the rest for another day."

Louise and Juliana agreed, so they scampered up the steps to the back of the house, chattering like a bunch of schoolgirls going to their first dance.

Juliana was about to go upstairs to change before meeting Helen at church, but Miss Margaret, who was coming out of the parlor, stopped her. "Juliana, there's someone to see you."

Juliana paused, wondering who it could be, since she wasn't

expecting Josh. "It's not Josh, is it? I thought I'd see him later at the art show."

"No, it's the sheriff. He wants a word with you." Miss Margaret took her hand and drew her into the room.

Juliana swallowed, anxiety causing her stomach to clench. She knew this had to be about her father. She took a deep breath and squared her shoulders, ready to face what he had to say.

Sheriff Wilson strode forward when she entered the room. "Miss Brady, thank you for your time. This won't take but a moment." The sheriff left his hat on and reached into his worn vest pocket, pulling out an envelope.

"What can I help you with?" Juliana asked cautiously.

Sheriff Wilson always breathed like he was out of breath, and his chest was tight. His shirt was stretched tightly across his stomach, and the buttons threatened to pop, apparently from one too many biscuits at Maggie's Café. But Juliana knew him to be a fair-minded and respected person in the community.

"There was a reward for the bank robber's capture and the return of the money from the robbery. Did you know that?" The sheriff cocked his head sideways.

"Yes, I did." Juliana's brow quirked upward. "Josh told me that he returned the money my . . . father stole."

"Indeed he did. That's what I'm getting to." He stretched out the envelope to her. "The reward is yours."

Her jaw dropped, and she started to protest. "I—"

The sheriff grinned at her. "No need to argue. That's the way the bank and I decided it after the money was returned. Please take it. There should be five hundred dollars in there."

Juliana was stunned. "I don't know what to say."

Miss Margaret, who was still in the room, said, "Say thank you."

"Yes . . . thank you." She stared at the envelope in her hands. "I really don't want any part of it because of my father's involvement."

"It's up to you. Do what you will, but put it to good use," the sheriff said. He walked toward the door to leave. "By the way, I'm really sorry you had to go through all that with your dad. Just remember that you weren't to blame, Miss Brady." He tipped his hat to them and promised to stop by the art sale later, then left.

Juliana turned to Miss Margaret, her eyes brimming with tears, and for once she was speechless.

Miss Margaret beamed at her. "God works in mysterious ways, doesn't He?"

36

Posing in front of the cheval mirror in her room, Juliana looked critically at her reflection. She was wearing a pale blue dress with splashes of delicate white lace trimming out the neckline and cuffs. Nellie, with her gift of the needle, had helped Juliana make the dress in the evenings after supper, and Juliana was quite pleased. During the process, she had learned a little about sewing and wanted to be taught more. Then she'd be able to make her children's clothes when the time came. That brought a vision of Josh's face uppermost in her mind, and she wistfully daydreamed of having his children. Perhaps a son just like him with those striking amber eyes.

She finished dressing, pleased with the way she looked. She swept her hair up but left a few curls to drape down the back of her neck. Would Josh notice her new dress? Probably not. Most men didn't take notice of those kinds of things.

Juliana had offered to help with the fund-raiser because she wanted it to be a great success. But she must hurry. Helen would need another set of hands. Miss Margaret and the rest of the women would be along directly, bringing the refreshments.

She hoped Jane would be there with Cynthia today. An outing would be good for her. She'd hate for her to miss the festivities.

As she was leaving, Juliana picked up her reticule. She slipped some of the money inside, then placed the envelope inside her top bureau drawer.

"Oh, I'm so glad you're here now." Helen hurried over to Juliana as she walked through the door of the fellowship hall. "Esther and I have hung a few paintings, but we need help with where to place the rest for the best possible exposure."

Esther nodded at Juliana and murmured, "Hello," looking down her sharp, bony nose at Juliana as though she had a disease. Juliana felt slighted, but she knew Esther hadn't liked her from the moment she'd first laid eyes on her, when Juliana had sat in on the Ladies Social Club meeting. Juliana decided if she wanted to be snobby, then that was her problem.

"Good to see you again, Esther," she said. Turning to Helen, she asked, "How can I help?"

Helen guided her to a long table where framed art was laid out. "These are our donations from local Montana artists. We've hung about seven." She swept her arm in the direction of the far wall.

"I'm impressed. These are very good. Do you know all the artists?" Juliana asked.

Helen smiled proudly. "Yes indeed. All were more than willing to donate for a good cause. It helps to be the mayor's wife. I have a little bit of influence." Helen's blue eyes danced. "Fanny Cooney donated several of her watercolors of children. Then there's a few of Charlie Russell's, and one Howard Stockton was kind enough to contribute. Some of the best are our own Esther White's paintings of various landscapes in oil."

Juliana was taken aback and looked over at Esther in surprise. "My goodness, Esther. I wasn't aware you were an artist. How delightful!" Juliana realized she knew very little about Esther or her life.

Esther had the decency to appear modest. "I've been painting since I was twelve."

Juliana exclaimed, "Well, they are quite beautiful. I'm sure these will sell."

Helen clapped her hands. "Ladies, we must get busy. At least we don't have to set up refreshments. But I think there's going to be a large crowd today."

They worked for two hours, lining the walls of the room with landscapes of flowers in oil and watercolors of children. Juliana suggested they not hang them in order of size. Instead, Helen took her suggestion of varying the placement of size to draw the eye of the guests to the different works of art.

"I must say, Juliana, for one so young you have quite an eye for this sort of thing. Esther will place a card at the corner of each piece with a suggested value, since this is her field. I've never held an art show, so I'm worried about its success. Of course, this will be just one of our fund-raisers. We'll have to come up with several ideas throughout the year to continue to raise money."

Esther glanced at Juliana. "Perhaps we should invite Juliana to be a part of our ladies club. It seems as though she has a lot to offer."

Juliana couldn't believe her ears. Maybe Esther had a heart after all.

"Excellent idea. I'm sure the rest would agree, and I'll tell them. We need fresh ideas."

Amusement touched Juliana's lips, and she forced back a giggle. *New, fresh blood?* she couldn't help but think. It was hard to think of herself in that light.

"Thank you, ladies. I'd be honored to be involved in the community work. Just think—I could continue to write the column but wouldn't need an invitation."

A small smile crossed Esther's lips. "Then it's settled. We'll vote on it."

Juliana felt her heart begin to warm toward Esther, and she was flattered that the women thought she would be an asset to their group.

Right before the guests would arrive, Juliana walked around and stood admiring all the artists' work. Upon closer inspection, she found the sketch that had hung in the Stockton Hotel. She walked closer, looking at Josh's eyes. The artist had captured the light of Josh's soul through his amber eyes, and Josh's love for his dog through the way he laid his hand on Shebe's head.

She loved the picture. She must have it! She looked at the suggested price and gulped. She could never afford fifty dollars, but oh, did she ever want it. Her mind was thrashing around with the idea of owning that sketch. Why not use some of the reward money? At first she hadn't wanted any part of the money, but now she realized this was the perfect thing to do, and it'd be for a good cause. She felt like hugging herself to think she would finally own the sketch, but she needed to tell Helen before someone else made an offer.

A flurry of activity at the door signaled that Natalie, Louise,

Miss Margaret, and Cynthia had arrived, laden with baskets of finger sandwiches and desserts. Marion came right behind them, carrying large tablecloths and a punch bowl. Juliana watched them all congregated in the corner, feeling left out while she stood deciding about the sketch. Natalie left the group and walked over to her, urging her toward the other ladies.

Louise drew her toward the group. "It gives me great pleasure to tell you that you're now a member of the Lewistown Ladies Social Club!" The ladies clapped and cheered, congratulating her as though it was the most enviable club to belong to, and Miss Margaret banged her cane on the floor.

Juliana stepped forward, expressing her thanks. It felt good to be a part of a group for the first time in her life. "I'm honored, and I will work hard to do what I can to further the good of our community." There was another round of applause.

Natalie tapped a punch cup to get their attention. "I want to further add that Marion has accepted the position to be the teacher once the new school is built."

Marion beamed and accepted the ladies' congratulations. "I hope I can call on each of you from time to time to help out with some of the specifics I'll be teaching."

Juliana was so tickled that her friend would now have something to center her life on. "I'll be more than happy to help with reading and literature, Marion."

"And I'll be taking you up on that! Thanks, Juliana."

Marion seemed quieter than normal. Juliana would try to visit her soon. She owed her a lot and hoped they would always be friends. She focused her attention back to Helen and her instructions.

"Things are shaping up nicely," Helen declared to everyone, looking around the fellowship hall. "I have a string quartet that will be using this end of the room and will be playing as our guests arrive." Her comment brought a rousing response from the ladies.

"It looks like you've thought of everything," Miss Margaret said.

"If you'd like, I'll stand next to the door and play the role of greeter," Natalie offered.

"Perfect. Louise, you take the clipboard and keep track of what we sell. Marion, you can serve the punch. Cynthia, you handle the snacks. The rest of us will play hostess."

Juliana touched Helen on the sleeve, pulling her away. "I want to be the first to purchase a piece of art," she said in a hushed tone.

Helen eyes widened, and she cleared her throat. "Dear, we simply *must* start at the suggested price."

"I understand, Helen. But I have the reward money from the bank, and I want to use some of it for that." Juliana's smile faded, and she looked away, exhaling slowly as she remembered how the money came about.

"Honey, I think that's a fine idea. I didn't mean to imply you couldn't own one. Which one are you interested in? I'll tag it sold. That should start things moving in the right direction when people see that one is purchased before we even start."

"I want the sketch of the sheepherder and his dog."

"Excellent choice! Russell is gaining ground as a popular Western artist. But something tells me by the look on your face that you know the subject." Helen stared at her.

Juliana hesitated. "Oh, all right. I do. His name is Josh McBride, and we're courting." It felt good to say it out loud.

Helen's eyes twinkled with mischief. "Ah ha, I knew there had to be a reason. I'll tag the picture, and you go mingle with our guests," she said, and scurried off.

The quartet arrived right on time, and lovely violin music filled the fellowship hall while guests perused the artwork. They dined on the delicate sandwiches and punch served from a beautiful etched glass bowl with matching cups. Marion had borrowed the dishes from the hotel, and along with the silver trays of food, they transformed the lowly room to a more formal one.

To be sure, Helen had a vast array of friends, some with lots of money, Josh thought. He'd worn the suit he'd quickly ordered right after the fire, but it was a tad snug on his thick chest and arms. The string tie at his neck was tight too, making him uncomfortable. He'd needed it fast to wear to church, but soon he'd have to find a tailor to make one that fit him right. He wasn't crazy about dressing up anyway. He was more comfortable in his jeans, chambray shirt, and a great pair of boots.

He strained to see over the heads of everyone in the room to locate Juliana. He walked among the people with a nod of his head to several. He said hello to Albert and Sally, then stood talking with them when he spotted Juliana. She was standing with Cynthia and Jane, who sat in her wheelchair alongside Mark. Juliana's head was slightly tilted, and when her laughter floated across the room, he felt a ping in his heart. Josh studied the outline of her shape in what appeared to be a new blue dress, which showed off every curve when she bent down to speak to Jane. She looked lovely and fresh as a flower. His hand holding the cup of punch shook, and he felt for the small box in his suit pocket, giving it a pat.

"I have my eye on that winter landscape," Albert said. "What do you think, Sally?"

Sally took Albert's arm. "Let's go have a closer look. Will you excuse us, Josh?"

"Yes, of course." Josh moved toward Juliana just as he saw Wes approach the group. He was surprised to see him here. He didn't appear to have a lot of money, or if he did, he spent it on his fine belt and boots. Josh figured Wes thought of this as just another way to meet ladies. He'd better go see what Wes was up to, but as he moved toward the cowboy, Miss Margaret used her cane as a hook to catch his arm. "Young man, come here a moment."

"Nice show going on here," Wes said. His tall, lanky form leaned in close to Juliana. "I don't know the first thing about art, but I know when I see a picture I like. What about you folks?" he said, addressing the small group.

Mark was the first to respond. "Art is subjective. Its beauty is in the eye of the beholder." He smiled down at Jane, who smiled back at him.

Wes had a quizzical look on his face. "Sub . . . what?"

"Mark means that everyone has a different way of looking at art. What one might like or see in a picture, others would disagree about," Juliana said. Mark cleared his throat, apparently stifling a laugh.

"Okay, I get it now." Wes grinned and stood staring at the art on the wall, his hip slumped to one side and his arms crossed.

Juliana noticed that today he'd actually pressed his shirt and slicked his unruly hair down. He hadn't checked his Stetson at the door but twirled it in his long, thin fingers. So he *could* try to be civilized when it suited him.

Cynthia turned to Mark and asked, "Shall we get some refreshments? I think Jane is thirsty."

"Sure thing," Mark said. "How about you, Juliana? Even a hostess needs refreshment."

"I'll be along in a moment. I'd like a word with Wes." Juliana decided she was going to be bold.

"Miss Juliana, are you still coming over next week?" Jane asked.

Juliana touched her hand. "You bet I will. How about I bring a board game?"

Jane's face lit up. "Oh, I'd really like that."

Mark pushed the wheelchair with Cynthia leading the way over to the table. Suddenly Juliana was alone with Wes, and she chewed her lip.

For the first time she noticed he had hazel eyes, a nice chiseled jawline, and a face bordering on thin. Why he ingratiated himself with their group, she hadn't a clue, but she would be civil, God help her. Wes *had* helped her pull the carriage out of the mud on the way to the funeral. She tried to remember what Natalie said, that he really wasn't all that bad. She'd have to see, but she was curious what he knew about her father. Something she'd read last night in Matthew came to mind—if she didn't forgive others, then her Father in heaven wouldn't forgive her. This was something Miss Margaret had repeated to Juliana more than once since her father had died. It wasn't easy to do, but Juliana was trying hard.

Wes had whirled around and now looked surprised. "*You* want to talk to me? Well, ain't it just my lucky day! I never thought you would be saying that to me."

Juliana sucked in a deep breath. "It's nothing personal, Wes, so don't get your hopes up. I wanted to ask you how you knew my father."

Wes leaned back on his boot heels, his grin suddenly gone. His gaze traveled over her with an admiring look. "I met Davin one day at Big Spring Creek. He was panning for gold, and I was on my way to Lewistown. He invited me to have a bite to eat, and we struck up an unusual friendship of sorts."

Juliana sighed. "What was he like?"

"I know what you're thinkin'." Wes shook his head. "But he seemed to be a decent, hardworking man as far as I could tell, who just took the wrong bend in the road of life. I think he was desperate to strike it rich, and then when he got back here, he found out his wife, uh, sorry—your mother—had died. He told me about the bank deal without really meaning to. It surprised me that he didn't spend the money but hid it. If it were me, I think I'd be hard-pressed not to have kept running with my saddlebags full, then find me a woman and have a heck of a time for sure."

"I'm sure you would, Wes. Thanks for telling me. I—"

Wes touched her arm, staying her. "Now see here, Juliana. I may not know art, but I sure know a good-looking woman standing before me. How about I get us some punch?"

She stiffened, trying to pull away. "I beg your pardon, please let go of my arm."

Suddenly Josh was standing next to her. He shoved Wes's shoulder hard, pushing him away from Juliana, and Wes tried to steady himself against the punch bowl table. Marion was unable to stop the bowl from shaking sideways, and the punch sloshed all over the damask white tablecloth. Cynthia grabbed a napkin to quickly try to soak up the mess, but it was too late. Half the sandwiches were now soaked with pink punch.

"Didn't our last talk teach you one blasted thing, Wes?" Josh gritted his teeth.

Wes straightened, glaring at Josh. "You don't own her, Josh! And I don't see no ring on her finger either."

"Maybe so, but that does not give you the right to touch Juliana in any way, especially when she tells you to let go. Why don't you get that?"

Juliana came between them, her hands up. "Please, keep your voices down or you'll cause a scene, and our guests will leave," she snapped. Josh's lips formed a hard line, and Wes looked mortified. Marion and Cynthia were watching the whole scenario.

Both men took a step back. Josh's face was full of thunder. Wes looked at Juliana, his Adam's apple bobbing, and said, "I've acted like a fool. I'm sorry. I wouldn't hurt you for nothin' in the world." With that Wes slammed on his hat and swaggered past them to get outside as quickly as he could.

Juliana turned to Josh, her hands on her hips. "I need to remind you that I'm able to take care of myself. *I* was the one who wanted to talk to Wes alone about my father."

He balked. "I'm sorry. I was trying to protect you. It looked to me like he overstepped his bounds again."

"What do you mean, again?" Juliana's bottom lip twitched. "Why don't you give it some thought first before you react next time?" she said tersely. As soon as the words fell from her lips, she was sorry for the way she'd spoken them.

His jaw dropped. "I'll just get out of your way then," he said hoarsely.

Juliana knew she'd hurt Josh by the deflated look on his face. Her lips parted to speak, but the words caught in her throat. She watched him disappear through the crowded room.

Miss Margaret stood next to her and touched her on the shoulder. "Juliana, let's go someplace we can talk."

Fighting back tears, Juliana nodded, and they walked out the back door of the church to the grounds outside, not too far from the cemetery. Juliana would not let herself look in that direction because she knew she would crumble. They walked in silence in the warmth of the afternoon among the cottonwood trees sporting their brand-new green leaves.

Miss Margaret stopped at a park bench. Juliana stared out at the serene countryside but could still hear distant chatter and laughter from the fellowship hall. She turned to Miss Margaret. "I'm afraid I've pushed Josh away one too many times."

Miss Margaret scooted closer to her on the bench, and Juliana smelled the delicate rose water mixed in with her mentholated cream that was ever present. Miss Margaret took Juliana's hand and looked into her eyes over the top of her spectacles. "Listen to me. Josh was just protecting you, though a little too strongly. He adores you, and he doesn't trust Wes. Wes has a lot to learn when it comes to manners and trying to get a lady to recognize he's alive. If he'd only observe Josh, he could get the hang of it." She paused, raising one gray brow. "At least, I think he could if he wanted to."

"You think so, Miss Margaret?" Juliana sniffed.

"I do. I think you're still angry with your father, but one day

318

you'll be able to let it all go. I know you don't want to depend on a man, and you don't have to, but man was meant to have a partner. That's God's design. Don't be angry with Josh. You must go find him. Don't let the sun go down on your anger or give the devil an opportunity," Miss Margaret said, patting Juliana's hand. "You love him, don't you?"

Juliana drew in a deep breath and exhaled. "More than anything."

Miss Margaret stood up and tapped her cane against Juliana's foot. "Then what are you waiting for?"

Juliana rose and gave Miss Margaret a peck on the cheek. "Bless you, sweet lady." Then she tore up the pathway to find Josh.

37

Josh stalked out the church's front door, his chest tight and his thoughts turning his anger into hurt. He had absolutely no interest in looking for art to buy now. He'd just make a donation to the new school, and he intended to make it in memory of the miners killed in the explosion. But that would have to wait. He just wanted to get away from everyone as fast as he could.

Now he chided himself for bringing the buckboard in hopes of whisking Juliana away. If he'd ridden his horse, Pete, he could've just hopped on him in a hurry and taken off. Now he felt silly at the plans he'd carried around in his mind all week. He didn't even say a word when Andy tried to stop him as he left. He waved him aside, leaving Andy staring after him with a frown.

Maybe Juliana was too young to understand how serious he was. Could be she didn't love him. His heart flipped over in his chest when he thought that might be the true reason for the way she'd spoken to him. Well, he'd never know, because he was going to be scarce from now on.

When he reached his wagon, Josh ripped off his new suit jacket, flung it onto the seat, and loosened his tie. He'd take the long way home to cool off.

Home. Where was that anyway? He didn't know anymore. He and Andy had found another suitable section of his property that had been spared from the worst of the fire to construct another house. But now he wasn't so sure he wanted to build the plans he'd spent every night drawing. He glanced at the rolled-up drawings on the seat. He had intended on showing them to Juliana today. Maybe all he needed was a cabin just big enough for him to live in.

He wasn't going back to Colorado with his tail between his legs. He'd found what he desired without looking—the Yogo sapphires—which would help him declare his independence from his father and establish his own path to success. But that was before he'd found Juliana, his Jewel, and decided to trade it all for a life with her, taking his chances at sheepherding.

Josh untied the horse's reins and stepped up into the wagon's seat. He turned around in his seat, glancing over his shoulder and hoping he'd see Juliana. Wishful thinking. He swallowed a huge lump in his throat.

With a "giddyap" and a snap on the reins, he left the church in the bright afternoon sun that dappled the lane with moving shadows.

Juliana stumbled on her way up the hill to the church's front yard. She fell hard on her hands, ripping the hem of her new blue dress, but that didn't stop her. Heavens above! She'd walked to church today, so she didn't have Choco. She caught a glimpse of Josh's back at the end of the lane as he disappeared around the bend through thick cottonwood trees. She looked about wildly.

Wes was saying good-bye to the reverend and mounting his beautiful chestnut mare to head out of the churchyard.

Swallowing her pride, she ran up to him. "Wes, please wait a minute. I want to apologize."

Wes pulled his horse up sharply, an odd look on his face. "What's that you said? I must need the wax cleaned outta my ears," he said, chuckling.

Juliana's chest was heaving from the run up the hill. "You heard me. Don't make me say it again. I see now that you weren't grabbing me to harm me." It was true and she knew it, and she just chalked it up to his egotistical ways.

He looked as if he didn't know what to say, so Juliana said, "How about we call a truce?"

Wes paused, rubbing his chin. "All right. All I wanted to do was have cup of punch with a pretty lady for a change, that's all. I know Josh is sweet on you. That's apparent, but I thought I'd give him a run for his money anyway."

"Then you should know that I care about him too. There *are* other pretty ladies here who you could have refreshments with," she said. She blew a strand of hair from her eyes, still breathing hard.

"They won't have a thing to do with me. I always seem to say just the wrong thing."

"Yes, Wes, you do, but you can change that if you really want to. And because of the way you talked to Josh, I'm afraid I wasn't nice to him either, and he took off, hurt."

Wes snickered. "Whatever you said to him was not my fault! But I'm sorry if I messed up your afternoon. Honest."

"I am too." Juliana stared wistfully down the lane as though Josh would materialize.

322

"Then go after him."

"It's too late. He's long gone. Besides, I walked to church today." Her voice cracked.

"One thing I know for sure, it's *never* too late," he said, sliding down off his horse.

Juliana, misunderstanding his intentions, took a step back. She was surprised when he held out his horse's reins to her. She stood staring back at him.

"You know how to ride?"

"Of course."

"You'd better. Dakota here is lightning fast, and a slight touch is what he responds to. Go after Josh. You can catch up with him if you hurry, but you'll need Dakota to do that." Wes shifted on his boots heels and watched her, a sheepish smile crossing his lips.

"But this is your horse." She wasn't sure why he was doing this.

"Yes, and the best piece of horseflesh around here. Anybody will tell you that. I don't let just anyone ride my horses, especially women. The horses are my pride and joy, but I'm willing to make an exception." Lifting her hand, Wes slapped the reins into her palm. "Well, are you just gonna stand there? Time's a-wasting! Come on, I'll give you a boost up." He practically lifted her up to the saddle, and she grabbed hold of the pommel, admiring the hand-tooled saddle. *Hmm, there's more to Wes than meets the eye*, she thought.

"Just bring him back here in awhile. I don't want to have to hitch a ride back home." Then he gave Dakota a slap on the rump, and the horse took off.

Juliana giggled. Miss Margaret would be horrified to see her in her new Sunday dress astride a horse that didn't even belong to her. But then, Miss Margaret *had* told her to go after Josh . . .

Yogo Creek gurgled, cutting its path across the bench lands with an inviting, rushing sound that always soothed Josh's spirit. Josh was tempted to take his boots off and wade in. The water would be chilly—it always was, no matter what the time of the year.

He looped the reins over a scrub and yanked off his boots and socks, then threw them into the back of the wagon. He trudged down the slope, feeling the cool grass under his bare feet. The water felt invigorating, so he rolled up his pants and waded in. The shock of cold water on his feet and legs made him suck in his breath. He waded further into the stream and found a large rock that jutted out. He sat down and rolled back his shirt sleeves. It was peaceful here.

He recalled the time back in February when he'd found the shiny blue stones and marveled at their translucent blue color. The last time he'd been to this spot was when he'd picnicked with Juliana. They'd enjoyed talking and discovering a little about each other, though she was bashful at first. The memory of him tossing her in the water brought a smile to his lips but an ache to his heart. He'd loved the sight of her that day, though she'd feigned anger with her pouting mouth.

Josh leaned back and closed his eyes to enjoy the sun's rays on his face. His heart thudded heavily in his chest when he recalled Juliana's warm kisses and the smell of her hair. This wasn't doing anything except making him feel lonelier than he ever had before. He should leave. He'd left Shebe to tend the sheep for long enough.

For a moment Josh thought he heard a sound, and he strained his ears to hear.

"May I join you?" Juliana lifted her dress cautiously and traipsed through the water barefoot, then shivered at the water's coldness.

Josh jerked around. Juliana dragged the hem of her dress in the water and walked toward him. He blinked hard, and as she drew near she saw his somber look and sad, weary eyes. He'd never looked more handsome. He was barefoot, with muscular legs dangling over the large rock, and he was leaning back on his strapping, tanned arms.

"Jewel," he whispered, "I was dreaming you'd come." The thickness in his voice when he called her Jewel in his incredibly tender way made her heart skip a beat. Still, he seemed to remain guarded, not moving toward her. Juliana knew he wasn't sure what to expect but was allowing her to make the first move.

"Josh, I'm sorry if I sounded mean," she said, drawing close enough to reach out and touch him. The water swirled around her legs in its icy grip.

"You're shaking," he said. He held out his arms to her, pulling her up to share his space on the huge rock. The look in his eyes made her heart flutter against her ribs. He drew her close to him and tucked her under the shelter of his strong arms. She laid her head on his broad chest and could hear his steady heartbeat. This was where she was meant to be, wrapped in the safety of his strong arms. She never wanted to leave here, ever.

"How did you get here?" he asked.

Juliana laughed. "You wouldn't believe it. Wes loaned me his horse." She felt him stiffen. Looking up at him, she saw his amber eyes narrow.

"Wes?"

"It's a long story, but let's don't talk about him. You don't have anything to fear where he's concerned, believe me. I like the soft-spoken, tenderhearted but strong type, and a man full of faith."

"And how did you tear your new dress, silly girl?" The impish grin teased her.

"So you *did* notice, but you never said anything." She folded her arms and pouted.

"I never miss anything about you," he said huskily, his hands stroking her forearms.

"Well, I tore my dress chasing after you, big guy," she said.

"Is that a fact? Well, this guy is looking for a lady who knows what her goals are in life, has determination to get them, has faith in God, and wants to spend her life with an adoring husband who's a little bit older. But she must be happy with the fact that he's a sheepherder and will never take up mining, no matter how good the odds are."

She leaned her head back to look up at him, surprised at his last comment. "Josh, I never want to hear you say another thing about age. And what do you mean about the mining?"

He took a deep breath and told her he'd sold his two claims to Hoover for a nice sum of money. "Mining is okay for some people, but it's not for me, not after what I saw at the explosion. I want no part of that. I was paid well enough to put me back on my feet and rebuild my home, but make it larger. Would you be interested in helping me do that?" His eyes burned with passion.

Was he asking her to be his wife? She knew what it took to have him sell his claims and give up the mining venture.

Their eyes met. His lips were parted, and she moistened her own, expecting his kiss. But he only continued to gaze down at her through smoldering eyes. Josh's fingers slowly traced the outline of her face while her heart beat wildly in her chest. She heard his breathing speed up.

"You are so lovely, my Jewel." Josh lowered his head to touch hers, and the familiarity of her flooded him, working its magic. "Did you know I dreamed several times that you were in trouble and I was to rescue you?" Those gorgeous blue eyes of hers flicked to his face, and his heart did a somersault. She made him feel like he was seventeen again, and he wanted to ride to Lewistown and shout from the rooftops that he loved her.

"You're kidding! I had a similar dream about you the night the wolf attacked Shebe. Isn't that strange?" She reached up and encircled his neck with her hands, interlocking her fingers, and it thrilled him to have her touch him with this kind of intimacy.

He bent down, and his lips touched hers in a lingering kiss, tasting their sweetness. "When two people are so connected, I think they instinctively know when the other one is in need. That's what we are—connected." Josh felt the tightness in his chest give way to peace and contentment while holding her this way, and he felt himself relax. He took one of her hands and circled her palm with his index finger. "You've been through a lot these past few months, and I've seen you become strong and independent. You were able to take care of yourself with determination, still hold your head high, and then begin to trust again. I admire that about you. I know how your father hurt you, but I promise I never will."

Juliana smiled. "I want you to be proud of me. That's important. I want to trust you with my heart, and I believe that I can do that now, Josh."

Josh breathed deeply, savoring what she said. "Would you like to see my new house plans?"

"I'd like that," Juliana answered, her hands still in his.

He pulled her up. "They're in the wagon."

They sloshed through the cold water again and ran up the bank to where the wagon was parked. He lifted her up onto the seat, sprang up to sit beside her, and unrolled his house plans. Their heads bent over the plans together while he explained the different rooms and how they would be laid out.

"I want your input on what should go where."

"You do? Why is that?" She peered up at him with a twinkle in her eyes.

Josh tried to control his nervousness and exhaled slowly. "Because I want this to be our house. I want to fill it with love, laughter, and our children," he said softly, blinking away tears. He reached over to his suit pocket and felt around for the box, but the pockets were empty. What had he done with the box? If he'd lost it, he was going to be worse than mad at himself. Suddenly, he felt sick to his stomach. This was the most important moment in his life, and he was bungling it.

"Josh, what are you looking for?" Juliana's brow lifted quizzically.

He twisted in his seat and reached for her hand. "I want to ask you to be my wife because I love you, and I can't imagine my life without you." Finally! He'd said it. He didn't have to wait a split second for her answer.

"Oh! Josh, I'm so honored you want me as your wife." He saw tears flood her eyes, making them sparkle just like the Yogos. "I love you so. I did from the first time you walked into the doctor's office the day my mother died." She started crying softly. "Maybe even before that, when I saw your eyes in the sketch at the Stockton Hotel. I bought it today, by the way." Tears streamed down her cheeks, and she reached up, touching his face, lips, and eyes, as if she couldn't get enough of him.

Josh's heart pounded once again, and he cupped her small face between his hands. How could he be so lucky? "You're the Jewel of my heart," he whispered tenderly.

He touched the hollow of her throat where her pulse beat, then leaned down to nuzzle her neck, showering her with light kisses. Juliana released a soft moan, and Josh heard her sharp intake of breath. He placed his hand at the back of her head, massaging her neck, then finally lowered his mouth to kiss hers with hunger and passion. Juliana returned his kiss with fierce tenderness, and he felt her tremble. When they embraced and he pressed against her, they nearly slid off the wagon seat. They pulled apart, laughing.

Just then Juliana stepped on something, and she reached down and picked up the small box. "What's this?"

Josh felt his face warm. "That's where it is," he said, snatching it out of her hand. "I guess it fell out of my pocket. I wanted to give you this." He snapped open the jewelry box, and lying against white satin was an exquisite silver ring set with a cornflower blue Yogo stone in its center.

Juliana cried out, "It's lovely! Oh Josh, I think I'm going to cry again." Her bottom lip quivered.

Josh chuckled at her reaction, then took the ring out and placed it on her left hand. It was a perfect fit. "You are now taken, Jewel. This is a commitment of my love for you until the day we're married." He felt his heart burn with love and desire as he looked into her eyes full of emotion. Tears slid down his face, and she kissed him slowly, lingering this time, until their tears united.

Lewistown Gazette, May 1896

Albert and Sally Spencer wish to announce the engagement of their protégé, Juliana Brady, to Josh McBride. Juliana is the daughter of the late Grace and Davin Brady of Topeka, Kansas. She is a journalist for the *Gazette*. Josh McBride is the son of Alice and Jim McBride of Steamboat Springs, Colorado. Josh owns a sheepherding ranch in Utica. After a fall wedding and honeymoon, the couple will reside at his ranch.

Miss Margaret laid the newspaper aside and expelled a sigh of relief. Her prayers had been answered, right on time. Not one minute too soon or one minute too late. Taking off her spectacles to wipe the tears from her eyes, she bowed her head in a prayer of thanksgiving.

Author Note

My brother was once the deputy superintendent of Glacier National Park in Montana. I visited Montana a couple of years ago to see his writing cabin after his death. There I discovered the story of the Yogo sapphire, and I was intrigued with the brilliance of the cornflower blue stone and the history behind it. Some of my story is loosely based on the sheepherder Jim Ettien, whose discovery would later become one of the largest and richest deposits of precious gemstones in North America—the Yogo dike. Though Ettien sold his share for a pitiful amount to Jake Hoover, who was the first to discover the unique sapphires in Yogo Creek, I took liberties in making it a profitable sale for the character of Josh.

Yogos are found and mined only in the state of Montana. Most historians agree the term Yogo was derived from an Indian word meaning "blue sky."

The Yogo Gulch mine was controlled by the British for thirty-five years. The stones can be found in the crown jewels of England and in the personal gem collections of the Duchess of York, Princess Mary, Queen Victoria, and Kaiser Wilhelm of Germany. The British Museum of Natural History in London also maintains a Yogo exhibit, and the Smithsonian Institution in Washington DC has the largest cut Yogo—10.2 karats. George Kunz's collections of Yogos are exhibited at the American Museum of Natural History in New York.

Yogos retain their brilliance under artificial light, making them unique from other gemstones. An estimated forty million dollars' worth of Yogos have been produced from the Yogo mines of Montana. Today commercial companies work those mines.

An interesting side note about sapphires: they were found in the breastplate of the high priest in the Old Testament (see Exod. 28:17–20). Their position in the breastplate was connected to religious beliefs.

Jake Hoover's partners, Mathew Dunn and George Wells, were historical characters as well. Charlie M. Russell, a Western artist, is the Charlie in my story. He was a protégé of Jake Hoover and resided in Great Falls, Montana, until he died. George Kunz of Tiffany & Co. was the true assayer who appraised the Yogos that Jake Hoover sent to New York in a cigar box. Kunz recognized the sapphires for their remarkable beauty and commercial potential.

Sapphires are a symbol of love and purity. I feel very fortunate to own a small Yogo and diamond ring set in silver.

Acknowledgments

To my agent, Tamela Hancock Murray, who is always available with her cheerful attitude and help at any time.

To my editor, Andrea Doering, and copyeditor, Jessica Miles, for their competent suggestions.

To Cheryl Van Andel, senior art director, and Dan Thornberg, for fabulous book covers.

To publicist Carmen Pease, publicity assistant Audrey Leach, and marketing manager Michele Misiak. I'm grateful for your tireless help in answering my many questions. You ladies are so gracious!

To my critique group for their feedback of every chapter in its raw form.

To all my writing friends of the ACFW. You rock!

To Sylvia for putting up with me in Montana for three weeks as I began to flesh out my story. Love you, girl!

To Dottie and gals at The Bookmark for their continual support. God bless.

To my readers, who have honored me with positive praise of my first book in this series—many thanks!

To my sisters, Doris and Dianne, who love me despite my flaws, and my brother Sam—the twinkle in your eye is your sweet confirmation.

And to my Lord, who meets my needs at every turn.

Maggie Brendan is a member of the American Christian Writers (ACW), the American Christian Fiction Writers (ACFW), and the American Fiction Writers Association. She was also a recipient of the 2004 Atlanta ACW Persistence Award.

Maggie has experience in media and print production and has a particular interest in and affinity with Christian radio. She also writes reviews for some of her favorite authors, which can be found on her blog, http://southernbellewriter.blogspot.com. She is a resident blogger on www.bustlesandspurs.com. A screenplay of her first novel, *No Place for a Lady*, book 1 of the Heart of the West series, has been optioned to Starz Media for production by Hallmark. She has led a writers' critique group in her home for six years and was quoted in *Word Weavers: The Story of a Successful Writers' Critique Group*.

Maggie is married with two grown children and four grandchildren. When she's not writing, she enjoys reading, singing, painting, scrapbooking, and being with her family. She lives in Marietta, Georgia.

Can a *Southern belle* tame the heart of a rugged cowboy?

Fall in love with the Colorado setting and the spunky heroine who wants to claim it as her own in book 1 of the Heart of the West series.

Ɍ Revell
a division of Baker Publishing Group
www.RevellBooks.com

Available at your local bookstore.